PEBBLES IN THEIR SHOES

PEBBLES IN THEIR SHOES

A Novel

Bud Simpson

iUniverse, Inc.

New York Lincoln Shanghai

Pebbles In Their Shoes
A Novel

Copyright © 2005 by E. A. Simpson, Jr

iUniverse books may be ordered through booksellers or by contacting:

iUniverse
2021 Pine Lake Road, Suite 100
Lincoln, NE 68512
www.iuniverse.com
1-800-Authors (1-800-288-4677)

ISBN-13: 978-0-595-34570-0 (pbk)
ISBN-13: 978-0-595-79409-6 (cloth)
ISBN-13: 978-0-595-79317-4 (ebk)
ISBN-10: 0-595-34570-0 (pbk)
ISBN-10: 0-595-79409-2 (cloth)
ISBN-10: 0-595-79317-7 (ebk)

Printed in the United States of America

CHAPTER 1

▼

Sookey plunged through the rain-filled night, clutching a small, tow-headed child to her black chest. Briars and low branches tore at her clothes and bare skin like bony fingers. Solid sheets of rain slammed against the leaves overhead, pushed through holes in the canopy, and stung her face and bare arms. She hunched forward. Her body sheltered the child from the rain. Her arms shielded it from the sharp foliage.

Shouts and gunfire moved closer. Lightning performed a crooked dance above her. The rifle fire posed a threat, but she feared the lightning more. The angry men chasing her through the darkness could kill her. But worse, God might feel the same way.

The throaty blast of a shotgun erupted at close range. A shower of steel pellets buzzed into nearby underbrush. She lurched forward. Her bare feet carried her swiftly through the dark mountain woods, narrowly avoiding rocks and roots. "Trust your feet," her grandmother always said, passing down the advice from a thousand campfires. "If your head is clear and your heart right, your feet will be true to you. Trust them."

She had no choice. But why had that failed those ancestors who tried to flee the neck shackles of the Moors? And those who tried in vain to board the Underground Railroad?

Sookey had thought her blackness would mask her presence in the dark, but the lightning reflected off her wet skin, each flash marking her position with a faint beacon.

"There she goes!" a voice cried out, followed by two quick pistol shots.

"Shoot low, or you'll hit the white kid," another called.

"It don't matter," the first one said. "He's just like 'em; cut his teeth sucking on those black tits." Four shots in rapid succession filled the night air.

A sharp twinge dug into Sookey's left shoulder. How badly was she hit? She was still on her feet, still running. A slight turn and she headed toward a narrow ravine split by a small creek. She had gathered crayfish there and fished for trout. No stranger to the woodlands of North Georgia, she had played in the mountains as a child, and when grown had retraced her childhood steps while foraging.

The boy child at her breast opened his pale mouth and cried. Sookey ignored her pain and tried to soothe and quiet him. Reaching the edge of the ravine, she hesitated, then rushed down its slope. The little boy howled. His cries might rise above the din of the storm. Stopping at the bottom of the ravine, she held the child up. With each successive flash of lightning, she saw an ever-increasing dark stain on the boy's right shoulder. Sookey ran her fingers over her own shoulder and felt the warm, stickiness of blood oozing from her. Was the blood on the boy hers? His right shoulder had been pressed against her left. Her fingers told her otherwise. The bullet had torn into the back of her left shoulder and passed completely through her and the child.

Sookey had to stop running soon or both would bleed to death. She pulled the boy tightly to her, using his shoulder to stop the blood flow. The palm of her right hand pressed hard against the hole in the back of his shoulder. She found her way to the creek. Her mountain wanderings had taught her that streams that flow downhill ultimately lead to civilization. The men chasing her were from civilization. She turned and ran. Uphill.

The ground steepened. She slowed. The howling of dogs rose above the voices of the men behind her. Keep moving. But movement drained life from her and the boy. His cries retreated to a soft whimper. Her strength ebbed with each step. If she kept moving, they would die. With the dogs added to the chase, she and the boy would die, if she stopped.

She remembered a trout pool halfway up the ravine guarded by the exposed roots of a large chestnut tree. Chestnuts, once plentiful in the mountains, were dying out. That tree stood out vividly in her recollection. She felt a kinship with it. Her own kind was dying out in the mountains, uprooted by the same men who now chased her.

The tangled base would hide her and the boy from the men, but not the dogs. Unless she could throw them off the scent. The tree stood nearby. The howling grew closer. Sookey plunged into the cold mountain stream and crossed to the other side. Running forward about fifty yards, she stopped, backtracked, and re-crossed the stream. Without squatting, she pulled up her loose dress, put her legs together, and peed. As urine coursed down her legs, she splashed her feet up and down in the growing puddle. Her legs and feet thoroughly saturated, she dashed uphill alongside the creek, until she reached the place where the stream widened near the chestnut.

Sookey waded into the pool at the base of the tree. She placed her hand over the nose and mouth of the boy and submerged. Surfacing in the darkness of a small hollow beneath the overhanging roots, she wondered what other creatures might also have sought refuge there. The water in the hollow covered her waist. She tore strips of cloth from her tattered dress and stuffed them into their jagged wounds. The strips and the cold water would help stanch the blood. Luckily, no bone or tendon had been hit in either of them. Stopping the blood loss was critical to their survival. Aside from the obvious reason, blood in the creek would give them away.

The dogs bayed approaching the creek. Sookey saw faintly through the maze of roots. The boy whimpered. She placed her mouth over his and sucked down his cry. She then breathed for both of them. He squirmed. She held him firmly, muffling his cries by breathing them. He quieted. She continued to supply his air, lest he cry out again.

The dogs reached the creek, dashing across without stopping. Their howls soon became disoriented barks and whimpers as the scent petered out. The men remained on the near side of the creek and urged the dogs on. The dogs milled around at the end of the scent trail. When the men called them back across, the dogs gathered around the urine-soaked ground, sniffing, whining.

"I smell piss. Don't you smell it?" one of the men said.

"Yeah," the other replied. "I guess we scared her so bad, she pissed her pants. Some people are so stupid, they don't know whether to piss or go blind."

"Let's go on back. From the way the dogs are acting, looks like we run Sookey Shanks plum out of the county."

"Isn't that what we were supposed to do?"

"You got that right. Let's go home."

Cracking the window open did little to prevent the glass on Sheriff Myron Turner's Model A from fogging. All it did was let the steady rain wet his already wrinkled khakis. He stretched his long legs, sore from their cramped space under the steering wheel. Parked across the street from the Fortune County courthouse, he had a view of most of the deserted square, as well as the two-lane street into and out of town. The only paved road across the county split Millersville in the middle and snaked its way north through the mountains to the Tennessee border and south to Atlanta.

Before the rain started, Sheriff Turner positioned himself to observe the torch-bearing crowd that gathered in front of the courthouse. One of the men recounted the claim of rape of a young woman by "a black Lucifer." The same speaker fueled the crowd's courage with an exhortation to "cast the demons from our midst."

The sole purpose of Turner's presence on the square was to stop any random acts of violence that might damage the white-owned homes or businesses of Fortune County. Ensuring that the crowd's energy was directed against the coloreds, was doing the job he, and his father before him, had been elected to do. A sudden squall dampened the frenzy of the throng and extinguished most of the torches. He breathed easier when the rain came. Whatever happened that night would be controllable.

He had heard talk around town earlier in the week about removing the black menace by running all the coloreds out of Millersville. The idea escalated to driving them completely out of the county. Though against that notion, Turner had not openly opposed it. The county's black population provided him with an instant source of suspects to pin crimes on. In some cases, it gave him a choice of people to accuse when he needed to cover for a crony, or for someone who could be of use in the future. Besides, he received a good cut of their moonshine purchases. He could not afford to sit back and let some overzealous citizens deplete a valuable resource. He called upon the Baxley brothers to focus the crowd's anger more narrowly; to single out one black to become the object of the crowd's wrath. "Give them Sookey Shanks," he said.

"It's the uppity coloreds that's got to go," Carter Baxley yelled.

"Yeah. Ones who think they're as good as whites," Carter's brother Caleb chimed in.

Sheriff Turner sensed a quieting of the crowd. Carter Baxley wasted no time reminding those assembled that Sookey Shanks was living in a white woman's house on Pea Ridge, had nursed and raised a white child by herself for the last five years, and was otherwise forgetting her place.

"It's that kind of example," Carter shouted, "that would make a black man think he could have his way with our women!"

The crowd abandoned the courthouse square with the Baxley brothers in the lead and headed, not toward Turnip Town where most of Millersville's blacks lived, but toward Pea Ridge instead. Turner smiled as the crowd departed.

Pea Ridge, a cluster of ramshackle shotgun shacks set precariously on the side of an eroded slope west of town, had been home to innumerable generations of poor whites. Even though her family worked a small farm in the northern part of the county, Sookey Shanks had lived for the past five years in Pea Ridge in the home of Cora Mae Briggs.

Cora Mae had been a favorite pastime of Sheriff Turner's before she grew up and headed off to Atlanta. She returned pregnant soon thereafter. He had not seen Cora Mae since Sookey acted as a midwife in the delivery of her son, Billy, five years before. Cora Mae headed back to her pimp in Atlanta as soon as she could, leaving Sookey to nurse and raise the boy. Turner did not mind Sookey's raising the boy. But staying on in a white woman's house, treating it and Billy Briggs as if they were her own, now that stuck in his craw. The crowd would take care of that.

The rain had stopped when Sookey emerged from the protection of the chestnut. Occasional droplets fell from the trees and splattered on nearby rhododendron. The only other sound left in the night was water sloshing down the rock-strewn creek. She shook from the cold of the mountain stream. Billy shivered. She pulled him closer to her breast.

"There now, Punkin. Sookey will get you warm."

She needed to find a place to hole up until daylight to conserve their body heat. She abandoned the creek and walked sideways around the steep slope. In her weakened condition, moving higher up the mountain was out of the question. The storm clouds cleared the moonless sky, leaving a canopy of stars behind. Sookey's eyes adjusted to the dim light, and she studied the prominent features in the dark woods.

Rejecting several possible shelters, she chose a fallen tree trunk lying against an outcrop of rocks. Its natural cover should keep them warm and dry. Sookey poked a stick into the darkness of the small cubbyhole to roust any sleeping critters. A faint rustle sounded in the vegetation under the tree trunk. Satisfied, she crawled in and moved as far to the rear as possible. She lay on her side on a bed of dry leaves, her back to the entrance, and pulled the boy tight to her body. The leaves beneath her felt warm.

"We can thank Mr. Rabbit tomorrow, Punkin, for the use of his bed tonight."

The silent boy had stopped shivering. He was asleep. Sookey smoothed his hair, kissed his cheek, and closed her eyes.

The Baxley brothers' truck circled the empty courthouse with its horn blowing. Men in the bed fired guns into the night air. The truck passed Myron Turner, blinking its lights twice.

He left the square and took the north road out of town, headed for the home of Zed and Flossie Rudeseal, and their teenage daughter, Nadine. Tuner had watched Nadine grow from a dirty-faced twig of a girl to a full-bodied young thing who didn't know what to do with her newfound breasts but show them off.

When Turner pulled into the Rudeseal's grassless yard, he found all three sitting in the dark on the front porch, Zed sprawled in a swing, Flossie crammed into a rocker, and Nadine on the porch floor with her bare feet dangling over the edge.

"Evening, Sheriff," Zed said.

Turner nodded at him. "Zed." He touched the brim of his tan Stetson. "Flossie."

"What brings you out so late?" Zed asked.

Turner approached the porch and stood in the yard facing Nadine. "Wanted to make sure I had Nadine's story straight. You mind?"

"No. Go right ahead."

"Nadine, if I recollect what you said, a colored man grabbed you from behind while you were hanging out the wash and dragged you into the barn."

Nadine did not look up. "That's right. In my own back yard in broad daylight."

"It was just you and your mama at home?"

She nodded. "Uh huh."

"Did you holler for her?"

Nadine, her eyes still hidden, picked at her elbow. "I couldn't. He had his hand over my mouth."

Turner rubbed his angular jaw. "Can you tell me what he looked like?"

Nadine's head jerked up, her dark hair washing across her face. She smoothed it away. "Like I said in town, he was real big and real black."

"And that's all you can say?"

"That's all."

Turner looked toward the porch. "Flossie, what can you tell me?"

Flossie repositioned her chubby body in the rocker and leaned forward. "Well, she left some pillow cases that needed drying, and I went looking for her, when she didn't answer me. I found her half-naked in the barn, crying."

"Did you see anyone?" Turner asked.

"No, but I heard a truck start up down the road and drive off that way." She pointed.

Zed straightened his broad shoulders and cleared his throat. "Flossie, you and Nadine go on inside and go to bed. I want to talk some more to the sheriff."

As the door closed behind them, Zed rose from the swing and tapped the ashes from his pipe on one of the porch posts. He turned toward the sheriff. "Myron, we've known each other a long time."

Turner nodded.

"I can tell by the look on your face that you don't believe Nadine."

Turner grimaced and shrugged. "Her description would fit any colored man in the county, Zed."

"That's probably why you haven't caught that boy yet. And ain't going to, so long as you're thinking that way."

The sheriff propped a foot on one of the porch steps. "She's got the whole county riled up against the Negroes. They're so upset, they ran the Shanks girl off tonight."

"Should've run 'em all off." Zed's thin lips set into a grim line. "That's a small price to pay for what they did to my Nadine."

Turner nodded. "But that don't help us catch the one that did it. Flossie said she heard a truck drive off from down the road apiece. It was headed away from the highway. There's not a colored man in the county that owns a truck, and only a few drive them for someone else. All those trucks are accounted for when it happened."

Zed returned to the swing, refilled and lit his pipe in silence, and flicked the glowing match out into the dark yard. "Maybe he was up here from Atlanta to buy shine or just stir up trouble."

Turner shook his head as he mounted the porch. "He would've stood out like a sore thumb, driving through town in broad daylight. Besides, y'all are so far off the main road, anyone coming this way would pretty much have to be coming to see you, or else be awfully lost." He sat in the rocker Flossie had vacated. "You got a few of your CCC fellas driving around the mountains in trucks. Any of them been trying to court Nadine?"

Zed rose abruptly, his huge frame towering over the sheriff. "Your welcome is wearing a might thin, Myron. I think it's time you left. We all know the coloreds should never have been let up here to start with. If you won't find the one who done it, I'll see to it they're all run off."

"Now, Zed,"

"Don't 'Now, Zed' me. It's just a few months to election. Folks won't take too kindly to your standing in the way."

Sheriff Turner excused himself and departed. Zed's comment about the coming election came as no surprise. Turner's concern about the election had kept him in the background when local tensions started rising earlier in the week. The Turners had always been successful politicians. They got that way by going with the flow.

Talk of ridding the county of all Negroes started slowly. Sheriff Turner heard it first whispered over coffee at Thelma's Café. Then folks mentioned it openly in his presence around the soda-cracker barrel at the dry goods store. They hotly discussed it at Elmer Duckett's barbershop and out on the sidewalk in front of the Roxy Theater. He learned that it had become an open topic at most supper tables and dominated all conversation at the Wednesday-night prayer meeting at Mt. Bethel Baptist Church. By Saturday, when everyone came into Millersville to shop and socialize, the town was at a flashpoint, needing only a spark.

It came dressed in the clothes of Zed Rudeseal.

As Zed strode along the sidewalk, people in his path parted. Some whispered as he passed. Others patted him on the arms and back. Mostly, they followed. A line two and three abreast formed and trailed him en masse to the courthouse steps. From there, he delivered a jerky and disorganized speech about how Nadine would never be the same, and how womenfolk would never be safe "unless every drop of the blood of Ham is purged from Fortune County."

Sheriff Turner stood off to one side, neither protesting nor approving Zed's ominous suggestion for the treatment of the colored population of Fortune County.

The flame lit, Zed Rudeseal left his granite dais to raucous cheers and back-slapping agreement.

The crowd crept in the direction of Turnip Town, with Zed out in front. Myron Turner watched alone from the courthouse steps, no longer concerned for the security of white-owned property, but only for the remnants of his own popularity.

CHAPTER 2

▼

When Sookey opened her eyes, long fingers of morning light crept across the forest floor. They eased their way to the den where she and Billy lay. Her eyes were the only things that didn't hurt when she moved. Morning had brought a new awareness of the wounds that the excitement and cold water of the night before had masked. Searing pain accompanied any movement of her shoulder, rendering her left arm almost useless.

She crawled out into the light, careful not to wake Billy. He would be hungry when he woke, but they needed a poultice more than food. She picked out several distinguishing landmarks to locate the den when she returned, then moved silently through the woods in search of something to soothe their wounds.

What little medicine that was available to treat such injuries was reserved for white folks. Her family used various remedies over the years, from plants to salt. Whenever necessary, Grandma Shanks made a poultice from a mixture of wild mustard, dumb plant, lichen, or north-side tree moss. Sookey recognized many plants and herbs and knew their qualities as servants of both man and beast. Mustard naturally heated up and reduced internal swelling. The juice of the dumb plant applied to a rash or open cut numbed the pain. Salt dried up a weeping wound, and along with lichen and tree moss kept down festering. Next to blood loss, festering was the biggest killer of injured folks. To her and to those who came before her, everything had a place; everything had a purpose.

As Sookey slipped through the forest, she made note of the edible plants, but focused on the healers. She knew of a deer lick, but it was too far. Mustard was easy to find. She spied the yellow flowers of several plants right away. Fallen and rotted logs provided an ample supply of fresh lichen.

Returning to the den, she stopped beside the rocky outcrop and crushed mustard leaves and lichen with a rock. After soaking the mixture in a small puddle, she crawled inside and applied the soggy mass to each side of Billy's shoulder. She held it in place with a few large leaves crammed into his shirt, then did the same to herself. He whimpered once or twice. She stroked his forehead and spoke softly to him.

Drained, Sookey returned to sleep, taking Billy with her.

Time marched by the den without stopping to wake Sookey and Billy. The hour of day or night played no role in their recovery. Only its passage did. Sookey would wake from time to time and notice light or dark outside. She placed her hand under Billy's nostrils, then felt his forehead. Satisfied, she rejoined him in sleep. Her body's demand for rest overpowered any craving for food or water.

When she awoke for good, she had no idea what day it was. Her dry lips and the gnawing in her gut said they had been holed up several days, but she felt strong and refreshed. Pain had left her body, settling only in her left shoulder. She checked Billy's wounds. They were closed, and the flesh around them red, but not angry. She applied a new poultice from what was left, using the last bit for herself.

Billy stirred when she crawled out into the midday sun. "Stay here," she said. "I'll find us some water and something to chew on. You all right?"

Billy nodded and smiled. She smiled back. He would stay put, hidden from danger like a wild kitten, while she foraged.

She shook her head. Before she could finish grieving over the child she had miscarried and the man who deserted her, this little boy was thrust upon her by a white woman. Maybe she should have walked away when she found herself alone with him, his mama gone God knew where. But who would have taken him in? When Cora Mae disappeared, Sookey was full of milk and had no other way to feed the baby. The whites on Pea Ridge made it plain they had no room for a whore's child, especially one being suckled by a colored woman. They told her so and slammed their doors in her face. It took only one trip to her home in the mountains to learn her family felt the same way.

"A white child in our house would be worse than a curse on us, Sookey," her father said, a deep frown joining his bushy eyebrows. "I don't care what his mama might've wanted you to do, she'll turn on you sooner or later. You got to stir whites with a long-handled spoon, or you'll be burnt for sure. And never forget that a lot of cute little white kids grow up to be mean white folks."

Her brother Noah was of the same mind. "You'd best bash its head on a rock," he said. "But if you're going to keep it, keep it at its own house. It's got a right to be there. It ain't got no right to be here."

Sookey's mother embraced her. "Do what you have to, child, until his mama comes back."

Sookey returned to Pea Ridge to live in Cora Mae's house, caring for Billy Briggs. She took in washing and ironing for the whites in Millersville, carting it and Billy back and forth in an old pull wagon she found and put back together. Sookey and Billy became a familiar sight on the road between Pea Ridge and town. She kept a few laying hens in a coop in the backyard and wandered the mountains in search of wild edibles. Adept at trapping small game, she took fish from the many mountain streams, as well. Strong, resourceful, and staunchly independent, she thought she got along with the whites on Pea Ridge, and was stunned when a screaming white mob drove her and Billy from their house and into the mountains.

Sookey now returned to the places where she had spotted edibles while tending their wounds. She filled the front of her dress with enough summer berries and watercress to satisfy their hunger. She brought back water in a discarded whiskey bottle.

She called Billy outside, and they sat atop the log and devoured their food. When Billy finished eating, he looked up. "Where we going now, Sookey?"

"Can't go back home right now. Something has riled up those folks against me. We best stay in the mountains for a spell. We'll be safe up here." She smiled. "Maybe we can find Mr. Rabbit and thank him proper by inviting him to dinner."

Billy grinned, took Sookey's hand, and they headed up the mountain.

Beaulah Jackson watched from her window as the good citizens of Millersville streamed through the dirt streets of Turnip Town, screaming epithets. Violence simmered in the crowd's agitation. Like the other residents of Turnip Town, she hid in her home, vulnerable and exposed. Beaulah was not caught by surprise. She had heard the talk. She felt the slights and digs that preceded. What happened to Sookey Shanks was only a prelude.

Shattering glass punctuated the night. Beaulah heard no cry of resistance or voice of protest from behind the flimsy walls and doors. Only silence—the deafening silence of submission. The residents of Turnip Town stayed out of sight. People in the crowd cast insults only at dark houses, not at objects of their wrath. The one-sided argument collapsed, when no one emerged to take issue.

The emotion of the crowd waned. A warm summer rain fell, gently at first, then harder. The streets emptied as the crowd scurried for cover.

The residents of Turnip Town slipped out of hiding to the drumming of rain on tin roofs. One by one, windows came alive with the soft glow of coal-oil lamps.

Beaulah Jackson turned from her window and struck a match against the side of a wooden table that dominated the front room of her two-room shack. The blaze of light reflected in the eyes of her daughter and granddaughter standing in the shadows. Beaulah lit the wick of a lamp in the center of the table and fitted the lamp chimney.

Her daughter rushed to the window. "Lord be praised for the rain," she whispered. She hid her face in her hands and cried softly.

The granddaughter reached for Beaulah's hand. "Did God come to save us, Grandma?"

Beaulah hesitated, studying the droplets coursing down the windowpanes. "No, child. He just come to cry with us."

CHAPTER 3

▼

At the top of the mountain, Sookey headed northeast along the tree-lined ridge. The best way to move on foot in the terrain of North Georgia was to keep climbing to a minimum, to follow the path of least resistance by walking the ridgeline. The mountains of the Blue Ridge, oriented northeast and southwest, afforded travel in four general directions. The traveler sometimes had to go out of the way a few miles, then descend and climb as necessary to get to a ridge going in a different direction.

She could follow the ridge about eight miles before reaching Wild Hog Gap. There she would have to descend. A forest-fire lookout tower recently built by the CCC for the new Chattahoochee National Forest stood on the near side of the gap. Perhaps she and Billy could get something to eat from the ranger there. Maybe they could get clean, white cloth for bandages, too. Movement made the poultices fall apart.

The cawing of crows got her attention. Black specks dotted the foliage of the trees to her left. Five or six fluttered in a thicket down a shallow ravine. She sat Billy on a rock and went to investigate.

The sentinel crow sounded the alarm as soon as she started down the slope. The others joined in the call and took flight. Sookey spotted muscadine vines growing in the thicket. She turned toward Billy and laughed. "Remember to keep your eyes out for crows if you want to find something to eat. And keep your ears tuned to them if you want to know when danger's afoot. It takes some kind of quiet to sneak up on a bunch of old crows, the way they look out for each other."

As suspected, the crows had been gorging themselves on muscadines growing in large clusters under the vines. Deep purple skins signaled their ripeness.

Sookey's mouth watered. She bit into a plump one and squeezed its pulp into her mouth, savoring its sweetness. She filled the front of her dress as if it were an apron and returned to Billy on the ridge.

"We can enjoy a few of these and save the rest for later," she said. "We'll even have enough left to trade." She gave a handful to Billy. "Now don't go spittin' out the seeds. They're good for you."

When Billy finished, Sookey took him by the hand and they continued. After a few miles, the pair emerged onto a bald spot on the ridge. Solid rock underfoot prevented the growth of anything but a few stunted bushes. The sun dipped on the horizon to the southwest. Only a few more hours of daylight remained. She wanted to reach the tower before dark. Whoever stood watch there would probably depart for the night. Maybe the ranger would not turn them away or cause them harm.

As Sookey and Billy crossed the bald, a clear view opened in several directions. As far as they could see, humpbacked mountains languished in a bluish haze. A solitary hawk hung suspended over a rock-strewn peak in the distance. Its shrill cry pierced the still mountain air. Sookey slowed to look, but did not stop. She took a deep breath.

Billy pulled on her hand. "Are we up very high, Sookey?"

A smile played with the corners of her mouth. "We're on the top of the world, Punkin."

They crossed the bald and reentered the forest. A few miles up the trail, Sookey spied the legs of the tower through the trees. An unsaddled horse tethered a short distance from the tower snorted as Sookey and Billy approached.

A uniformed man descended a section of the zigzag stairs. He stopped on a platform about halfway down when he spotted them. "What are you folks doing way out here?" he asked.

Sookey briefly explained their dilemma, then offered to trade fresh muscadines for meat or bread. He studied the two for a moment. "Come on up to the lookout. I've got a tin of corned beef and some cold biscuits."

"That'll be just fine," Sookey said.

"I'm Roger Bentley with the Forest Service. What do you two go by?"

"I'm Sookey Shanks. This here's Billy Briggs. Say 'hello' to the ranger, Billy."

"Hello," he said softly.

Sookey and Billy started up the stairs behind the ranger. He opened a trap door in the floor of the walkway around the lookout and held it for them as they climbed through. Once inside, the ranger studied Billy. Poultice leaves protruded from the neck of Billy's shirt. Bentley knelt down, opened the top of Billy's shirt, and bent the leaves away from his shoulder.

"My God. This boy's been shot."

"We both been." Sookey pulled the top of her dress aside.

"Dear Lord. Who did this?"

"The same folks who ran us out of Millersville."

"I'd heard there'd been trouble in town because of that rape. I didn't know anything about it, though." Bentley turned toward a cabinet and removed a small first-aid kit. "Don't have anything to treat gunshot. I can bandage you up, and that's about it. What's that stuff you've put on yourselves?"

Sookey removed Billy's shirt. "It's a poultice. I wish you wouldn't take it off of him. Just put the bandage over it."

Bentley peeled back a portion of the mustard leaf mixture and examined Billy's wound. "You're very lucky, little fellow. I don't see any infection. I guess this mess your nanny put on you won't harm you none." He used a roll of gauze to wrap Billy's shoulder, then did the same to Sookey. "There. That should hold you both for a while."

Sookey helped Billy put on his shirt and button it, while Bentley returned the first-aid kit to the cabinet. "We thank you," she said.

Bentley pulled a tin of beef off a shelf and rummaged through a brown paper bag. He dropped the tin in the bag and handed it to Sookey. "There's some biscuits in the bag. No need to trade for this."

"Got to," Sookey said. "Can't carry these muscadines and the meat and biscuits too. I'll just leave them on the counter for you to enjoy tomorrow. They're real sweet."

Bentley thanked her and looked out the west side windows toward the setting sun. "I'm headed down to Millersville by way of Wildcat Mountain. If you're up to traveling, my horse can carry me and the boy, and you can walk and hold on to a stirrup strap. We got a good hour before dark, and the horse knows the way after that."

Sookey glanced sideways and cleared her throat. "I...I wasn't meaning to go back to Millersville. I—"

Bentley shook his close-cropped head. "You can go on, if you want, but I'm taking the boy to be looked at by a doctor and report your gunshot wounds to Sheriff Turner." Bentley lifted Billy and moved outside to the trapdoor. "You coming?"

Sookey nodded and followed. "You're new to Millersville, aren't you?"

"Yeah. How'd you know?"

"Because the only doctor in the county is Doc Whitley, and he won't be sober when you get there. He loves his conversation-juice too much."

Bentley laughed and started down the stairs.

"Of course, I got no problem with Doc Whitley looking at Billy, sober or no," Sookey said. She followed him down the stairs. "But complaining to the Sheriff might just stir up more trouble for me and Billy. The same kind of trouble that got us run off in the first place."

Bentley reached the bottom and stepped toward his horse. "How so?" he said.

Sookey stayed close behind and held Billy while Bentley saddled up. "There was a whole crowd of folks that came to our house, raising sand and screaming at us. We took off out the back, and they chased us what seemed like forever, hollering and shootin'. The sheriff's not going to know who shot us, but the folks who did it will know, and may shoot us again. No, Sir. I just as soon see Doc Whitley and be on our way, if you don't mind. We don't need more trouble."

Bentley mounted and reached for Billy, placing him in the rear astride the saddlebags. "We'll deal with that in Millersville, but right now we've got to get moving." He glanced over his shoulder. "Hold on tight when we go up and down. Okay?"

Billy's blue eyes could not have gotten any wider. He nodded. "Okay," he whispered and grabbed Bentley around the waist.

Bentley grinned and clicked his tongue. The horse plodded down the trail, with Sookey alongside.

Carter Baxley pulled his flatbed off to the side of the dirt road and killed the engine. He stretched his arms and broad shoulders and ran a hand through his tousled brown hair. "That damn generator must've gone out again," he said. "And there's not enough juice in the battery to keep the lights on much longer. It'd be best to stop right here and save enough battery to start her up when the generator's fixed."

Carter unlimbered his lanky frame and stepped out of the cab. "I'll check the load," he said. He reached back and retrieved a double-barreled shotgun.

"I'll come with you," Caleb said. He climbed halfway down from the passenger's side, then jumped. Though bearing a facial resemblance, he lacked his brother's height and muscular build.

A light brown tarp covered a load of boxes on the front half of the truck bed. A rope secured the tarp to the sides. The brothers moved down opposite sides, tugging on the lashings.

"Looks okay over here," Caleb said.

"Same here," Carter replied.

They returned to the cab. Carter placed the butt of the shotgun on the floor-board between him and Caleb and leaned the barrel against the seat. He pulled a can of Prince Albert from his shirt pocket and rolled a cigarette. "Want one?" He offered the fixings to Caleb.

"Naw."

Carter lit up and took a deep drag. "One of us has to hoof it into town, and one of us has to stay with the load. I'll keep the shotgun here with me."

"Why do you always get the cushy jobs?" Caleb asked.

"Because I'm the oldest and the smartest. That's why. Now start walking."

Before Caleb could move, Carter grabbed his arm. "Wait a minute. Do you see that?"

"What?"

Carter pointed across the road and up into the woods. A faint light flickered through the thick trees.

"Looks like a campfire," Caleb said.

"Yeah. I wonder who'd be camping up here." Carter picked up the shotgun and eased out of the cab.

Caleb climbed out on his side. "Could be coon hunters."

"We'd have heard the dogs by now. No, it's someone else. We can't let this load sit here with someone we don't know up in these woods. Come on."

The two slipped through the trees toward the fire. The pungent smell of onions and potatoes frying in bacon grease hung in the air. A lone figure squatted close to the fire, his slender back to them. As they neared, Carter could make out a shirtless black male in overalls. He was humming.

"Well, I'll be," Carter murmured. "Aren't we close to the Rudeseal place?"

"Yeah," Caleb whispered. "It's about five miles from here."

"Come on," Carter said. He trotted into the clearing, the shotgun raised waist high. He growled at the camper, "Hold it right there."

The man jerked to his feet, stumbled forward, and sent a small pan tumbling into the fire. The grease sizzled. A burst of flames ignited one leg of the man's overalls. He screamed and beat his leg with his hands. He jumped backward away from the fire and whirled around in Carter's direction.

"Hold it, I said," Carter yelled, as the frantic man continued to beat at his burning pant leg, his gyrations bringing him closer to Carter.

The report blasted. The man's chest exploded from a tight pattern of dou-ble-ought buckshot. The man's body propelled backward and landed across the fire.

Who shot the man? Carter looked around to see who had entered the clearing behind him. All he saw was a wide-eyed Caleb, his mouth gaping open, trying to form words but uttering only guttural noises. A wisp of smoke rose lazily from one barrel of the shotgun in Carter's hands. Only then did he realize what he'd done.

"Oh, sweet Jesus." Caleb rushed forward and rolled the dead man's body out of the fire and into the dirt, where it lay smoldering. "What're we gunna do now, Carter? What on earth we gunna do?"

Carter propped the shotgun against a nearby tree and sat on a log close to the body. "Let me think." He wiped sweat from his forehead with one finger and flicked it into the dirt at his feet. After a moment, he looked over at Caleb, who stood gawking at the smoking black corpse. "You know this was the one that raped Nadine, don't you?"

Caleb's curly head snapped around. "No. How would I know that?"

"Because he confessed to us when we caught him hiding out here in the woods. Then when he tried to get away, we shot him." Carter smiled.

Caleb backed away. "But you shot him flat in the chest, Carter."

"Okay. He was charging us, and I had no choice. Either way, we just killed ourselves a guilty colored man. Myron won't care, and we'll be heroes."

Caleb sat down beside his brother. He stared into the dirt and slowly shook his head. "Don't know. I just don't know."

Carter struck Caleb's shoulder hard with his elbow. "Get hold of yourself. Don't leave me hanging. I didn't gun that fella down on purpose. It was an accident. But I'd just as soon folks not know that. You need to back me up on this."

"I will. You know I will."

"Good. Now get to town and find another truck. We can't talk about this killing to anyone but Myron, until we transfer that load of shine and haul it out of here."

Caleb struck out on foot for Millersville. Carter settled back and rolled another cigarette.

Sookey was pleased that the three of them had made it to the old logging road along Bear Den Creek without incident. Having a surefooted horse in the mountains after dark was a pleasure.

On the way down Wildcat Mountain, Billy's grip on Bentley loosened. Sookey presumed the little boy was drifting off to sleep. She helped move him up front where Bentley could hold him in the saddle. Sookey moved to the other side of the horse to even the strain. Now that they were on the logging road, the rest of the trip would be easy.

As the trio plodded down the old road, Sookey was jolted by what sounded like a shotgun blast echoing in the mountains. Someone must be hunting. A truck sat off the roadside ahead. Firelight flickered in the woods.

"I'd better investigate," Bentley said. "Whatever's going on is being done on Forest Service land." Bentley guided his horse into the woods. He stopped and handed a sleeping Billy to Sookey. "Y'all stay quiet and out of sight. I need to see what's happening up there." He nudged the horse back onto the dirt road and approached the truck from the rear.

*   *   *   *

Carter never heard the mountain horse until it entered the clearing behind him. He whirled around to face a mounted ranger looming high overhead.

"That load of shine out there is a federal crime. Consider yourself under arrest," the ranger announced.

His surprise subsiding, Carter studied the ranger momentarily and saw no weapon on him or on his horse. Carter's shotgun was only three feet away, leaning against a tree. He doubted the ranger could see it. If alerted, the ranger could maneuver his horse between Carter and the tree and cut him off from his gun. Carter had to plan his move.

"At least you won't be taking that one over there to jail," Carter said, motioning with his head.

The ranger turned his head toward the prone figure lying by the fire. "Is he dead?"

"As a doornail."

The ranger's eyes widened as he stared at the mutilated body. When the man's jaw dropped, Carter sprang for the gun and brought it up toward the ranger's face.

The ranger straightened in the saddle and raised his hands. "I'm not armed," he said. His voice trembled.

"That was your first mistake. Do I know you?"

"I'm Roger Bentley. I moved over a few months ago from Dahlonega to work in this district. Please don't kill me. I have a wife and kids."

"So do I." Carter pulled the trigger.

The blast knocked Bentley from the saddle. His wife was widowed before his limp body slammed into the dirt. The horse reared, then bolted, disappearing into the woods.

When Caleb arrived later with another truck, Carter met him out on the road. He didn't say anything about killing Bentley. He simply helped Caleb transfer the boxes of moonshine-filled fruit jars and cover them.

As he tied the last knot, Carter said, "Where'd you get the truck?"

"From Sheriff Turner. It was his daddy's."

"Did you tell him about us catching and killing that raper?"

"Yeah. But I don't think he believed me. He's on his way up here."

The two of them walked toward the front of the truck. "Well," Carter drawled, "he's going to have a harder time believing that dead boy back there killed a forest ranger before we got him."

Caleb froze. "What?"

"Yeah," Carter continued. "I found a ranger's body over in the bushes right after you left. I dragged him into the clearing, but wasn't nothing I could do for him. That boy had a shotgun in his bedroll. He would've gotten us, if we hadn't gotten him. So, you see? We did the right thing by killing him when we had the chance. Why don't you start the truck and get that load to the house. I'll handle the sheriff when he gets here."

Caleb crawled into the cab. "This is terrible."

"Yeah, I know it."

The big eight-cylinder engine roared to life, and the truck moved out into the night. Carter watched the taillights disappear down the narrow dirt road.

Sookey recoiled at the roar of the shotgun blast. She shivered, but not from the chill of the night air. She had heard such a blast up close days before and escaped it. This time she might not be so lucky. A sense of foreboding overcame the chill. Forest rangers were new to the mountains of North Georgia. Moonshiners didn't cotton to outsiders and had absolutely no use for government men. Shiners were a dangerous lot who came to the mountains armed. Ranger Bentley had no gun.

Sookey sat in the dark and waited, straining to hear anything that would tell her what was happening. The woods around her were strangely silent. Normal night sounds were missing, seemingly stifled by the blast. Billy slept soundly in her arms. Unless Bently had run into bad trouble, he should have returned by now.

After a while, the clatter of a truck arriving and departing shattered the night's stillness, but Sookey couldn't see anything from her hiding place. Unwilling to wait and worry any longer, she propped Billy against the base of a large gum and moved cautiously through the woods to the edge of the tree line. The outline of the truck still sat off the side of the road. The dim light of a small campfire shone through the woods on the other side. She heard no voices.

Her instinct was to grab Billy and disappear into the night, to flee back into the mountains and make her way north to her family's farm. That way, she would avoid knowing what was happening in the small clearing up ahead, if it was bad. She would avoid having to go back into town, if it was not. Her intense curiosity overcame her instinct.

Sookey crept across the road and entered the woods. Inching toward the clearing, she kept the fire in sight to avoid walking into a tree. She crawled the last fifty feet on hands and knees. A sickening smell of something burned filled her nostrils. It reminded her of the time her daddy cauterized a bad cut on her brother's leg with a red-hot poker.

When Sookey got as close as she dared, she raised her head and peered through a low bush. Carter Baxley sat on a log on the opposite side of the clearing, nonchalantly smoking. He held the barrels of a shotgun in his left hand, its butt resting in the dirt beside his foot.

A jolt coursed through her. Two bodies lay in front of him, one face down, the other face up. The ranger's green uniform glowed in the firelight. Bentley. The dirt was stained around his misshapen head. He was dead. Run! But she mustn't be detected. Running would only alert Carter Baxley, and the race she had won once would start anew. No, stay calm. She remained still.

Is that steam rising from the body of the black man lying near the fire? No. His overalls and parts of his body have been badly burned and are still smoldering. She got another jolt when she recognized him. Bailey Turnage, the son of an old friend, had been a slow child who never fit in. But he grew up at home in the wild, and was quite happy there. He was a gentle spirit, known to roam the mountains. He and Sookey had often traded information on medicinal roots and herbs and the best places to find them. Now, no remedy in the world could help poor Bailey. His dancing eyes and flashing smile were forever still.

Sookey closed her eyes and muttered a hasty prayer for the souls and families of the two dead men. She then asked for safe passage for herself and Billy. The chatter of an automobile engine interrupted her prayer. Carter stood and walked out of the clearing.

She heard voices, but could not discern what they were saying. Carter returned to the clearing, accompanied by Sheriff Myron Turner. She listened in awe as Carter told the sheriff that Bailey Turnage had confessed to the rape of Nadine Rudeseal, and that Carter had shot Bailey when he attacked him and his brother, Caleb. Her awe quickly turned to disbelief when Carter told the sheriff of finding the ranger dead at the hands of Bailey.

The sheriff removed his hat and smoothed his sandy hair before putting it back on. "I'm going to report what you say happened, Carter. But you know the feds are going to come up here and check it out. They won't care about that colored boy over there, but you don't get a free bite on a ranger. They'll be asking a lot of questions. You up to it?"

Carter nodded and mopped the perspiration from his forehead. "There's not much to it. It happened the way I said. But just remember, half that load is yours, and I'm sure you don't want anyone going to jail over all this."

Turner's mouth formed a straight thin line as he looked Carter in the eyes. He shrugged and walked over to the dead ranger and rolled him over with his foot. "I'll take his body down to Doc Whitley. You can throw the boy and his things on the back of your truck and bring him in when it's fixed. In the meantime, get some mules and a float up here and get rid of those truck tracks on the road north of here. We don't want the feds following them up to Raven Cliffs."

Turner picked up the ranger's body and started toward his car. After a few steps, he stopped and turned around. "If that boy's shotgun hasn't been fired in the last year or so, I strongly suggest you do it before it gets to town."

Carter's jaw dropped. He nodded.

CHAPTER 4

▼

Myron Turner pushed away from his untouched breakfast at Thelma's. Acid rose in his throat as he walked to his office in the courthouse. He sat hunched over his desk, staring at a full cup of coffee grown cold. He struggled to keep down just one sip. A twinge shot through his stomach as he recalled the bodies of Bailey Turnage and Roger Bentley. Moonshining was a victimless crime and a respected mountain tradition. Killing was never part of it. Chasing folks off with guns, yes, but never killing. In all Myron's years as a lawman, he never killed a man. Didn't think he could, unless in mortal danger.

He paid lip service to Carter's story and repeated it in his report of the events of that evening, but the truth gnawed at his gut. Was the price of silence worth it?

As Turner suspected, the account of the killings electrified Fortune County. Many agreed that swift justice had been meted out, but Turner knew the whites were far from satisfied. While the U.S. Forest Service was viewed as an intruder in the lives of the mountain folk of North Georgia, the killing of a ranger by a colored man would not be tolerated.

Turner abandoned his office for the front of the courthouse and leaned against a column. Lighting one cigarette after another, he watched white men and women arrive in Millersville in droves just hours behind the news. Hundreds milled in downtown streets and on the courthouse square. People talked in agitated tones. All they needed was a leader. Merchants quick to make a sale sent young boys through the crowd, hawking sandwiches, lemonade, and soft drinks.

The continuous blaring of a truck horn quieted the multitude. Heads turned to the north road. Carter Baxley's flatbed hove into view, its horn blasting the still air. When it turned to circle the courthouse, Turner saw Zed Rudeseal standing behind the cab, his fist raised. A roar went up from the crowd. As the truck neared, Zed kicked at a motionless black figure lying on the rear of the bed. The body of Bailey Turnage, a rope tied around his neck, fell to the pavement and was dragged around the square. The crowd cheered and clapped, some giggling at the flailing of Bailey's arms and legs as his body bounced along behind the truck.

The cheering of the crowd subsided after several turns around the courthouse. The gruesome dance of Bailey Turnage had ended, and the dragging of an unrecognizable piece of meat commenced. They grew strangely silent. Some continued to watch in horror, but many turned away, attempting to cover the eyes of their children.

Myron Turner stepped away from the column, raised his pistol over his head. He fired twice. The gunfire got Carter Baxley's attention, and Turner motioned for him to leave.

Zed Rudeseal leaped from the back of the slow-moving truck as it drove away. He headed for the courthouse steps. As he approached, the sheriff went back inside and watched from his office window. The crowd began to chant for Zed, who beamed as he took the sheriff's place at the top of the steps. "No longer will blacks be able to rape our women and kill our men!" he yelled.

The crowd roared its approval.

"It's time to finish what we started. Let's do it now, and do it right this time."

The crowd roared again.

"Half of you follow me to Turnip Town!" he shouted. "The rest of you spread out throughout the county. Don't let the sun set on a colored person in Fortune County tonight."

Beaulah Jackson heard them coming. She parted the flour-sack curtains in her unpainted cabin and watched the angry men burst onto the streets of Turnip Town. They smashed windows, kicked doors open, and dragged bewildered residents into the dirt streets. The men permitted the coloreds to hitch up their wagons, because wagons would get them out of town faster. Residents took only those few possessions they loaded while the horses and mules were being harnessed. The few coloreds with old cars left immediately, if they could get them started. They abandoned those that would not crank. The unfortunate owners departed on foot with what was on their backs and in their hands.

A young man appeared on the front steps of a cabin across the street from Beaulah's with a single-shot .22 rifle in hand. He stood between the crowd and his family inside. He died where he stood, shot in the head. A grinning white man kicked the young man's body into the side yard.

The shooter held up the rifle like a trophy. "Wouldn't you know? It wasn't even loaded."

Beaulah Jackson expected the mob. As soon as she heard the sad news about Bailey Turnage, she packed a small bag of clothes for her daughter and granddaughter to carry. She packed a lifetime of memories in family photos, some of her mother's lace, and enough food for several days.

When hustled out onto her porch, she had her bag in one hand and the family Bible in the other. The large book slipped from her grasp and fell to the porch floor. As she stooped to retrieve it, one of the men forcing them from their home pushed her from behind. She fell to her knees.

"Leave it be," he growled.

Beaulah ignored him and reached back for her Bible. The man stepped on her hand.

"Leave it be, I said."

Beaulah grimaced and pulled her stinging fingers from under his boot.

"What's the matter, George?" a woman said.

Beaulah looked up. Birdie Zell, the wife of Reverend Clint Zell, pastor of Mt. Bethel Baptist Church, sat in a buggy in the street.

"She's trying to take a big old family Bible with her, Ma."

"Mrs. Zell," Beaulah said. "It's me. Beaulah Jackson. I do ironing for you, and sometimes help clean up your church. Tell him to let me have my Bible. Please, Mrs. Zell."

Birdie Zell straightened her bonnet, chewed on her lip, and then clicked her tongue. "Oh, go ahead and let her have it, George. It's the Christian thing to do."

George Zell kicked the Bible. It slid across the porch floor and stopped in front of Beaulah.

"Thank you," Beaulah said softly. She grasped the big book in both hands and dusted it off. She struggled to her feet, raised her head high, and walked off her porch and into the street.

Down the Atlanta road they streamed, in small groups, as families, as individuals separated from friends and loved ones. Some rode, many walked, but all moved south. Those who tired were helped by others. When what they carried became heavier than their desire to keep it, they tossed it into a ditch beside the road.

Slowly they moved, as in a funeral procession, mourning the death of dignity.

Those who joined Beaulah south of Millersville confirmed that things were no different out in the county. Armed men in cars and trucks, they said, pulled into farmyards, firing into the air, and rousted families out into the open. The men pushed, shoved, and gun-butted black men, women, and children down dirt roads. If they had transportation of their own, the white men allowed only enough time to hitch up a cart or wagon or crank an old vehicle. They left homes filled with a lifetime of possessions, some with hot food still on the table. A few acted fast enough to free their livestock, lest they perish in their pens or end up on a white man's table. Others abandoned their farms, wondering who would milk their cows or feed their pigs and chickens. Family after family emerged from country roads and wooded trails onto the main road, headed south. They came from every direction and formed a long line, like ants on the move. The black exodus from Fortune County, Georgia had begun.

Sookey stirred from a deep sleep under a small evergreen. The low-hanging branches touched the ground, sheltering her from the heat of the noonday sun. She ached from an all-night trek with Billy asleep in her arms. They had collapsed on a bed of pine needles at the base of the tree, Billy curled up beside her. She rolled over to wake him. He was gone.

Sookey leaped to her feet and cried out for Billy. No answer. She plunged into the underbrush alongside the trail and trotted in ever-increasing circles around the tree, calling for him as she went. Her third circle took her to a creek that split two large rock formations to the east. She waded across the stream and climbed the higher formation. From there she could see the narrow creek for several hundred yards in both directions.

As she scanned the banks for any sign of movement, she heard splashing and Billy's laughter coming from downstream. Thank God. She climbed down from her perch. As she reached the bottom, she heard more laughter and the unmistakable bawling of a bear cub.

The hair rose on the back of Sookey's neck. A chill shot through her as she raced toward the sound, catapulted by fear. Black bears were plentiful in the mountains and were not dangerous unless surprised or protecting their young.

Sookey rounded a bend in the creek and spied Billy sitting in a shallow pool near a cave a few yards from the bank. He splashed water at a bear cub standing in the cave entrance. Its mother must have stashed it there while searching for food. Much like she had done Billy some days before.

When the little bear saw Sookey coming, it bawled again and darted into the cave. Sookey swooped down on Billy, snatched him out of the water, and sprinted away from the den. She never looked back. Billy offered no resistance. Sookey measured his shock by the lack of color in his round face and the way his mouth hung open. He made no sound as she carried him along, which suited her just fine. The last thing she wanted was for her own cub to start bawling and draw mama bear's attention to their proximity.

Sookey did not stop running until she reached the tree shelter where they slept the night before. She put Billy down and stayed just long enough to retrieve the paper bag of food Roger Bentley had given her. Taking Billy by the hand, Sookey resumed her trip north. If they kept a steady pace, they would reach the family farm before nightfall. She looked forward to a warm meal and a soft quilt to ward off the night chill.

"You gave old Sookey a scare back there, Punkin," she said as they walked along. "You ought not be playing with a bear cub. Its mama will come and eat you up."

"I wasn't going to hurt it."

"I know that. But, she doesn't know that. It's sorta like you and me. If I thought someone was going to hurt you, I'd eat them up, too."

They both laughed.

After traveling less than a mile, Billy spoke up. "I'm hungry."

"I figured you would be. There's a good picnic place up ahead a ways. We can stop and eat when we get there."

Soon, they arrived at a small clearing beside the trail. A table-like rock stood in the middle of the open space. Sookey emptied the bag and ripped it apart, spreading it out like a petite tablecloth on the flat surface. She placed the biscuits on it and opened the tin of beef. The biscuits were hard, but they split evenly. She made them into several sandwiches and let Billy eat his fill before she took one.

The spot Sookey chose commanded the view on the north end of the ridge they had been following. As far as she could see, the round tops of mountains folded into others just beyond them. Various hues of green covered the near ridges, but they faded to blue in the distance, until sky and mountain became one. She pointed off to the northeast. "Look just beyond that next mountain over there. See that small valley with the road coming in from the right side of it?"

Billy nodded.

"That's Shanks Cove."

"What's Shanks Cove?"

"That's where Sookey's mama lives. You'll see her tonight."

Billy's blond head snapped toward Sookey. "Is she going to eat me up?"

Sookey cackled. "No, Punkin."

A lightness came into her feet the closer she got to home. When Billy tired, she had no problem hoisting him and carrying him the rest of the way. A dull ache filled her shoulder, but her back felt strong, her legs stronger. The thought of home invigorated her. Nothing could stop her or even slow her down. Nothing.

The last half-mile of the ridge sloped downhill. The entirety of the cove lay below. A hundred acres of flat farmland formed a fat crescent oriented north and south, its two rounded prongs facing east. The cove was protected on all sides by gentle mountains. Cornfields lay on the far end, the home and farm buildings on the near end facing south. The garden grew east of the house.

Her grandfather, Ezra Shanks, had settled in the cove sixty-five years earlier, clearing and tilling the land. He tended the fields and raised a family, until he died of consumption when Sookey was just a young girl. Her father took over when her grandfather grew ill, taking care of his parents and raising his own family on the place.

Except for the five years Sookey stayed in Millersville with Billy, Shanks Cove was the only home she had ever known. Her father and brother still farmed the original fields. The home and barn of massive hand-hewn logs and the accompanying outbuildings were as sturdy now as the day Ezra Shanks erected them.

They would arrive in time for supper. She could already taste fried pork chops, collards, hot biscuits, and gravy. Nothing compared to her mama's hot biscuits, cooked on a wood-burning stove older than mama. Heading home down the high winding trail at suppertime reminded her of the many times she came that way after foraging all day in the mountains for roots and herbs. She could always tell that supper would be on the table from the wisps rising from the chimney and the smell of wood smoke in the air.

Sookey stopped abruptly.

"What is it, Sookey?"

"There's no smoke rising from the house. A cold stove at suppertime means someone's sick or hurt, or—"

"Or what, Sookey?"

"Or there's other trouble afoot."

Sookey placed Billy on the ground and stared at the quiet scene below, looking for anything that would indicate what was wrong. Being chased, shot at, and seeing the gruesome remains of Bailey and the ranger made her jumpy. Nothing looked out of the ordinary. A pile of fresh-cut firewood sat in the side yard, her father's ax imbedded in the stump used for chopping kindling. Stacks of wood cured under the eaves of the house. Chickens wandered around the barnyard, and pigs rooted at the edge of the woods. Her mother never let her chickens wander, and her father's pigs were not allowed to roam the woods. Bears would kill them for sure.

"You need to be real quiet, Punkin. Something's bad wrong at my mama's house, and I need to slip down there and find out. Hold on to my hand, and don't make a sound. Okay?"

"Okay," he whispered.

Sookey slipped down the trail, Billy in tow, keeping as close to the edge as she could to stay hidden by the foliage. As the trail flattened out on the valley floor, she stepped behind a stand of blackberry bushes and remained out of sight. She watched the farmhouse from that vantage point for about ten minutes before deciding that the farm was abandoned.

"Hello? Anyone home?" she cried. She called out again. No answer. "Mama? Daddy? Gertie? Noah?" Still no answer.

A pig up in the woods grunted and moved into view. Something stirred in the woods where the pig had been. She remained still.

"Sookey? Is that you?"

Her brother emerged from the woods above the house. He looked around. Sookey took Billy by the hand and stepped out into the open.

"Over here, Noah," she said.

Noah nodded and trotted toward her. She moved in his direction, and the two embraced in the middle of the yard.

"Where's Mama, Daddy, and Gertie?"

Noah put his head in his calloused hands. Tears started down his cheeks. "Some men came and ran them off."

"Who?" Sookey demanded.

"Three truckloads of white men with guns. They came and dragged them out of the house. Said they had to leave or they'd kill them. Said they was making all the colored folks leave Fortune County."

Sookey put her arm around him. Muscles rippled under his cotton shirt as he sobbed. She walked him to the covered porch that extended across the entire front of the house. They sat on the porch edge. Sookey waited until her brother regained his composure.

"Where were you when they came?" Sookey asked.

"I was just up there in the woods, robbing some hives for Mama. I heard the commotion and hid out. I could hear everything. Mama and them didn't let on that anyone else was here. I watched Daddy hitch up Jake to the wagon. He turned Maude and the pigs and chickens loose. They pulled out of here about seven or eight hours ago. I've been hiding ever since."

Sookey rose and extended her hand to Noah. "Come on. Let's go inside."

Noah took her hand and stood, but looked at the ground and hunched his broad shoulders. "What're we going to do, Sookey?"

Sookey started inside the house. "I'm not going to do anything but stay right here. They've already run me and Billy out of Millersville. They're not going to run me out of Grandpa's cove."

Noah followed her to the kitchen.

"Is there anything to eat around here?" she said.

"I put fresh milk and butter in the springhouse this morning. Mama and Daddy weren't able to take anything with them. There's plenty of food here. You'll just have to put something together."

Sookey lit a fire in the stove and looked for food to cook. Noah sat at the kitchen table and watched. Billy played on the floor.

She turned to Noah. "Why don't you go see if you can gather up the animals before it gets dark. I'll fix supper. And see if you can call Maude in. That old mule can't make it on her own out there. I'll be needing her, too, if I'm going to keep this old place going. Daddy knew what he was doing leaving Maude behind. The way she hated old Jake, she would have kicked him silly before they got half-way to Atlanta."

Noah headed for the door. "I'll be leaving in the morning. I guess Mama and Daddy went to stay with Aunt Phoebe down in Albany. I plan to join them down there."

"Do as you must. I'm staying put."

He turned to face Sookey. "They'll kill you if you stay."

"Let them kill away. Some things are worse than being dead. Giving up our home is one of them. A person without a place to come home to has already started dying. He just don't know it."

CHAPTER 5

▼

Sheriff Turner was dead set against running the coloreds out of the county, but if he wanted to stay in office, he knew better than to oppose it. Besides, he could do nothing about it. They were all gone. He knew it would not be long before the citizens would be fighting among themselves over the abandoned houses and land. He would have his hands full, if violence broke out.

His plan was simple. He would have the county clerk make up quitclaim deeds to all colored land, with him as grantor, and the grantee's name left blank. He would hold a public auction on the courthouse steps and sell each parcel to the highest bidder. Folks didn't have much to give, and he didn't expect to get much, but whatever he got he could keep, after giving the clerk his due. The Depression still had a stranglehold on the South, but other than depriving folks of cash in hand, it hadn't affected people in the mountains much. Most already owned their farmland outright and were not beholden to the banks. Few people were employed to start with, and those worked for local or state government. Others lived off the land or owned small businesses. Trading goods was common and food, plentiful. While he was sorry for the treatment the coloreds had received, he saw no reason to pass up an opportunity to profit from it.

Sheriff Turner advertised the auction for three weeks in a row in the county's only newspaper, *The Fortune Teller.* When auction Monday rolled around, the courthouse square filled with serious buyers and curious onlookers. A few dissenters of the auction also appeared. They were the ones who had already claimed certain abandoned property as their own by right of possession. They came to defend their claim.

Turner wasted no time getting down to business. He read the street address and name of the former colored owner for Turnip Town property and gave the acreage, location, and the former owner's name for farmland. He knocked down parcel after parcel without much discussion. Turner sold shacks for forty and fifty dollars apiece, but refused to accept bids on farms for less than seventy-five dollars. Several people in attendance purchased farms for that price, and in some instances the bid rose to one hundred dollars. Turner took the money from the highest bidder, and the clerk filled in the purchaser's name on each deed and duly recorded it in the county deed book right on the spot.

Only Dwayne Hutchins raised a fuss when the sheriff put on the block a Turnip Town house he already occupied. "What gives you the right to sell that house to me, Sheriff?" he cried out.

"Because I'm the sheriff, and because I'm the one who's going to keep anyone from taking that house away from you, if you pay for it and record the deed."

"What do I need a deed for?" Dwayne replied. "Daddy says it can be mine if I claim it as mine and live in it as mine."

"Your daddy only told you the half of it. For it to be yours by possession, you've got to stay there twenty years. You've never stayed anywhere two years, much less twenty. If you take it by deed, you claim under color of title, and you only need to live in it for seven years. You think you can make that?"

Dwayne grumbled.

"Let me put it this way, so you'll understand," Turner said. "I'm going to personally let whoever buys that house live in it. I'm going to personally escort out whoever is in there now. Do you want to buy that house, or don't you?"

Dwayne Hutchins bought the house. By midafternoon, all the houses and lands had been sold and all the deeds recorded.

Myron Turner smiled. He had avoided almost certain confrontation and potential violence and turned a profit in the process. Yesiree, 1935 had turned out to be a good year after all, especially if you were white.

*   *   *   *

Sookey wasted no time introducing Billy to life on the farm. She started his day before sunup, having him carry her morning milking to the springhouse. He fed and drew water for the animals and carried wood from the woodpile in the yard to the wood box in the kitchen, all before breakfast. After breakfast cleanup, he picked vegetables while Sookey and Maude turned under weeds in the garden. If he finished before she did, she occasionally let him ride Maude.

"The softest place is on her rump," she reminded him. "So, hold on real tight and slide back as far as you dare. Otherwise, you'll be straddling pure bone."

If Billy became restless, she sent him off to the edge of the woods to pick the last few blackberries of summer. She pointed out the white lace-like flower clusters of elderberry bushes up in the woods and told him to watch for them to turn to purple berries when the weather cooled.

"We can make good things from those berries," she said. "Jams and jellies for you, wine for me, and a good cold-and-flu tonic for the both of us."

In the evening after supper, the two of them sat on the front porch. The summer sun slipped from white to orange to red, as it lowered in the southwestern sky and disappeared behind undulating hills set against a background of ever-deepening shades of pink and gray. They shelled peas or snapped string beans for the next day's meal, until darkness squeezed the last drop of light from the cove. Because fresh vegetables were being harvested every day, Sookey made ready for winter by blanching and canning some each night before bedtime.

Before long, both of them settled into the routine of farm life. On Saturdays and Sundays, she and Billy rode Maude into the mountains to forage. Sookey was eager to pass her knowledge to Billy, just as it had been passed to her. He, too, seemed eager to learn.

"See that bush with the red stalks, dark green leaves, and purple berries." She pointed. "That there's poke. The young leaves cook up into a fine mess of greens in the spring. But it's too far along now." She turned and wagged her finger. "But don't ever eat the stalk or the berries. They're poison. My granny used to color clothes with the berry juice, and my daddy used it for writin'."

"I see some nuts on the ground. Want me to get 'em?"

"No, Punkin. Them's last year's walnuts." She motioned toward the branches hovering over them. "See the green ones clustered up there. They'll fall when it gets a little cooler. The meat of the ripe ones makes good eatin', and we can use the hull juice from the green ones to cure the ringworm, or if we want, to color our clothes brown."

"I'm getting hungry," Billy said.

Sookey nudged Maude under the canopy of a young tree with reddish brown bark. She popped a handful of tender twigs from a branch and handed one to Billy.

"That smells nice," he said.

"Chew on it."

"It's good. What is it?"

Sookey put her knees into Maude's sides. "Sweet birch. Won't fill you up, but it'll tide you over. You can eat the whole thing, and I'll make us some tea with the rest of it, when we get home. Speaking of tea, you can boil the bark of that red oak over there to stop the green-apple-quick-step." She chuckled. "Heaven forbid that you ever get it."

They spent delightful hours touching, sniffing, and tasting all manner of growing things. The only trick Sookey ever played on Billy was allowing him to taste a wild persimmon before it ripened. After he got his lips un-puckered, she was sure he would always be careful when identifying edibles in the wild.

Their first three weeks on the farm were undisturbed, but Sookey anticipated the inevitable. No matter what she was doing, she stayed alert for visitors she knew would come.

She was splitting kindling at the woodpile when engine clatter invaded Shanks Cove. The only road into the cove wound down a steep slope on the east side, proceeded through a dense hardwood thicket on the valley floor for about a mile, passed through a cleared area between the woods and the farm, and ended in the dirt farmyard in front of the house. She had plenty of time, before the vehicle arrived, to move into the house, load a shotgun, and place it just inside the door by the jamb. She wanted no trouble. She was ready, if it came calling.

A black two-door sedan with a lone driver pulled into the yard and squeaked to a stop near the porch. She moved into the door opening and stood, her hand resting on the doorframe, only inches from the barrel of the hidden gun.

An overweight, pockmarked man emerged from the car and slammed the door. "What're you doing on my land?" he demanded.

"I don't know who you are, or where you think you are, Mister, but you're standing on three generations of Shanks land."

"My name's George Zell. I bought this here land at public auction, because it was abandoned."

"Well, Mr. Zell. I'm Sookey Shanks, and I think you bought yourself a pig in a poke. There's been a Shanks standing on this land every day of the world since eighteen hundred and seventy. It's not been abandoned, and it's never been for sale."

Blood rushed to George Zell's rough face. He stepped abruptly toward the porch. "I paid a hundred dollars for this farm!" he shouted. "And I won't be cheated by a damn—"

Sookey reached inside the door and grabbed the shotgun. "By a damn what?"

George stopped dead in his tracks when he came eyeball to eyeball with the open ends of two steel barrels.

Sookey continued calmly, "I think all your hundred dollars bought you was a thousand dollars worth of trouble. Now git."

George backed slowly down the steps and to the car, eyeing the shotgun all the while. "I'll be back, and I'll bring help."

"You'd better bring Cox's Army," Sookey said down the gun barrel.

He opened the car door. "You haven't heard the last of me."

"I know. That's why I ought to shoot you right now." Sookey fired one barrel after the other into the air.

George leaped behind the wheel and backed frantically out of the yard, smashing his rear fender into a small dogwood near the edge of the road. He roared away in a cloud of dust, weaving erratically out of sight.

Sookey sat down on the steps. "He's right about stirring up more trouble," she said, sighing. "Maybe I should've gone ahead and shot him, anyway, and fed him to the bears." She laughed. "He'd a probably made them sick, though."

When the excitement of her encounter passed, acrid shotgun smoke filled her nostrils. She shivered at the thought of killing another human. It ran against the grain of everything she believed. Her best protection was that George Zell and his kind didn't know she felt that way.

Sookey called Billy out onto the porch. "We have work to do before dark, Punkin."

He followed her out to the barn where she hitched Maude to a middle-buster plow. With Billy on the mule's back, she drove the animal up the road, dragging the plow on its side, so as not to slice open the soil. When they reached the halfway point on the road through the thicket, Sookey set the plow in the earth and cut a narrow but deep trench directly across the road. She covered the trench with leafy branches, and the branches with pine straw. Satisfied, she returned Maude and the plow to the barn.

Back at the house, Sookey rummaged through an old trunk in an upstairs bedroom and removed a moth-eaten bearskin. "This here's Methuselah," she said, holding up the huge skin for Billy to see. "My grandpa ran this bear out of the backyard once, and then chased it for years all over these mountains."

Billy stared at the great expanse of black fur, the watermelon-size head, the gaping mouth, and sharp incisors. When he reached out to touch it, Sookey let out a fake growl. Billy recoiled. Sookey laughed, and Billy soon joined in. She laid the skin on the floor, and Billy pounced on it, laughing and giggling. Sookey watched in amusement as he crawled over the full eight-foot length of old Methuselah.

"Did your grandpa kill it, Sookey?"

"No, Punkin. The story goes that when he finally had the bear dead to rights in the sights of his rifle, he didn't have the heart to do it. The bear had never done him any harm, and he hated the taste of bear meat, anyway. He just couldn't bring himself to kill such a magnificent creature."

Billy's blue eyes shone. "Who killed it, then?"

Sookey sat down on the trunk. "Nobody. It lived out its life and died of old age. My daddy found it dead in the backyard the same day Grandpa died. It was as if it had come to get Grandpa, so they could go off to heaven together. Daddy was so touched that it came home to die that he skinned it and kept it here ever since."

Billy stroked the fur.

"I used him as a rug for years. He was always warm and cozy in front of a winter fire."

Billy stepped off the skin and walked around its perimeter in awe. "Poor old Methuselah," he said.

"He's not poor, Punkin. He got to be inside all these years, out of the rain and cold, and all. Think about poor Grandpa, still out there in the cold, cold ground. We couldn't rightly skin him, you know."

At first she gave Billy a serious look, but when she burst out laughing, he joined in.

Sookey rose and marched around the bearskin, with Billy on her heels. She sang as she went:

> "Poor old Methuselah, you've forgotten how to hug.
> Poor old Methuselah, you're nothing but a rug.
> Poor old Grandpa, you cannot hear a sound.
> Poor old Grandpa, you're lying in the ground.
> Grandpa and Methuselah, each quiet as a mouse.
> Now Grandpa's in the backyard, and Methuselah's in the house."

When they finished their march, Billy asked, "What're you going to do with Methuselah now that you've let him out of the trunk?"

Sookey picked up the great skin and threw it over her back. It engulfed her, with only her black face shining under Methuselah's open maw. Billy's mouth snapped open. He backed away.

Sookey put on her best bear smile. "He's going to introduce himself to that peckerwood, George Zell and his friends. That's what."

When darkness came, Sookey took Billy to the springhouse where he would be safe, then moved down the road to await the men who would come in the night like bugs and scavengers do. She took Methuselah's hide with her. She also took two shotguns, in case her plan failed. She propped one behind a tree on each side of the road. She waited in the bushes, with the trench between her and any approaching vehicles. She didn't wait long.

The lights of three vehicles appeared on the ridge road and wound down the slope toward the thicket. When they hit the straightaway on the floor of the valley, they bunched up with only a few yards separating them. The black sedan from earlier in the day was in the lead, with a Model A coupe behind it, and a small truck bringing up the rear.

Sookey pulled the bear skin close around her and put her hands under the front claws. When the lead car was about twenty feet from the trench, she leaped into the middle of the road behind the trench and stood as tall as she could, raising the front paws of old Methuselah into the air. The sedan jammed on its brakes and slid forward, straight toward her. When it was almost on her, its front wheels slammed into the trench. The vehicle stopped so abruptly that the two front occupants crashed through the windshield, landing on the ground at Sookey's feet. The two rear passengers flew forward, as well. One ended up on the hood, the other entangled in the steering wheel.

The coupe could not stop and crashed into the rear of the sedan. The sedan could not be forced forward out of the trench. The impact demolished its rear end and the front half of the coupe. The coupe gas tank, located up front, caught fire, setting the rear of the sedan ablaze. The truck almost stopped, but slid hard into the back of the burning coupe.

The men in the sedan lay still, either unconscious or dazed. The men in the coupe staggered out and away from the fire. After several attempts, the driver of the truck disengaged its front end and fishtailed backward. Seeing the coupe's occupants bleeding but staring at her in the darkness, Sookey reared up under her bear rug, emitted a blood-curdling growl, and advanced. Shock registered in the men's faces. They bolted for the truck that was still backing away.

Sookey turned her attention to the four men in the sedan. Three of them were stirring, but the fourth hung motionless in the steering wheel. Sookey jerked open the door and snatched the trapped man out of the burning car and onto the ground on the side of the road. She spied several rifles and pistols on the floorboard and threw them into the bushes for later use.

She snarled and circled the two burning vehicles, making whatever animal noises she could think of.

When the four men who remained came to their senses, horror widened their eyes. They limped and dragged themselves back up the road, bleeding and bewildered. They grew smaller in the dimming headlights of the truck as it backed away.

She let the fire burn while she went to retrieve Billy. The two sat on the porch for hours, watching the glow grow fainter. They did not talk much, just enough for Sookey to explain why the men came and why their cars were on fire. She answered Billy's questions, then rocked and thought. Maybe what happened on the road through the thicket was Methuselah's way of paying Grandpa back for sparing him so many years before. At least there would be no more trouble that night. Old Methuselah had seen to that.

✳   ✳   ✳   ✳

"Why didn't you come tell me Sookey Shanks was on her father's place instead of stirring up more trouble?" Myron Turner stood in his office, his hands on his narrow hips.

George Zell stood in front of him, his head bandaged and his left arm in a sling.

"Is it broke?" Turner asked.

George nodded. "Charlie and Cooter are more stove up than me. The rest of them are just cut and bruised a little."

Turner slipped behind his desk and sat down. "Have a seat and tell me one more time about this giant bear that destroyed two cars and beat a truck and eight of your best friends all to hell." Turner opened a penknife and cleaned under a fingernail.

George remained standing in front of Turner's desk. "It's the gospel truth, Sheriff. I wouldn't have believed it myself, unless I saw it with my own eyes. But I did. I swear I did."

Turner looked up and stared at George for a moment, then went back to his nail cleaning.

"We were coming down the road to the Shanks place, when all of a sudden this giant, I mean giant, of a bear leaped out in front of my car. It must've stood ten feet tall. Its eyes were blazing, almost like they were on fire. It wasn't afraid of nothing!" George's voice grew louder and his gestures more graphic. "It dared me to run into it, so I rammed it as hard as I could with my car, but it stopped me dead in my tracks."

Turner spoke when George stopped to catch his breath. "I said sit down. You're going to knock something over."

George pulled a wooden chair closer to the desk and sat on the edge of it. "It was like hitting the side of a mountain, only worse. Hitting it only made it madder. It pushed my car back into Henry and Will, who were following me."

Turner looked up, closed his knife, and laid it on the desk. He shook his head and exhaled through his mouth.

"It smashed my windshield and ripped me and Cooter out of the car and threw us on the ground. Then it jerked open the door and pulled Charlie and Woodrow out and threw them over into the woods. All the time it was snarling, and growling, and slobbering something awful. By that time the cars were burning, and we got out of there when it started acting like it was going to eat all that burning metal and us along with it. Sheriff, it was a sight to behold."

Turner rose from behind his desk, shaking his head. "I wouldn't tell anybody this, if I were you."

"You think it might scare them?"

"No. They'll think you went plum loco. A ten-foot bear wrecking three moving cars and offering to eat the lot of you? Horsefeathers. I don't know what happened out there, George, but if I buy into this, I'll be as crazy as you seem to be. Now, go on home."

George grimaced as he lifted his heavy frame out of the chair. "What about my farm? What about my hundred dollars?"

Turner ushered George toward the door. "You still want that farm, don't you?"

"You know I do."

"Well, I still want your hundred dollars. So, don't fret about it. I'll get to the bottom of all this, and I'll get Sookey Shanks off that land."

George shuffled through the door and into the courthouse hallway. He turned back toward Turner. "Don't take your sweet time about it, or I'll just have to take matters into my own hands."

Turner stood in the doorway, one hand on his thin waist. "Seems like you already tried that and came up short. Now, if you want another go at it —"

"No. No," George said. "I can wait."

Early the next morning, Sookey took Maude back up the road to the burned-out hulks. She had the mule pull them back about three feet, and she filled in the trench. She broke off a leafy branch and smoothed the dirt where the trench had been, as well as around the cars, removing any sign of Maude's or her own presence. The lack of bear tracks would have to remain unexplained, adding to the mystery of George Zell's encounter with the giant bear of Shanks Cove.

She retrieved the weapons and returned Maude to the barn. When she got home, she wiped the guns clean and placed them in the trunk under Methuselah's skin. After helping Billy feed and water the animals, she fixed breakfast for the two of them, then sat on the porch with Billy to await the arrival of Sheriff Myron Turner.

Turner didn't get to the cove until late in the morning. When he did, his car was blocked by the two burned-out ones on the road through the thicket. He had to walk the last three quarters of a mile. When he reached the porch, his khaki shirt was dark-stained under his arms, around his skinny neck, and for a short distance down the front. He mounted the steps.

"Got some cool water, if you want some," Sookey said.

"Don't mind if I do," he replied.

She turned to Billy. "Get the sheriff a dipper of water, Punkin."

Billy disappeared into the house.

Turner turned toward Sookey. "Seems like an obedient child. Does he do everything you say?"

"Everything. And he's right smart, too. He holds his own around here."

Turner raised both hands. "Speaking of around here, I heard a time back that you'd left the county. Something about a disagreement with the folks up on Pea Ridge."

Billy reappeared with a blue enamel dipper dripping water and handed it to the sheriff.

"Thank you, son." Turner emptied it and handed it back. "Go on inside, so Sookey and I can talk."

"You stay put, Billy." Sookey lowered her eyelids at the sheriff. "Anything you have to say to me, you can say in front of him. He's in this as much as I am." She reached over and pulled Billy close.

Turner removed his Stetson and wiped his forehead with the back of his hand. "I don't know what you mean."

Sookey shook her head. "You know that all the colored folks have been driven out. And, if you're really the sheriff of this county, you ought to know that they tried to run me and Billy off first."

Turner chewed on his bottom lip. "I heard you'd left Millersville and took Billy with you. I didn't know anyone had run you off," He adjusted the ribbon on his hat and put it on.

"Not only did they run us off, they shot us both."

Turner's face clouded over. His deep-set blue eyes narrowed. "Shot you? The boy, too?"

Sookey pulled the left side of Billy's shirt over his shoulder, exposing a scab. Turner's eyes widened. She spun Billy around, revealing a larger scab on his back. Turner stepped forward to touch the wound, but Billy ducked away and straightened his shirt.

"What about you?" Turner said. He stood over Sookey.

She pulled the neck of her print dress off her shoulder, so he could see her wounds as well.

A frown creased Turner's tanned forehead as his thin lips went slack. "I had no idea," he said. He backed away. "Who did it?"

"I thought you might know better than me, Sheriff. And I was thinking you didn't drive all the way out here to pay a social call on a Negro." Sookey studied Turner's face.

His furrowed brow relaxed, and his squint disappeared. But she didn't trust him as far as she could spit.

"What do you know about that Zell fellow's claim to my land? He said he bought it because it was abandoned."

Turner's gaze rose from the wound in Sookey's shoulder to her eyes. "Well, he did."

Sookey rocked back and forth. "Who said it was abandoned? And who on this blessed earth did he buy it from?"

"He bought it from the county. Since all the coloreds left Fortune County, the county auctioned off their land to keep the peace."

Sookey pressed her body against the back of her chair, stared at the porch ceiling, and pushed with her feet to keep moving. Her voice took on a quizzical tone. "How is selling something the county don't own to someone who don't have a right to buy it keeping the peace?"

"Because they would've all fought over it. That's how."

"I thought keeping the peace was your job, Sheriff."

"It is."

The only sound on the porch was the soft wood-on-wood squeak of the rocker. She looked into Sheriff Turner's eyes and stiffened her upper lip. "Why didn't you keep the peace when the whites were driving all the colored folks off?"

Turner backed away and leaned against one of the porch posts. "That's no concern of yours, Sookey."

"What *is* my concern, Sheriff?" Sookey stopped moving and glared at Turner.

"You have several. First, George Zell has title to this land. It's recorded at the county courthouse, all neat and legal. Second, there's the assault on him and several other citizens of Millersville, and the criminal destruction of their vehicles." Turner stopped long enough to light a cigarette. "Third, there's the theft of several weapons they say they left in their cars, and I saw no trace of them in the wreckage back there."

"Do those boys say I had anything to do with all that?"

"Well, no."

"Then why come way out here and accuse me of it?"

Turner picked at a piece of tobacco on the tip of his tongue. "Because even though I don't know what happened, I sure don't believe that story they're telling around town. I suspect that whatever really went on out here last night, you were right in the middle of it."

"I don't know what tall tales those boys are spreading around, but it looks to me like they got wild-eyed drunk and went ass over tea kettle out there on the road. I don't know who they're trying to blame it on, but it's good to know they're not blaming me." Sookey resumed her rocking.

Turner hesitated, then spoke. "They're blaming it on a bear."

Sookey broke into such hearty laughter, that even Myron Turner joined in. "A bear?" Sookey wiped her eyes.

"Yeah, a bear. Ain't that a hoot?" His laughter subsided as quickly as it had come. His eyes narrowed at Sookey, pencil-thin lines formed at the corners. "What do you know about a large bear roaming these parts?"

Before Sookey could respond, Billy broke in. "I know about a large bear named Methuselah."

Sookey's heart rose in her throat. She leaned forward and tried to get Billy's attention to stop him, but he was gazing at Turner.

Turner's head snapped toward Billy. "Oh you do, do you? And what do you know about this bear, son?" Turner's blond eyebrows rose.

Billy's eyes lit up, and he began to sing:

"Grandpa and Methuselah, both quiet as a mouse.

Now Grandpa's in the backyard, and Methuselah's in the house."

Turner exhaled loudly and frowned at Sookey. "Here I am supposed to be looking for a vicious killer, and he's singing about his grandpa and a teddy bear. I should've known better."

Sookey sighed and sat back. "He meant well. He was only trying to be helpful."

"Yeah."

"Is there anything else we can do for you, Sheriff?"

Turner stared at her again. He licked his dry lips. "Yeah. I'm afraid that you and the boy are going to have to leave this place. Like it or not, you're the only colored person left in Fortune County, and I don't need any more trouble like we had last night."

"We didn't cause any trouble last night," Sookey said. She chuckled. "If I heard you right, a bear did."

Turner stepped in Sookey's direction. "Don't you get it? They wouldn't have come out here last night, if you hadn't been here. If you don't leave, more will come, and you and the boy may end up dead. If you don't care about yourself, what about Billy?"

"Seems like I'm the only one around here who *does* care about him. If I die, he might as well die with me. No one's willing to take care of him with me alive. I don't see that changing any if I pass."

Turner flicked the butt of his cigarette out into the yard. "If you don't agree to go, Sookey, I just might arrest you."

Sookey laughed. "For what? For living on my own land?"

"George Zell said you fired a shotgun at him yesterday."

"Did he say I fired it before a bear wrecked his car, or after a bear wrecked his car?"

Turner nodded and smiled. "You do own a shotgun, don't you?"

"I own several of them." She looked over at Billy. "Go get Sookey's shotgun, Punkin. The one leaning against the wall just inside the door."

Billy went inside.

"Is that safe?" Turner asked.

"It's not loaded," Sookey said, shaking her head. "But he doesn't know that."

Billy reappeared in the doorway, just barely able to hold level the long, double-barreled gun. It pointed directly at Myron Turner. Tuner tried to move out of the field of fire.

Before he could, Sookey said, "Now, shoot the sheriff, Punkin."

Without hesitating, Billy pulled both triggers. Turner dived off the porch, as both firing pins clicked home. His hat flew from his head when he hit the ground. He lay motionless for a moment, breathing hard, then rose from the dirt. He stared at the open end of the gun, still pointed in his direction.

Sookey nonchalantly took the shotgun from Billy, broke it open, reached into her dress pocket, pulled out two shells, and inserted them. She snapped the barrels into place. "I guess I'll have to cut these barrels off some, so Billy can handle this gun better, since it looks like we're going to have more visitors, like you say." She laid the loaded gun across her lap, her hand cradling the trigger guard.

Turner picked up his hat and used it to beat the dust from his clothing. He thrust his red face toward Sookey and gritted his teeth. "Why in hell did you do that?" he fumed.

"To show you that the boy'll do what I say, like I told you he would. Why did you go and jump off the porch like that? I told you it wasn't loaded."

Turner took a deep breath and started back toward his car. "Never mind that. You and the boy aren't going to be able to hold off the folks who want you off this land and out of this county, Sookey Shanks. Mark my words."

"You may be right, Sheriff, but you go back and tell the good folks of Fortune County that they best come loaded for bear, for Billy, and for Sookey. And be sure and tell them, especially that George Zell, that the first ones to hit our front porch are going to be dead white folks." She looked at Billy. "Run out to the tool shed, Punkin, and fetch me the hacksaw."

CHAPTER 6

▼

As Myron Turner drove past Thelma's in downtown Millersville, he spied Carter Baxley sitting in his truck in front of the cafe. Turner stopped in the street and killed his engine. When Carter looked up, Turner motioned for him to come over. "I thought you told me you ran Sookey Shanks off."

"I did, Sheriff. Right out of the county."

"You did no such thing."

Carter's mouth flew open. "Did she come back?"

"No, Carter," Turner said. "She never left. She went straight to her daddy's place. Now, she's holed up there and not likely to ever leave."

Carter flashed a yellow-toothed grin and shifted a toothpick from one side of his mouth to the other. "I'll just go up there and take care of it."

"Go, if you want to get your balls shot off. All you did was make her mad. I'm telling you, a mean, nasty mad. No, I think you'd better leave her alone. And speaking of getting shot, why'd y'all go and shoot her and the boy? I didn't want anyone to get hurt."

"I didn't know we'd shot them. But they're still kicking, I take it."

"Yeah."

Carter dug between two of his teeth and made a sucking sound. "Well, everything's all right, then. You sure you don't want me to go up there?"

"I'm sure," Turner said. He cranked his engine. "We don't need any more problems around here. And she's not going to hurt anyone." The image of blue-eyed Billy Briggs wielding a sawed-off, double-barreled shotgun flashed across Turner's mind. "Leastways, not those who don't go up there spoiling for trouble."

Carter shrugged and headed back to his parked truck.

"Where you going?" Turner said.

"Up to the cliffs. We shut down, you know, when the Forest Service investigated that ranger killing. When they cleared out, we had to change the operation around some, since all the coloreds are gone. I want to go check on how things are coming along. Wanna come?"

Turner slipped his car in gear. "I've got an errand to run. I may come up later."

He pulled away and headed for the parsonage of the Mt. Bethel Baptist Church, the home of the Reverend and Mrs. Clint Zell and their slug of a son, George. Turner checked a folder on the seat for a quitclaim deed and a hundred dollars. He was not looking forward to his visit. Like any Bible-belt preacher worth half a lick, Clint Zell was a force in the community and would be outspoken come election time. Turner had his work cut out for him.

A graying Birdie Zell met Turner on the porch with a glass of tea and held him there with mindless chatter until her stout husband and their son George came out of the house. George's head bandage was gone, but his arm was still in a sling.

After they were all seated in porch chairs, Turner got right to the point. "I don't have the authority to force Sookey Shanks to leave her father's land. I tried to persuade her to go, but that didn't work, so I brought George's money back."

Turner pulled five twenty-dollar bills from the folder. The three Zells stared at it.

When George reached for the money, Reverend Zell slapped his hand. "That's mine, remember?"

When the reverend stretched his stubby arm toward it, Turner pulled back. "Of course, George will have to quitclaim the property," he said. He removed a deed from the folder and handed it to George.

"What's that for?" Reverend Zell asked.

"It puts the property back in Sookey's father's name."

Reverend Zell's eyes receded into fleshy sockets connected by a deep frown line. "Why do that? Why can't we just leave it in George's name? Who knows? Anything can happen. The Lord works in mysterious ways."

"We can do that, but then I keep the hundred dollars while he's working."

"But Sheriff," Reverend Zell sputtered. "How can you keep our money if George doesn't have the land?"

Turner took a sip and set his glass on a small wicker table close to his chair. "This is very good," he said to Birdie. He looked toward Reverend Zell and

George, who were sitting close together. "He'll have legal title to it. He can't have both. So, what do you want, the money or the title?"

Reverend Zell leaned forward in his chair. "Are you going to help us move her off that place?"

Turner rubbed his chin and the corners of his mouth before he answered. "No, but I won't stop you, either."

The reverend rose. "That settles it. Keep the money. The Lord helps those who help themselves."

Turner thanked Birdie for the tea, put the money and deed back into the folder, and headed for his car, grinning as he went. "God help you, then," he muttered as he walked away.

Driving out of town along the north road, he smiled and patted the folder lying beside him.

Turner pulled off the pavement a few miles out of town and bounced along an ever-worsening series of dirt roads. Upon reaching the old logging road along Bear Den Creek, he backed his Model A into the trees and cut the engine. For the next twenty minutes he remained concealed, making sure no one was around to track his movements.

Since the death of Roger Bentley brought the feds to his county, Turner had been jumpy and overly cautious. They left a couple of weeks before, but where was the harm in looking over his shoulder? Satisfied that all was well, he pulled out of the woods and eased up the road. The presence of only one set of truck tracks calmed him. Carter's Speedwagon had made them.

He bumped along the old logging road as it wound its way deeper into the mountains. The last three miles were so steep he had to drive in first gear to the whine of his transmission. Carter's old truck, its narrow, doorless cab and massive solid wheels showing through the trees, sat parked where the road ended at the bottom of a sheer rock face. When Turner pulled up beside it, his radiator thermometer was on boil.

Two short and one long tap on his horn caused a man atop the rock face to lower a rope fitted with a wooden bosun's chair. Turner climbed into the seat as one would a swing and gripped the rope with such force his hands ached. He yelled for the man to hoist him and gritted his teeth when the chair jerked upward. During the short trip up the rock face, he wished for an easier way to get to the top of the highest point of Raven Cliffs. The only other route required a mile and a half hike through the forest to a place where the cliffs could be scaled.

He dangled precariously from a wood beam extending over the edge. He breathed easier once on top, though he tried never to show his apprehension. He still had to endure the return trip.

The sour stench of fermenting cornmeal clawed at Turner's nostrils. A wind shift burned his eyes with wood smoke from the mash-cooking fires. The use of well-seasoned wood kept smoke to a minimum, reducing the possibility of detection by the forest-fire towers that had sprung up in the mountains. Whether rising from green or dry wood, the acrid smoke made his eyes water.

Only two of the three stills were in operation. The cold one shut down, he presumed, because of the decrease in production. Sam Clewiston, his wiry frame swallowed by baggy overalls, tended the two cookers, while his skinny wife Lessie prepared the raw mash. Their two barefoot children hauled wood and water as needed. The Clewistons were a rugged mountain family displaced from their home, which had become federal land. They lived in a shanty atop the cliffs and spent their time cooking juice for the Baxleys and Myron Turner.

Their rickety home was built against a rock face and opened into a large cave that extended deep into the mountain that formed the cliffs. The cave had several entrances and stored supplies and finished shine.

In the cave Turner spied Carter Baxley bent over boxes filled with jars. Turner walked up behind him. "You know, one day someone's going to take you in for this, don't you?"

Carter whirled around, his shotgun pointed toward Turner. "You know they'll have to kill me first," Carter said.

"You're never too far away from that shotgun, are you?"

Carter lowered his gun and leaned it against a box. "Not since little Rachel Ann killed herself with it."

Turner held out his hands. "Look, I'm sorry…uh…didn't mean to bring that up."

An audible sigh escaped the huge man. "It don't matter. I never quit thinking about it anyway. If I'd not left it under my bed, she'd be alive today."

"You and your daddy never got along after that, I take it."

"That's when it all started. Rachel Ann was daddy's only girl, and me being thirteen and the oldest, he expected me to watch over her. She was a curious sort, into most everything. But she was napping when I took Caleb off to catch tadpoles. I never dreamed—" Carter hung his head. He trembled.

Turner placed a hand on his shoulder.

"He took a cane to me that day. Beat me til I passed out. I was so stove up, I couldn't go to the burying. But I swear, Myron. I never felt a lick. All I could think of was that sweet little girl with no face." A single tear eased down Carter's pockmarked cheek. He swatted it away like a pesky gnat with a flick of his massive hand. "He beat me regular after that for no reason at all. Even after I was full-growed and could have taken him on. I never did. He was my daddy. Until the day he died, he never let me forget what I'd done. Say what you want to, but God can't punish me in hell. He's already done it in Millersville."

Carter pushed Turner away, and cleared his throat. "Sorry about that."

"It's okay," Turner said.

Carter turned his face away and pointed to the boxes of jars on the cave floor. "What do you think about all this extra shine?"

Turner scanned the inventory, then turned toward Carter. "I think we can sell it to those scratch-dirt fools still trying to find gold in Dahlonega and to the boys at the CCC Camp in Union County near Woody Gap."

Carter cocked his head and rubbed the back of his muscular neck. "But I thought you never wanted to distribute outside Fortune County, where we know we're protected."

Turner nodded. "But with all the coloreds gone, we're losing a lot of money. We can probably sell enough over there to fire up that other still. Besides, Zed Rudeseal is lead foreman at the camp. He's one of us."

Carter picked up his shotgun. "Okay. Let's do it."

They shook hands.

The farm provided most of Sookey's needs, except for flour, cornmeal, sugar, and salt. As much as she hated to, she would have to go into town for staple goods and other necessities. Having no money should not be a problem. She could trade.

Early one morning, she loaded a feed sack with garden produce and another one with a cured ham, a couple of jars of honey, several dozen eggs packed in straw, and something to eat along the way. She tied the two sacks together at the top and hung them over Maude's neck. She and Billy climbed on Maude's bare back, and the three of them headed for Millersville.

"Slide back there on her rump where it's nice and soft," Sookey said. "But don't slip off, now."

They left Shanks Cove at daybreak and moved at an easy pace down dirt roads swept smooth by wind and rain. Dappled light filtered through the trees, and feeding birds warned each other of their presence on the road. The only other sound in the cool morning air was the soft clop of Maude's hooves in the dirt.

Sookey mentally thumbed the pages of a worn hymnal until she found a song she liked. Soon, the woods around them resounded with her strong, clear voice.

"This world is not my home. I'm just a passing through.
My treasures are laid up somewhere beyond the blue.
The angels beckon me from heaven's open door,
And I don't feel at home in this world anymore.
Oh, Lord, you know I have no friend like you.
If heaven's not my home, then Lord what will I do?
The angels beckon me from heaven's open door,
And I don't feel at home in this world anymore."

Billy hummed softly behind her. A broad smile flashed across her face. She urged him to join in, especially on the chorus. He did, and at one point Maude emitted a raucous snort, adding some bass to their rendition. They both laughed.
"Come on, Punkin. You know this one. Sing with me." Sookey sang,

"Jesus loves the little children."

Billy picked right up and joined in.
"All the children of the world."
Together they sang,

"Red and yellow, black and white,
They are precious in his sight.
Jesus loves the little children of the world."

They plodded on in silence for a while. Finally, Billy spoke up. "I wish I was red and yellow, black and white."
Sookey chuckled. "Why would you say a thing like that?"
"Because if I was all those colors, Jesus would love me, too."
"What makes you think he doesn't love you?"
"Because I'm pink," Billy said.
Sookey laughed. "The meaning of the song is that Jesus loves you no matter what your color is. Red or yellow, black or white. It don't matter. You just happen to be white."
Billy started crying. "But, I'm not white. I'm pink."

"Yes, Punkin, you are pink. And we can include you in the song, too." Sookey sang,

> "Red and yellow, black and pink,
> They are precious in his sight.
> Jesus loves the little children of the world, including Billy Briggs."

Billy laughed, and Sookey turned around to look at him. "There, now. Is that better?"

Billy nodded, and Sookey pushed her heels into Maude's sides to speed up the pace. They moved steadily for several more hours. The sun rose higher and got hotter. Sookey reached into one of the bags and retrieved two straw hats.

She handed one to Billy. "Put this on," she said. "Or you won't be pink anymore. You'll be red, just like in the song." She laughed again.

They reached the main road to Millersville at a place where a small stream passed under a metal bridge. Sookey guided Maude under the bridge and stopped to rest out of the sun. She slipped down from the mule and tied her to a bridge support away from the water, then lifted Billy.

"Don't we need to give Maude some water?" he asked. "She looks thirsty."

"Don't ever water a hot mule. They'll puff up so, you'll think they're going to bust."

Maude strained at her rope halter.

"Hold your horses, mule," Sookey said. "You'll get water soon enough."

Sookey partially untied one of the feed sacks around Maude's neck and took out a white cloth containing their food. They sat in the shade of the bridge and ate. When they finished, they drank from a small spring feeding the creek, then rested.

Ready to leave, Sookey allowed Maude to drink from the creek. They climbed on and moved along the shoulder of the paved road. Billy was full of questions. He asked why the sun was hot, why the clouds moved, why they changed shape, why some birds hopped and others walked.

"You sure have a bad case of the whys," Sookey said.

Billy was quiet for a moment, then asked, "When is my face going to turn black like yours?"

"It's not ever going to turn black, Punkin."

"Why not?"

"It's just not, that's why. When God makes up his mind what color a flower's going to be, that's what color it is. And it's never going to change. We're God's little flowers, you and me, and he picked me for black and you for pink, which is what most folks call white."

Neither spoke for a while, then Billy broke the silence. "Was your mama black like you?"

"Yes, she was."

"And your daddy?"

"Yes."

"And your brother?"

"Yes." She anticipated and dreaded the next question.

"Are you my mama?"

Sookey spoke slowly and looked straight ahead. "If cutting your cord with a butcher knife and breathing air into your lungs with my own makes me your mama, then that's what I am." She took a deep breath. "If giving you breast milk from your very first drop to your last, and wiping your forehead with a cold cloth all night when you was sick with the fever makes me your mama, then that's what I am."

Sookey's voice cracked. She stopped talking for a moment to regain her composure. "If giving you food and making your clothes and keeping you clean and teaching you all about nature and the God who created it makes me your mama, then that's what I am."

A tear crept down Sookey's cheek. She brushed it aside with one finger. "If loving you more than life itself makes me your mama, then I'm your mama, Punkin. But all those things don't make a body a mama. God didn't give you to me. He gave you to someone else. He just loaned you to me to raise. And that's what I've been doing. Praise the Lord."

Billy's arms encircled her waist and he lay his head against her back. "You're my mama, Sookey. Yes, you are."

People stopped what they were doing and gawked. A black woman and a white child riding a mule bareback down the main street of Millersville was worth a look, especially when no one had seen a colored person in the county for more than a month. People talked quietly to each other as Sookey passed. Occasionally, someone on the sidewalk called them a name or yelled at them to get out of town. Sookey kept her head up and focused on the empty street ahead, moving steadily along, as stubborn and determined as the farm mule that carried her.

"Why are they yelling at us?" Billy asked.

"Pay them no mind," Sookey said in a gentle voice. "Keep your eyes straight ahead, and don't give them the satisfaction of a look."

An automobile overtook them, and a young front-seat passenger snapped his head around and cursed as the car passed. It proceeded up the block a short distance, then reversed its course. As it returned, Sookey pressed both knees into Maude's sides to keep her moving in a straight line.

The automobile bore down on them on Sookey's side of the street, its horn blaring. People on the sidewalk stopped to watch. A few gasped and turned away. Sookey kept Maude plodding forward in the direct path of the car. As the gap between them closed to just a few yards, the car veered away. It almost overturned as the driver tried to avoid the mule first and then the sidewalk on the opposite side of the street. Neither Maude nor Sookey flinched.

Billy had hid his head and was out of breath when he was finally able to speak. "Didn't you think he was going to hit us?"

"Never did," Sookey said. "I think he knew what the front end of his car would look like after butting heads with an eighteen-hundred-pound mule." Sookey guided Maude to the front of Truett's, the only general store in Millersville. She and Billy slid off, and she tied Maude to a post.

Clyde Truett waited on two women at the main counter. A slender male customer wandered through the store. Mrs. Truett fussed with some boxes on a shelf near the back wall. When Clyde looked up and saw Sookey in his store, he stopped talking to his customers in mid-sentence. The two women turned in her direction.

He studied Sookey for a moment. "If you're here to sell something, I'm not buying."

"I'm here to trade," Sookey said. She held up a feed sack in each hand.

Clyde Truett shook his head. "I'm not trading today."

Sookey lowered the sacks. "All I need is sugar, salt, flour, and cornmeal. And maybe some candy for the boy." She nodded toward Billy.

"We're all out," Truett said.

His wife spoke up from the rear of the store. "But Clyde, we got plenty of—"

"I *said* we're all out." His eyes narrowed.

The two women watched intently, but said nothing. The male customer stopped beside a display table in the center of the store and peered toward the front.

Mrs. Truett walked toward the main counter where her husband stood. "At least find out what she's got for trade."

Before Truett could respond, Sookey spoke. "I got eggs, fresh produce, a cured ham, and some sourwood honey."

The male customer slipped past Sookey and out the front door.

Mrs. Truett put her hands to her face. "Oh, Clyde. We could sure use—"

"I'm not going to say this again. I'm not trading today. Even if I was, we're out of everything she wants." He stepped out from behind the counter. "Now, get out of my store. Do yourself a favor and get out of town. I don't know what you're doing here anyway. And take that young 'un with you."

Sookey shrugged. "Come on, Billy."

By the time they got outside, curious onlookers had gathered on the sidewalk in front of the store.

The tall man who had left earlier approached Sookey. "How many eggs you got?"

"Two dozen."

"I'll give you five cents for the lot," he said.

Sookey paused for a moment. "That's not rightly enough, but I'll take ten."

"Ten cents it is." The man reached into his pocket and gave Sookey two nickels.

She removed the packed eggs from one of the sacks and handed them to the man. She handed one of the nickels to Billy. "Go back inside and tell the man you want a penny's worth of candy."

Billy took the nickel and scampered inside, as if the rest of his body was trying to keep up with the smile that was racing toward the candy jar.

"Don't forget your change," Sookey called out, before he disappeared through the door. She chuckled while she tied the two feed sacks together and placed them over Maude's neck. She was loosening the rope that held Maude to the post, when Billy reappeared at the door. His shoulders drooped. He stared at the floor.

She noticed a redness in his face, when he got closer. "What is it, Punkin?"

"The man said he didn't have any candy." Billy buried his face in the front of her dress.

Sookey stroked the top of his blond head and lifted his chin. His soft, blue eyes were filled to the brim. Cradling his head in her hands, she leaned over and brushed his cheek with her lips. She felt his shortened breath on her face and tasted the salt of his disappointment. "I'm so sorry," she whispered.

"But Sookey, I saw candy in the jar."

"I know, Punkin. Let's go on home." She dried his tears with the folds of her dress.

She placed him atop Maude and climbed on in front of him. They moved out into the street. When they had traveled only a few yards, a raw egg slapped Sookey in the head, splattering all over one side of her face. She reached up in disbelief to clear the mess from her eye, and another hit her. Suddenly, she, Billy, and Maude were enveloped in a shower of eggs thrown by the crowd on the sidewalk. It stopped as quickly as it had started. Laughter broke out at the sight of the egg-covered riders on an egg-covered mule.

"It was worth ten cents, woman," the man who had bought the eggs shouted. The crowd roared again.

Sookey held her head high and urged Maude to keep moving. Billy whimpered. "Don't fret, Punkin. Everything's going to be fine. Sookey will clean you up good as new. In the meantime, don't give them any satisfaction. Keep your chin up like Maude and me. Come on, Maude. Take us home."

They moved slowly out of Millersville, not bothered by anyone else as they went. They were soon well out of town and into the countryside. Sookey guided Maude into the middle of the first creek they saw. She and Billy slid into the water and sat in it up to their necks. Maude stood knee deep and watched curiously as the two of them laughed and splashed each other clean. When it was Maude's turn, they attacked from both sides, laughing, splashing, and combing shells and egg goo out of Maude's hair.

As Sookey and Billy lay side by side on the creek bank drying, Billy reached over and touched Sookey's hand. "That was a bad thing they did to us, wasn't it?"

"Look at it this way, Punkin. We got a fair price for our eggs."

The road home was long. They stopped once to eat along the way. When they started up again, the sun hung low in the sky. The deep red hue that engulfed the western horizon signaled fair weather for the next day. If they were not too tired, maybe they could try trading their goods over in Dahlonega. No black folks ever lived in Lumpkin County, so no trouble had arisen over there. They just might be welcome to visit.

As they rode along in the gathering darkness, Billy asked, "Why were those people so mean to us today?"

"I think me being black and you being pink makes them uncomfortable."

"What does uncomfortable mean?"

Sookey drummed her fingers against her temple and pursed her lips. "You know how it feels when you get a pebble in your shoe and can't get rid of it?"

"Uh huh."

"Well, that feeling is uncomfortable. You and me make them feel uncomfortable."

Billy was silent for a moment. "Are we pebbles in their shoes?"

"You know, Punkin, now that you put it that way, I guess we are. You and me are nothing but pebbles in their shoes. And they can't get rid of us."

CHAPTER 7

▼

Carter Baxley nursed the lumbering Speedwagon up the steep seven-mile grade toward Woody Gap. Once through the gap, he could coast most of the way to the CCC Camp. Zed Rudeseal had initially refused Carter's suggestion that he look the other way when Carter appeared at the CCC Camp with a load of shine, criticizing Carter's gall at wanting to sell non-federally taxed liquor on federal land. Without explanation, Zed sent word through his most trusted truck driver, Jimmy Mack Jones, that Carter should haul a load of shine up to the camp on payday. What had changed?

As Carter approached, he saw the lanky frame of Jimmy Mack leaning against the camp gate. The boy was hard to miss with that shock of red hair that refused to surrender to the confines of a cap. He was the spitting image of his late father, Red Jones. It was only natural that Zed was partial to the rangy mountain boy. Zed and Red Jones, close friends since childhood, had grown up in each other's shadow in Millersville. When Red died, Zed kept his eye on Red's only child. When he wasn't driving throughout the mountains on CCC business, Jimmy Mack was never too far from Zed Rudeseal's coattail.

The brakes on the old truck complained loudly as it jerked to a stop in front of the gate. Jimmy Mack walked over.

"Mr. Rudeseal wants you to set up out here. Told me to tell you he needed forty dollars a month up front."

"That's fair enough," Carter said. He pulled into the bushes on the side of the road, stepped out, and counted eight five-dollar bills into Jimmy Mack's outstretched hand.

Jimmy Mack started to walk away.

Carter stopped him. "Just a minute. Do you know why he changed his mind? Is someone sick?"

"Oh, no. He's decided to send Nadine off to a boarding school in Atlanta for a year. Said the change would do her good. And the extra money will come in handy."

"I see." Carter hopped onto the bed. "Hold on. I have something else for Zed." He pulled back the tarp and slid an apple crate to the edge. "These are the first of the season. But be careful. There are also several quarts of my best shine in there for his personal stash."

Carter rubbed his hand over his mouth as Jimmy Mack disappeared into the camp. A struggling mountain family sent a daughter off to Atlanta for very few reasons. Nadine wasn't smart enough for more schooling, and she sure wouldn't take to any finishing. He smiled.

The camp whistle blew, and men streamed out of the camp. Carter busied himself dispensing jar after jar to those who lined up behind his truck.

Zed's coupe emerged from the camp, headed in the direction of Woody Gap. He nodded at Carter as he passed and held up an open fruit jar.

*   *   *   *

Sookey and Billy made a quick turn around. A good night's sleep, a hot breakfast, a new supply of eggs, and they were on their way to Dahlonega. Because Sookey wanted to avoid having to go back through Millersville, most of their trip would be overland along the ridges. She would pick up the Dahlonega road at Turner's Corner. The trip would take a full day's travel each way. She expected good weather for at least the first day. After that…

She loaded Maude with extra food, bedrolls, and some canvas for shelter. The bedrolls and canvas provided a soft seat. The extra weight was not a problem. Maude was a strong mountain mule, unflappable and surefooted. Sookey trusted her on the roughest terrain and committed her own and Billy's safety to Maude's slow but steady gait.

Summer would soon be abandoning the North Georgia Mountains. It didn't normally hang around and jaw with autumn. Most times, it just packed up and left in the middle of the night without so much as a by-your-leave. The normally cold summer nights would become cold mornings as well, and they would hang around all day. Color would swarm over the trees, devouring everything green, replacing it with brilliant reds, ambers, and a multitude of yellows. An early fall was fast approaching. She could not see or feel it, but like the wild critters around her, she sensed it.

"You'd better get those last few nuts to home," she called out to a gray squirrel rummaging through leaves at the base of a large hickory. "They just might be what tides you over." She used her knees to guide Maude past the tree and onto the trail heading southwest away from the cove.

The rising sun was just below the horizon, but the creatures of the mountain forest were awake and well into another day of foraging. They paid scant attention to the passing mule and its two riders. As was her custom, Sookey identified for Billy the mountain flora and extolled its many uses and benefits. She was also quick to caution him of the many dangers that lay in wait for the unwary. Even Maude had the presence of mind to avoid the low-hanging branch with the hornets' nest, and to allow the timber rattler enough time to slither off the trail ahead.

They moved steadily throughout the day, stopping occasionally to rest or eat, then moved again. When they were only a few miles from Turner's Corner, Sookey stopped atop a ridge overlooking a small cove on the northwest side of the trail. She decided not to try to make it all the way into Dahlonega the first day and arrive so late that nothing would be open. They'd spend the night in the woods and get an early start the next day. The cove would provide good shelter, and they could make camp in a stand of poplar and walnut trees that were abundant throughout the cove.

She coaxed Maude off the trail. They descended a gentle slope toward a small stream at the bottom. They traveled only twenty or thirty yards through the trees when Sookey exclaimed, "Well, I'll be. Look down there, Punkin." She pointed to some plants scattered across the slope in front of them. "See those five leaves spread out like the fingers of your hand with the red berries raised up on a stem like that? That's sang. Oh, Lordy mercy. It's sang for sure. And it's everywhere."

Sookey leaped from Maude's back and fell to her knees in front of one of the plants. She stroked it as if it were fragile crystal that would break at a touch. "This one here is a five-pronger." She shook her head, trying to loosen the disbelief from her mind. "I've heard tell of five-prongers, but this is the first one these old eyes have ever seen." Sookey gently picked all the berries off the stem that topped the plant and put them in her pocket. She dug around the base of the plant until she had exposed the root. She pulled it from the ground and broke it from the main stem. "Look at that grizzled old thing. It must weigh a quarter pound." She held up the root for Billy to see.

"What is sang, Sookey? And, why you so excited?"

"Sang is gold, Punkin." A brilliant smile flashed across her face. "At least it's worth its weight in gold if sold to the right folks. These mountains have almost been picked clean of it, but this here cove is plum full of it. I've never seen so much in one place. It doesn't look like it's ever been touched. A lot of these plants have three, four and five prongs on them. Most I've ever seen is two. These are old plants. Some as much as eight to ten years."

"Can I get down, now?" Billy asked.

Sookey put the root in her pocket and went to where Maude stood patiently. "I'm sorry." She lifted Billy to the ground. "Let's go to the bottom of the cove and set up our camp near that stream." She took the boy by the hand and led Maude down the slope. "This sang has kept for years. It'll keep til we've had supper."

Billy helped stretch the canvas over a rope tied between two trees to make a shelter for the night. Sookey built a fire, fried bacon, and cooked potatoes and eggs in the grease.

Their hunger satisfied, she took Billy back up the slope to dig several more roots, telling him all the while how to identify the plant and tell its age. She wrapped the roots and berries separately in pieces of soft cloth and put them in a small cotton bag, which she hung around her neck with string. She stuffed the bag out of sight down the front of her dress. When darkness came, they sat by the fire for a while and talked.

"That root we been digging is ginseng, but I grew up calling it sang. It's good for what ails you. You can chew it or make it into a tonic. It's a might bitter, all right, but it'll cure the colic in young and old alike. It helps your appetite. It helps you digest what you eat. And if you're not digesting too good, it'll help you with the stomach ache. It gives vigor to your blood and stimulates your spirits. It's good for particular ailments of us women, and it makes men and women cotton more to each other."

"What does that mean, Sookey?"

"I'll be explaining that to you someday." She chuckled.

She told him how ginseng hunters had searched for it since colonial days, almost denuding the forests of the most desired plant in the mountains, not so much for their own use, but to sell the roots to those who would pay the most for it—the Chinese.

"What are you going to do with the berries?" Billy asked.

"Before we leave in the morning, we're going to plant some to replace the ones we dug up. We're going to take the rest back to Shanks Cove and plant them in the woods near the house. I know a nice shady grove that they should take kindly to. That way, we can have sang growing right under our noses in a few years."

When the fire burned low, Billy snuggled close to Sookey for warmth. "Why don't we plant them in our garden?"

Sookey stirred the embers with a small stick until they flamed up one last time. "Because sang's much like you and me. It don't like being tamed. And if you succeed in taming it, it's not as good as it was when it was wild and free. You can be sure, the ones who know sang best know the difference between wild and tame. They won't pay you near the same for that what's tamed."

As she tried to keep the small fire going, she felt Billy's full weight against her shoulder. She picked up his limp body and carried him to their lean-to. When he was snug in his bedroll, she climbed into hers. She lay there, watching the coals glow red for a long while, then extinguish one by one. A new worry replaced her concern over whether anyone would trade with them in Dahlonega. She had a gold mine at her disposal, and that brought with it a host of other dangers. She had to find the best way to convert the ginseng root into cash without arousing suspicion. Most of all, neither she nor Billy could reveal their discovery. Some folks would kill to have the ginseng patch for themselves. She had no idea what the going rate for the root was, but before the bad times hit, it was as high as thirty-five dollars a pound.

When morning came, they broke camp early and breakfasted on honey and day-old biscuits. After they planted the berries, they continued through the woods toward Turner's Corner and the Dahlonega road. Her grandfather told her that when he came to the mountains, Turner's Corner was a way station along the treacherous wagon road between Blairsville and Cleveland. The road to Dahlonega branched off the Blairsville road at Turner's Corner, starting at the bridge that crossed Waters Creek. From there the road meandered southwesterly past Porter Springs, then south to Dahlonega. The store and old mill at the bridge had long since been abandoned.

Maude's hooves beat a hollow tattoo on the bridge planks. It reminded Sookey of the sound of Indian drums her grandfather had imitated for her as a child. She even imagined she heard the cries of wild Indians in the distance.

Billy straightened and grabbed Sookey's shoulders. "Who's that crying out?"

Sookey laughed. "Do you hear Indians, too?"

Billy took a deep breath. "Is that an Indian?"

Sookey cocked her head and listened intently. Was that a faint cry? She was not daydreaming. She forced Maude to pull up before reaching the end of the bridge. There was no mistaking it this time. Someone was calling for help from under the bridge.

Sookey guided Maude toward the creek. A dark coupe sat in the water, its door jammed against a bridge timber. The rushing water was pushing against the other door. Water filled the interior of the car.

A man inside waved frantically. "Help me," he cried weakly. "Please help me."

Sookey called out. "Can't you get your window down?"

He shook his head. "It's stuck. They're all stuck. Please get help. I can't last much longer."

Sookey leaped from Maude's back. She pulled Billy off and made him sit on the bank. She stripped Maude of her load, saving only the rope that rigged their shelter the night before. Sookey plunged into the icy water. She submerged and tied one end of the rope to the coupe's rear axle. Gasping for breath, she crawled ashore and formed a loop with the other end. She threw the loop over Maude's neck.

"Pull, Maude. Pull!" she urged.

Maude strained forward. The rope grew taut and vibrated. Water slung from its many twists and turns. Sookey feared it would snap and lash out at her, so she moved in front of Maude and tugged on her halter. "Pull!"

The man trapped inside stared wide-eyed through the rear window. Both of his hands pressed against the glass. Maude lurched forward. The half-submerged car crept toward the bank. It drew away from the support timber and out of the main flow of the stream. Sookey stopped Maude and leaped into the water on the downstream side. When she opened the door, water and apples gushed out into the creek and floated away.

Sookey pulled the man from the car and dragged him up on the bank. Although he tried, he was unable to walk.

"Get me a blanket, Punkin," she said. "This is the whitest white man I've ever seen."

Billy brought both blankets. Sookey wrapped the man in one blanket and herself in the other.

"You're not going to like this very much, mister," she said, "But I got to take your clothes off. You've been in the water so long, you're going into what they call shock. Your wet clothes will kill you for sure, if I don't get them off."

The man did not answer or put up any resistance as Sookey stripped him and tucked the blanket close around him. He sat down beside his pile of soggy clothes and hunched forward.

Sookey stood over him. "If you wasn't half dead, I'd say you have a strange way of bobbing for apples. But seeing that you don't feel so good right now, I won't comment on it."

The man fell over on his side and rolled into a fetal position.

Sookey put her hands to her head. "Oh, Lordy, Lordy. He's going to die on us for certain, if we don't get him to a doctor. Stay with him, Punkin. I'll be right back."

Sookey grabbed a knife from one of her bags and sprinted toward the nearest thicket, where she cut two slender poles and two short stubby ones. Returning to the creek bank, she cut a length of rope and lashed the poles together to form a frame, over which she secured the piece of canvas. She attached the makeshift litter to Maude and placed the man on it.

"You and me will be walking to Dahlonega, Punkin. We'll have to leave our trade goods behind. Maude can drag this fellow all the way, but we can't ask her to haul anything else. You take her reins and lead her down this road. I'll walk alongside and keep my eye on him."

Billy nodded, and they started off. Sookey expected the man's color to return as he warmed up, but it didn't. She added her own blanket to his, but it did no good. She called for Billy and Maude to stop. She felt his pulse. Weak. She pulled the blankets back and put her ear to his chest. The heartbeat was faint. Worse yet, it sounded irregular.

"We need to keep moving, and we need to be on the lookout for some foxglove. Grandma Shanks swore by it when Grandpa had his heart trouble. She always claimed it gave her at least ten more miserable years of him." She burst out laughing.

"What does it look like?" Billy asked.

"It'll be easy to spot. It's my favorite color—purple, and it has long spikes with little flowers shaped like thimbles attached to them. Just sing out if you think you see one."

They plodded steadily for another hour. The man went into and out of consciousness and barely clung to life.

When they reached the road to Woody Gap, Billy yelled, "I see one, Sookey. Over there." He pointed to a pile of rocks near a spot where the two roads joined.

The foxglove stood tall in the sunshine beside the rock pile.

"Good boy," Sookey said. She raced over to the rocks and rummaged around the base of the plant. She laid a few dried leaves on a flat rock and with another rock ground the leaves into a fine powder, then scraped the powder onto a piece of cloth and folded it. "Now to find some water to mix this with."

Sookey returned to where Maude stood. "Grab a stone for each of us out of that ditch over there, and throw them on that pile, Punkin."

Billy did and then asked, "What are the rocks for?"

"That rock pile is Trahlyta's grave. Throwing a stone on it for each of us will bring us all good fortune."

"Who's Trahlyta?" he asked.

"A Cherokee princess who used to live with her people back there on Cedar Mountain." Sookey pointed to the north. "She was taken away against her will, and the one who took her didn't bring her back until she was dying. He buried her right here, so she'd be close to her home and near some springs the Indians said was magic. We passed Porter Springs back up the road a piece. I could use some of that water right now, magic or not, but we can't be backtracking. Let's keep going."

Billy took Maude by the reins, and they resumed their trek toward Dahlonega.

"Will we all have good fortune?" Billy said as they moved along.

Sookey nodded. "Seems as if it started for you and me late yesterday when we found that sang patch. It started for this poor soul here when you found that fox-glove growing close to old Trahlyta's grave. Yep, Punkin. I think we will. But right now, we need water. Wouldn't you know it? A while back, we had more water than the law would allow. Now, we need more."

They kept the same pace for another mile and came to a spot where the product of many mountain springs leaked from around mossy rocks along the side of the road. Sookey mixed some of the powdered leaves with water and forced the mixture down the semiconscious man's throat. He coughed once or twice, but accepted it all.

They continued toward the town. In less than a half hour the man's pulse and heartbeat returned to normal. His color came back a short time later.

A mule dragging a litter attracted considerable attention on the courthouse square in Dahlonega. The townsfolk directed Sookey to the home of the only doctor in Lumpkin County. He met them at the door and took the man inside. Sookey told the doctor what she had done to get the man there, and the doctor nodded and patted her on the shoulder. She left without ever learning the man's name.

When Sookey and Billy left the doctor's home, their only possessions were two blankets, a piece of canvas, some rope, and a knife. Everything else had been dumped on the ground back at the bridge in Turner's Corner. They had no food or money. Sookey still had the bag of ginseng root, but trying to trade or sell it outright would attract unwanted attention.

With nothing she could trade or sell to get the staples they needed, Sookey headed home.

They traveled a little lighter on the way back, and she made Maude pick up the pace, not an easy task. When they reached the bridge over Waters Creek, Sookey slowed Maude and looked for the trade goods they left behind. She found nothing on the ground or on the bridge, not even the pile of wet clothes of the man they rescued.

A bearded figure leaped from behind a bridge abutment and grabbed Maude's halter. "Whoa, mule!" he cried.

The barefoot man had a shock of tangled brown hair. He wore torn, dirty clothes. A length of rope held up his pants. He was not carrying a gun, but a knife handle showed above his rope belt.

"What do you want?" Sookey said in a stern tone.

He showed two rows of scattered, rotten teeth. "Whatever you got."

"We don't have anything," she replied.

"We'll see about that," he said. "Get down off that mule."

Sookey climbed down slowly without turning her back on him. She kept her eyes on his hands and on the knife. "I'm telling you, we have nothing to give you. We're poor ourselves."

"What's that lump under your dress?" he demanded.

Sookey put her hands under both breasts and pushed upward. "You mean these?"

"No, *this*." He grabbed at the cloth bag hanging beneath the front of her dress. The string around her neck broke, and the bag came free in his hand.

"That's gold," Billy said from atop Maude.

The bearded stranger's black eyes lit up as he plunged his hand into the bag. His narrow shoulders sagged, and his face fell when he pulled out the large ginseng root. He turned it over several times, his mouth hanging open. He glared at Billy. "Why'd you lie to me, boy?"

Sookey said, "He didn't lie to you, mister. He said 'it's old.' Can't you see how wrinkled and gnarly it is?"

The man stuck the root in Sookey's face. "What is this thing?"

Sookey didn't flinch. "That's my bitter root."

"I never heard tell of such a thing," he said.

"I'll bet you've never been to Atlanta, either," Sookey replied.

He turned it over in his hand once more. "Is that where you get 'em?"

"It's where I got that one."

He put the root to his nose and sniffed it. "What do you do with it?"

Sookey smiled. "You eat it."

The man brushed the root on the leg of his trousers, which had more dirt on them than the root, and bit into it. His eyes closed and opened rapidly. He grimaced and spit out a large chunk. "Oh, that's bitter."

"I told you it was bitter root." Sookey grinned.

The man stuck the root back in Sookey's face. "Why would you eat something that tastes so bad, woman?"

Sookey shrugged. "It's for my monthlies."

"Your what?"

"My monthlies," Sookey replied. "You know. That woman thing."

The man spit and flung the root into the creek, followed by the bag. He continued spitting and wiping his mouth as if he had eaten poison. Sookey watched in dismay as the root and bag floated downstream, disappearing in a swirl of white water. The man glared at Sookey, then moved to the rear of Maude and felt around in the blankets and the piece of canvas Billy sat on.

Sookey reached up and pulled Billy down. "Come on, Punkin. Let the nice gentleman look through our things." She placed Billy on the ground beside her, then put her hand on Maude's halter and said, "Jake's behind you, Maude."

Maude's ears perked up. Her nostrils flared. And both hind legs flew backwards. One foot caught the man in the chest and the other in the face. Blood, spit, and teeth went in one direction, and the man went in the other.

"Maude never could stand that old mule, Jake," Sookey said.

She walked over, got the man's knife, and cut the rope that held up his trousers. She threw the rope and knife into the creek. "When you wake up, you'll be too busy holding up your pants to cause any more trouble."

Sookey calmly replaced Billy on Maude's back and climbed on.

The man groaned and rolled over onto his back.

"Is he going to be all right?" Billy asked.

"Oh, he'll do fine in time," she said. "He just won't ever eat corn on the cob again." She clicked her tongue. "Come on, Maude. Take us home."

CHAPTER 8

▼

The field of feed corn Sookey's father planted was ready for harvest. The ears had hardened in their dry husks, and the stalks rustled with the slightest breeze. The opportunistic crows helped themselves at first light, and deer were surely doing the same at night. If she worked steadily, she could get the crop in. Certainly not in the same time as her father and brother could, but there was no hurry. It wasn't going to spoil and didn't need to get to market, only to the barn for the animals. She and Billy could do it together.

She hitched Maude to their only wagon and let Billy drive it slowly down the side of each row. She walked alongside, stripping the ears from each stalk and throwing them into the bed behind Billy. The wagon filled quickly, even though Maude poked along.

On one of their many trips to empty the load in the corncribs, Billy touched Sookey's arm. "Who are those people?"

Sookey looked toward the house. A portly man and woman stood together on the porch. "I don't know, but whoever it is, there're all decked out in their Sunday-go-to-meeting clothes." She steered Maude toward the front of the house and stopped close to the porch. "Can I help you?" she said, as she climbed down.

Billy followed close behind.

The man nodded. "I'm the Reverend Clint Zell." He made a slight gesture toward the stout woman. "This is my wife, Birdie."

"Nice to meet you," Sookey said. "I've heard about you." She nodded at Birdie. "Ma'am." She turned back toward Reverend Zell. "I'm Sookey Shanks. This here's Billy."

"Hello," Billy said softly.

Reverend Zell ignored him and grunted at Sookey, while carefully looking her over. "I've heard tell of you, too."

"Won't y'all have a seat?" Sookey said, trying to break the awkwardness of their meeting.

Without a word, Reverend Zell took the porch seat closest to him, leaving Birdie to fend for herself. He pulled a crumpled handkerchief from his hip pocket and mopped perspiration that oozed from his fat neck and under his double chin. He remained silent, except for a grunt or two and the sound of air escaping over his bottom lip.

Sookey took the only remaining chair. "Can I offer you some cool water from the springhouse?"

The reverend's pig eyes lit up, but Birdie's hard gaze met his. Her head moved ever so slightly from side to side. "No, thank you," he said. He licked his dry lips.

"You sure? I have a special dipper for my white guests."

Reverend Zell's gaze darted toward Birdie. She nodded.

"On second thought," he said. "Don't mind if I do. Got kind of hot walking. We had to leave our car up the road. Couldn't get past those wrecks back there."

Sookey smiled. "I know. It is an inconvenience." She turned to Billy. "Go get a bucket of cold water. And be sure to bring the dipper we use for our white guests."

Billy stared at Sookey with a blank expression. "But, Sookey—"

"You know, Punkin. Our best one." She put her hands on his shoulders and nudged him in the direction of the front door. "Go on, now. Our guests are thirsty."

Billy left the porch. Birdie sat stiffly on the edge of her chair, not making eye contact with Sookey. Reverend Zell continued sopping moisture from his neck with the dingy handkerchief. He stopped only when Billy reappeared with a wooden bucket in one hand and a dipper in the other. He grabbed the dipper from Billy and plunged it into the bucket. Two full dippers quenched his thirst. When he finished, he belched and handed the empty dipper to Birdie.

Birdie scooped water from the bucket and drank from the side of the dipper not used by her husband. When she finished, she handed the dipper to Billy without saying anything. She reached into the sleeve of her frilly dress, pulled out a lace handkerchief, and dabbed her ample lips. She smiled weakly in Sookey's direction.

Sookey motioned to Billy. "Come give Sookey a drink, Punkin."

Both Zells leaned forward in their chairs. Their mouths flew open as Sookey drew a full dipper from the bucket and drank it.

When she was through, she looked at the blue enameled dipper in her hand. "That boy can't ever seem to get it right. He brings me the colored folks' dipper every time."

Sookey watched in amusement as both Zells tried to retain their composure while wiping their mouths with their handkerchiefs. She was sure they would never mention this story to anyone. Before they finished, Sookey said, "How's Mr. George doing? I hear he wrecked his car and got himself stove up."

"He'll be just fine," Reverend Zell said quickly and without emotion. "He's the one we came all the way out here to discuss with you."

Birdie nodded.

Sookey cocked her head to one side. "How so?"

Reverend Zell continued, "Well, it seems that he has legal title to this land, but you refuse to get off it. Is that right?"

"I don't rightly know about the legal title part, but you're right as rain on the not leaving part. This has been my family's land for sixty-five years. I don't intend to leave it."

Reverend Zell rose and stood over Sookey. "You realize, of course, that you're the only colored person left in Fortune County?"

"That I've been told, and I know I haven't seen any around lately." She looked at Billy. "Have you?"

He shook his head.

"That must be right, then," Sookey said. "But, what does that have to do with me leaving?"

"Well," Reverend Zell stammered, "it must mean that God has a purpose for all you folks somewhere else." He smiled. "Just like when all the children of God left Egypt. Yes, just like that."

Sookey pursed her lips. "The way I been reading that story out of the good book to little Billy over there, is that all his children wanted to leave Egypt in the worst way, and God helped them do it. But I hear tell that the colored folks of Fortune County weren't too happy about leaving." She looked directly into the reverend's deep-set eyes.

A blank look came over his face as he stared at Sookey.

Suddenly, he lit up. "When it's God's will, we all have to do what he wants us to, whether we want to or not."

Sookey stroked her chin. "Let me see if I have this right. Are you saying that it's God's will that all the colored folks leave everything they own and get out of Fortune County for good?"

"Yes."

"And that I go with them?"

"That's right."

Sookey leaned back. "How do you know what's going on in God's head? I hardly know my own mind sometimes."

Reverend Zell smiled, placed the tips of the fingers of both hands together, and looked toward the rafters of the porch roof. "I'm close to him. I spoke to him last night."

Birdie folded her hands and bowed her head momentarily. "Praise the Lord," she whispered.

Sookey rose and walked to the edge of the porch. She stopped and turned around, facing Reverend Zell. "What time was that?"

"What time was what?" he said.

"When you were talking to God."

He thought for a moment, then looked over at Birdie. "About 7:30?"

Birdie nodded.

He looked back to Sookey. "It was about 7:30 last night, during our home Bible study and prayer time."

Sookey cocked her head and closed one eye. "You sure about that?"

"God as my witness," Reverend Zell said and smiled. "Why?"

Sookey straightened, and looked at him. "Because it was exactly that time last night that I was walking across that field over yonder." Sookey pointed toward the cornfield she and Billy had been picking. "And, I said, 'Thank you, Lord, for this bountiful harvest.' And God said, 'You sure are welcome, Sookey.'"

Blood rose and changed the color of Reverend Zell's pasty complexion. "He said no such thing!"

Sookey continued calmly, "Oh, that's not all. He said, 'Sookey, you and your family have sure taken good care of this land and all my creatures since I gave it to your grandfather so many years ago. I can't think of anyone else I'd rather have own it.'"

Reverend Zell's face glowed beet red. He opened his mouth, but nothing came out. He tried again. "That's blasphemy!" he finally managed. "My God doesn't talk to, to—" He lowered his volume and narrowed his eyes. "God talks only to his blessed servants, and you are certainly not one of them. He has revealed his plan for this land to me, and you're not part of it."

Sookey smiled. "That is so strange," she said. "Because when he was talking to me out in the field, he said, 'Girl, you watch out for that hypocrite Clint Zell and his fat wife. If they ever come 'round pretending to speak for me, you ask them to leave. If they don't, you have my permission to run them off your land. They quit representin' me a long time ago.'"

Birdie leaped to her feet. "Well! I never."

Reverend Zell reached for Birdie and took her by the pudgy arm. "That's devil's talk. That's what it is. There's no need to run us off. We'll leave peaceable." He moved Birdie toward the porch steps, then turned toward Sookey. "You are a blasphemer and an agent of Lucifer. And that little suckling of yours is the spawn of the devil's seed."

"You best be leaving *now*," Sookey said, fire in her eyes and ice in her tone. "You can call me anything you want, but you can't talk about my Billy that a way. I'd be careful of God's wrath, if I was you. It's plain to see you don't recognize one of his little angels when you see one."

Reverend Zell started down the steps with Birdie in tow. "I'll go, but I'm not through with you. Before this is over, I'll show you how God punishes evil and rewards his children."

Sookey raised her eyebrows. "You wouldn't be thinking about sending that George fellow back, would you?"

"Yes," Reverend Zell replied over his thick shoulder as he started up the road toward his car. "And he'll be accompanied by some Christian soldiers, too."

Sookey smiled. "Have you talked to him lately? Seems like he tried that once before and couldn't get past an old bear out there on the road."

She watched until the couple was out of sight, before she and Billy resumed their corn picking. It took them two more days, working dawn to dusk, to pick the field clean.

As they drove the last load from the field, Sookey bypassed the barn and headed the wagon up the road through the thicket. When they reached the two burned-out cars in the road, Sookey carefully turned the wagon around and stopped. She pulled the husks back on some ears that were piled close to her seat. She pointed to the peeled ears. "As I shuck them, you throw them out into the woods on each side of the road."

Billy tossed several ears out of the wagon. "What are these for?"

"For the crows," she said. "And it's going to be your job to come here once a week with a few more ears."

"Do you feel sorry for them now the field's empty?"

"Oh, no, Punkin. I want them to get used to coming over here to eat. That way, those old crows will give us a call if any Christian soldiers come sneaking down this road."

CHAPTER 9

▼

Myron Turner located Cora Mae Briggs with only one call to Atlanta. Her string of prostitution arrests had earned her considerable recognition with the Atlanta Police Department. He learned that she had two notorious places of abode. When not entertaining a client in one, she was doing time in the other.

Turner had enjoyed Cora Mae's charms when she was too young to be legal, but lost interest when she up and left Millersville to sell them in Atlanta. He refused to see her when she returned briefly to birth a son. He later learned through local gossip that she had left the infant behind and gone back to the bad life. Good riddance. Though he reluctantly admitted that with times the way they were, what was a poor Pea Ridge girl to do to make it on her own in this world?

Finding Billy's mother might just be the answer to his mounting problems with Sookey Shanks. He felt pressure from the townsfolk to take action. Clyde Truett was distressed about her disrupting business at his store. Clint Zell demanded that his son have possession of the farm. He also complained that she insulted and threatened him and his wife for no reason. Zed Rudeseal suspected her of stealing forty dollars from him. At least, he thought it was her. He said it was taken by a strong colored woman with a white child. Who else could that be?

The impending election heightened his concern. It was only two weeks away, and he had opposition for the first time. If he could get rid of Billy, he might be able to get rid of Sookey as well.

He didn't recognize Cora Mae at first. The jail dress hung on her like a sack, masking her femininity. What had once been long, light brown hair had been replaced by a Harlow blond bob. Whatever she used on her hair had to be as harsh as the life she had chosen.

The jailer who led her into the room would never suspect that they knew each other. She neither voiced recognition nor gave any visible sign. Neither did he, but Turner saw the dilation of her soft brown eyes.

"Leave us," he said to the jailer, then added as an afterthought, "please."

When the jailer shut the door to the small cubicle, Cora Mae said, "Hello, Myron. It's been a long time." She tried to smooth the wrinkles of her ill-fitting dress.

"It has been."

"What brings you to Atlanta?"

Tuner gestured toward a chair. "Have a seat."

When she was seated, he took one as well. "I wanted to talk to you about Billy."

She stared at him blankly. "Billy? Billy who?"

"Your son, Billy."

Cora Mae stood. Color drained from her face. "What happened? Is he all right?"

Turner patted her hand. "Sit down, please. He's fine."

She sat. "What is it about him that we need to discuss, then?"

"It's about the way he's being raised," Turner said.

Cora Mae's blond head dropped. She stared at the floor. "I don't know much about that," she mumbled.

He put his hand under her chin and raised her head. "I know," he said softly. "That's why I'm here." He looked into her brown eyes. "Did you know that he's been raised all these years by that colored woman, Sookey Shanks?"

"I had no idea." She rubbed her tongue across her top row of teeth and pushed at her hair.

Turner chewed on his bottom lip. "Your good neighbors on Pea Ridge wanted to take him in after you had to leave, but that Shanks woman refused. She kept him to herself, all the while living in that house your grandma left you after she died. The way I figure it, keeping him was her way of being able to live high on the hog on Pea Ridge."

Cora Mae shook her head. "You don't say. Is she still living in my house?"

Turner moved his chair a little closer. "Your old neighbors finally got their belly full of her and run her off."

"Billy, too?" she asked.

He nodded. "They tried to make just her leave, but she took the boy off in the middle of the night."

"Where are they now?"

He dragged his chair even closer and spoke in a grim, measured tone. "She's got him up in the northern part of the county on her family farm. Preacher Zell tells me she works him pretty hard in the field, then after that, hauling water and such. I for one have seen him playing with guns. Damn near shot himself one day."

Cora Mae jumped to her feet. "Oh, that makes me mad."

"It should. And, that's not all," Turner added. "She hauls him all over the mountains on the back of a mule. No fit place for such a tender child. She don't teach him nothing, and the worst part of it is…" He looked around the room and said in a half-whisper, "He's beginning to talk like a little colored boy." He raised his eyebrows, and drummed his fingertips on a nearby table.

Cora Mae paced the room. "What can you do about it, Myron?"

"Nothing. That's why I'm here."

She stopped pacing and turned. "You're still the sheriff, aren't you? You're wearing the uniform."

"Yes, I am. But, you're the mother. Only you can put a stop to this."

Cora Mae made a sweeping gesture down the front of her jail dress. "I'm not exactly dressed for it, now, am I?"

Turner studied her. He looked right through her baggy garb and recalled every inch of the body he had known so many years before, but the desire it had once stirred in him was gone. Her body had become a commodity, sold cheap, cleaned up, then sold again. He shivered. "I can take care of that. The powers that be have agreed to release you to my custody."

A smirk nibbled around the corners of her plump mouth. "And what do I have to do? Jazz one of those powers that be, like I did the last time someone let me out of here for free?"

Turner rose and walked over to her. "You don't have to do nothing but come with me to Millersville and take Billy away from that colored woman."

Cora Mae frowned. "I mean about the charge against me."

"Oh," he said. "You'll have to appear in court a week from Monday."

She shook her head. "No deal. You get them to drop the charge, or I'm not going. Besides, what good will it do if I get the boy and come back in here?"

"I'll talk to the chief," Turner said. He started toward the door.

Cora Mae put her hands on her shapely hips. "One more thing. You're not suggesting that I keep the kid, are you?"

Turner stopped and turned around. "Well, I thought you could if you wanted to. Don't you have room?"

She grimaced and shook her head. "I work out of a studio apartment with one bed. The only way I can make it is to keep it occupied. That's no place for a kid. Hell, it's no place for me." She hesitated and shrugged. "But, what else can you do nowadays?"

Turner looked at her in silence, chewing on his lower lip. "We can work that out," he said finally. "The Henry Grady Benevolent Society helps locate foster homes. We can work with them."

"You mean *you* can work with them. My part is to get the kid away from that Shanks woman." She raised her head. "As is my God-given right. After that, the rest is up to you."

Turner gritted his teeth, but agreed and left to make arrangements for Cora Mae's release. He did not like the deal, but he could live with it. If the ploy got Sookey Shanks out of his county, the election should be his.

Sookey was robbing a beehive when she heard the un-muffled engines of two winch trucks roaring down into the cove from the road on the ridge. She slipped through the woods to a place where she could observe without being seen and watched as the winches hoisted the two burned-out hulks off the ground and hauled them away. She summoned Billy, who was picking elderberries nearby, and took him to the house.

"It's time to get ready, Punkin. We can expect some unwelcome company tonight. Do you remember the things Sookey showed you how to do when bad folks are coming?"

Billy nodded. He stood straight with his hands at his sides and recited, "Hide behind the big oak tree. Pull the first string when the first car passes the poplar by the side of the road. Pull the second string when the last car passes the big pine."

Sookey cocked her head. "Then what?"

He licked his lips. "Sit down behind the oak and shoot the pistol at the first car until all the bullets are gone."

Sookey put her hands on her hips and raised her eyebrows. "And?"

"Run to the springhouse and wait for you to come get me." He smiled.

Sookey smiled back. "Good boy. And remember to always keep the tree between you and the men in the cars. Don't ever let any of them see you. Okay?"

Billy nodded. "Okay."

Sookey led him to the bedroom and took Methuselah's skin from the trunk. She also removed the guns she confiscated from George Zell and his friends. She and Billy hauled the guns to the thicket.

Sookey secured two shotguns to the trunks of two small trees about twenty yards apart on the roadside. She lashed the guns about a foot off the ground and pointed them at an angle in the direction the cars had to approach. She tied twine to the trigger of each shotgun and unrolled the two lengths of line along the ground to a spot behind the big oak where Billy would hide. She fastened a small stick to the string leading to the first shotgun.

"Remember, the first one you pull is the one with the stick on it."

He nodded.

She handed Billy a small double-action revolver. "This isn't loaded yet, but I want you to point it toward the road and show me that you remember what I taught you."

Billy held the pistol at arm's length and pulled the trigger six times.

"Good," Sookey said. She recovered the pistol from him and took all the other guns and laid them on the ground on clean pieces of cloth at predetermined spots in the bushes on both sides of the road.

"We have time for one last practice," she said, as she loaded Billy's revolver. "I've taken the lead out of each of your bullets and stuffed them with wads of cardboard, so you can shoot at the car and not hurt anybody, but they won't know that."

Sookey loaded the two shotguns with shells filled with rock salt. The rock salt was hard enough to puncture a car tire at close range, but it would melt away without a trace in the morning dew. She loaded all the other guns with card-board-wadded shells and took her place on the opposite side of the road from Billy.

When Billy was ready, she yelled, "Pretend the first car is at the poplar tree, Punkin."

The first shotgun roared.

Sookey grinned and waited a moment. "Now, the last one's at the pine."

The second shotgun fired. After about ten seconds, pistol shots rang out on Billy's side of the road. When the sound of the sixth one died away, she fired her rifle several times and then moved to a new location. She picked up another shotgun, fired it, and moved on to where she had placed a pistol. After taking several shots with it, she crossed the road behind where the cars would be and began firing a rifle from Billy's side of the road.

When the smoke cleared, she reloaded all the guns with wadded shells and retrieved Billy from his hiding place in the springhouse. After a quick supper, she pulled Maude out of the barn and draped Methuselah's skin over Maude's back. Though the bear was long since dead, his smell was still strong. With the huge skin draped over the mule, the animal grew skittish.

Billy looked at Maude, cocked his head and wrinkled his nose. "Why is Methuselah riding Maude backwards?"

"Because I'm going to tie Maude to a tree beside the road, so the men in the cars will see Methuselah just before you shoot their tires out. You know we can't go running folks off our land without letting old Methuselah in on the fun."

Billy grinned. "Yeah, I know."

The weather turned cold when the sun went down. The crisp, evening air marked every breath with smoky puffs. Maude's labored breathing was especially pronounced.

Sookey hitched Maude to a nearby tree with her head facing away from the direction Sookey expected the cars to come. She wrapped Maude's halter rope a few times around a low branch, sufficient enough to hold her in place for a while, but loose enough for her to break free.

Sookey double-checked all the guns. She handed the two strings and the pistol to Billy. "Remember, just like we practiced it, okay?"

"Okay," he said.

Sookey smiled. They were ready. They sat quietly in the dark. Only Maude moved nervously in the bushes nearby. In less than an hour, lights bobbed on the ridge. Only two cars showed up this time. *Please Lord, let my plan work.* She hated to resort to her loaded shotguns back at the house. *If push came to shove, she might not be able to avoid it.*

"Here they come, Punkin," she called across the road.

"I see them," he said softly.

"If anything goes wrong," she said, "I want you to forget about our plan and hightail it to the springhouse.

These men will kill you, if they get half a chance."

"I will."

The two sets of approaching headlights nudged her back to the task at hand. She had to act just a few seconds before Billy. She watched closely, as the first car neared the poplar. When it was about five car lengths from the tree, she called out, "Jake's behind you, Maude."

Maude snorted and shifted her weight to her front legs. She lashed out in a series of furious kicks and bucks, and old Methuselah arose from the darkness.

The headlights of the approaching car bathed him in a yellowish glow. The sight of his front paws frantically clawing the air sent a chill down Sookey's spine.

The lead car slowed and coasted past the poplar. To Sookey's delight, the first shotgun fired right on cue. The car wobbled, then veered to its left. In a blink, it ran off the narrow dirt road and crashed into a tree. Its lights went out. A hissing billow of steam escaped the crushed radiator.

The second car slowed and stopped before it reached the pine. Its headlights barely illuminated the rear of the wrecked car ahead. Sookey's heart was in her throat. The plan would not work unless the second shotgun disabled the second car. If Billy fired too soon, they were in trouble. If he thought the plan wasn't working and headed for the springhouse, it was all over. Hang in there, Billy. We still have a chance.

One of the rear doors of the wrecked car popped open. The bloodied figure of a man staggered out into the road. He was barely visible in the faint glow of the headlights of the second car. When he called for help, Maude kicked and bucked again. The man looked in Maude's direction, then screamed.

The stopped car accelerated toward him and passed the big pine tree. The roar of the second shotgun was deafening. Sookey grinned and watched with amazement as the second car repeated the actions of the first.

The dark road grew still. Only the hiss of steam and the whimpering of a grown man pierced the night.

A car door opened. Before Sookey could discern where the sound was coming from, the darkness erupted with gunfire. Shot after shot rang out at close range. She hit the ground, but almost laughed aloud—Billy! The sound alone was scary, but the muzzle flashes leaping out of the darkness were enough to bring someone to his knees. For an instant, Sookey's mind raced back to her rainy escape into the mountains.

She was so engrossed in the scene unfolding in front of her that she forgot to count the number of shots. Silence once again prevailed in the woods. During the lull, car doors creaked open and out came the muffled voices of desperate and confused men. She fired three shots from a rifle. Then she crept up the side of the road to a shotgun. She fired it and moved to the pistol. After several quick shots, she crossed the road behind the cars. As she prepared to fire another rifle, one of the men yelled, "Run!" Feet thudded through the bushes. Movement appeared on the road. She fired several more shots. And waited.

All remained quiet around the wrecked cars. Maude headed for the barn, and voices faded in the distance in the direction of the ridge road. She raised her rifle high into the air and shouted toward the dark sky, "Hallelujah! Praise the Lord!"

When the echo of her joy faded away, the only sounds remaining in the cool stillness of the night were the muted sobs of Sookey Shanks.

"If I hear that giant-bear story one more time, George, I'm going to puke." Sheriff Turner stood at a wall mirror in his office and patted his sandy hair in place.

"I wasn't driving this time, Sheriff," George said. "I was in the back seat of the first car watching, and I saw it plain as day. Rising up out of the bushes. It was as big as a mule. God is my witness."

Turner shook his head and grimaced in the mirror.

"Cooter was the first one out of the car and into the road," George continued. "It towered over him like a building. Some of his hair done turned white. I don't care what you say. He ain't ever going to be the same."

Turner checked his teeth, then turned around. "Hell, he wasn't right to begin with. And what's all this bull Charlie over there is spreading around about y'all being surrounded and shot at by a horde of renegade Indians armed to the teeth? He never mentioned a bear. Seems like y'all could at least get your stories straight before you come in here."

Charlie moved away from the door and crossed to the center of the room. "I said, 'Honest Injun. We were shot at by a bunch of renegades.' But, it couldn't have been blacks. Ain't none of them left. It <u>had</u> to be something."

Turner picked up his gun belt and buckled it around his waist. "Charlie, there haven't been any Indians in these mountains for over a hundred years. But you say that a whole bunch of somebodies shot at you?"

Charlie's pin head bobbed up and down like it was on a spring. "They was right on top of us. So close I could see fire coming out of their gun barrels."

"How many you figure there were?" Turner removed his revolver from its holster and methodically turned the cylinder, checking each chamber for a shell.

Charlie's head snapped in George's direction. "At least ten. Wouldn't you say, George?"

George nodded. "That and maybe more. There were more guns firing than you could shake a stick at."

Turner holstered his gun and looked directly at them. "And none of you boys were hit."

George and Charlie answered as one, "That's right."

"And, they were firing at close range?" Turner said.

They both nodded. Charlie said, "Uh huh."

"Did y'all hit any of them?"

They hung their heads.

"Well?" Turner said.

George lifted his large head. "If that bear hadn't stopped us, we'd have busted right through their ambush, but he roared out of nowhere and pushed us right off the road."

Turner tapped his foot.

George looked back toward the floor. "Well, that's what it seemed like."

Turner addressed Charlie. "What about you? You never saw no bear. What's your excuse for running your car off into the woods?"

"Somebody must've shot out my tire, Sheriff. That's all I can think of."

Turner walked over to the door of his office and opened it. "I had both your cars hauled in this morning. They're out back. There's not the first bullet hole in either one of them. Your front wheels are so busted up from hitting those trees, I couldn't tell a thing, but there was no buckshot or slugs in the casings." He made a gesture toward the open door with one hand. "I think you boys had better peddle your bear-and-Indian story somewhere else. I got more important things to do."

Charlie hurried through the door, followed closely by George. As an afterthought, Charlie turned around and asked, "Are our guns still in the cars?"

"Didn't see any," Turner said. He pushed on the door.

"Damn," George whined. "Daddy's going to kill me."

Turner returned to the mirror and continued sprucing up. When finished, he wiped the toe of each shoe on the back of his trouser legs, then headed for Pea Ridge to pick up Cora Mae.

When she was in his car, they drove in silence up the north road toward Shanks Cove. Turner wasn't well suited to small talk, and apparently Cora Mae wasn't prone to it, either. She seemed preoccupied and constantly straightened her long skirt, nervously picking lint from it. The dark skirt and long-sleeved white blouse were quite appropriate, almost like a citified schoolteacher would wear, but the small black hat perched to one side of her head was a bit much for the mountains.

Did she think she had to have Sookey's approval before she could take her son? Or was she simply trying to portray an image that fooled no one in Fortune County?

When she spoke, she appeared out of breath. "He won't know me, will he?"

"No. But, he won't know anything about you, either." Turner hesitated for a moment. "Unless that Shanks woman has poisoned his mind against you."

Cora Mae closed her eyes. She rode in silence for another mile or two, then blurted out, "I need a drink."

Turner kept his eyes straight ahead. "This is a dry county. Have you forgotten?"

"When did that ever stop *you*, Myron Turner?"

Turner simply shook his head and kept driving. The only sound was the steady thump of the tires crossing the expansion joints on the cement road.

Cora Mae's round face reddened. She gritted her teeth. "I'm telling you, I can't do this without a drink."

"That wasn't part of my plan," Turner snapped. "You don't need to be liquored up when we get there."

She threw her head back and let out a haughty laugh. "What is she going to do? Report me?"

"No. I want you on your best behavior for the boy. I don't want any trouble out of him. He can be a handful. Believe me."

Cora Mae ran a finger down Turner's right arm. "Please," she cooed. "Just one. I'll be good. I promise."

Turner rubbed his cheek. She'd been mighty tense throughout the trip, and now might screw everything up if she were too nervous when it came time to take Billy. Maybe a drink would calm her down. "What'd you have in mind?" he asked.

Cora Mae grinned. "Some vodka would be nice."

"I don't know why I asked." Turner laughed. "All I can get you way out here is shine. The real liquor is locked up in a cabinet at home."

Cora Mae shrugged. "I'll take it, as long as it's not rot gut."

Turner slowed and eased the car off the pavement onto a dirt road. "Oh, no. It's good stuff. It's the Baxley boy's fixings."

She cocked her head. "Are you talking about Carter Baxley?"

The car hit a hole in the road. The springs bottomed out and released with a groan. The jolt tossed them almost into the headliner. Cora Mae came down close to Turner, her thigh against his.

"Was this part of the plan?" she asked.

He moved his leg. "No, it wasn't. I'm a married man. Remember?"

"Oh, I remember, all right. But that never stopped you before." She moved back toward her window.

"Things were different then," he said.

Cora Mae put her well-manicured hand to her chin. "You can say that again."

They slumped back into the silence that had marked most of the trip, with Cora Mae acting distracted and Turner looking straight ahead. When they reached Bear Den Creek Road, Turner pulled the car into the woods to see if anyone was about. Satisfied that no one had seen them, he continued toward Raven Cliffs.

A few toots on the horn, some yelling back and forth, and a bucket with a quart of clear mountain whiskey came down. Turner unscrewed the lid, then passed the wide-mouth jar to Cora Mae. She sipped daintily, but Turner knew it was tracing a fiery path down her throat. He reached for the jar, but Cora Mae pulled back and kept taking baby sips.

"Give me a minute," she said in a husky voice. "It's been a while."

Turner started the car, and Cora Mae wiped her mouth with the back of her hand.

She pointed back down the mountain road. "No more bumps. I don't need to be wearing this."

Once back on the main road, they soon approached the ridge road into Shanks Cove. Cora Mae put the jar aside and fretted with her clothes again. "How do I look?"

"Just fine," Turner said without looking.

Cora Mae clicked her tongue. "You men are all alike."

Turner drove slowly through the thicket. He looked carefully on each side as they inched along, noting crushed underbrush and two damaged trees on his left.

"What in the world are you looking for?" she asked.

"Nothing. Just looking."

She rolled her window down and leaned her head out. "What's all that racket?"

"Seems like we stirred up a bunch of old crows," he said and sped up.

Sookey was sitting in a rocker on the front porch, as if she expected him, when Turner pulled into the yard. She held a large knife in her right hand. The knife and both her hands glistened with a red, sticky substance. Billy was nowhere in sight.

"Stay here," he said to Cora Mae. "Let me check this out." He released the strap that secured his gun in its holster and stepped out of the car. He left his door open and walked toward the porch.

"Good morning, Sheriff," Sookey said. She pointed toward the car with the knife. "Who you got in the car?"

"Is everything all right, Sookey?" He stepped up on the porch and stopped.

"Everything's just fine. Why?"

Turner kept his distance. "Well, you're a mess. Whose blood is that?"

Sookey looked at her hands, then stood up.

Turner stepped backward.

"Oh, this," she said, looking back at her hands. "Billy and I were butchering a hog out back when we heard somebody coming. Let me go clean up." She rose and stepped inside.

Turner took a deep breath and motioned for Cora Mae to come to him. They both sat on the porch and waited. Cora Mae played with a small, white handkerchief. Turner lit a cigarette.

When Sookey came back through the door, she stopped abruptly when she saw Cora Mae. Her jaw went slack. Her mouth flew open. She tried to speak, but words did not come. The slamming of the screen door behind her broke the awkward silence.

Turner smirked. "You remember Cora Mae, don't you?"

Sookey nodded.

Cora Mae faced Sookey. "Where's my son?" she demanded.

Sookey's hand trembled as she motioned over her right shoulder into the house.

Turner studied Sookey's face. Her strength and resilience melted away before his eyes. Her emotions lay exposed, ready for the gutting, just like the hog out back. He knew when Cora Mae agreed to come that he would defeat Sookey Shanks. He smiled.

"Billy," Cora Mae called out. "Come to your mama, Honey."

No response. She called again, this time louder. "Billy! This is your mother. Come outside."

Still no answer.

Sookey stirred and regained some of her composure. "Punkin, your mother is out here. She's come to get you." She looked at Turner and raised her eyebrows. He nodded. "Come on out, now," she said softly, her voice cracking.

"You're my mama, Sookey," Billy said from inside the house.

Sookey looked at the porch floor. Two wet streaks glistened on her cheeks. Turner nudged her and motioned with his head for her to continue. He looked over at Cora Mae, who stood gawking at the cabin door, her mouth open.

Sookey swiped at her face with one hand and cleared her throat. "You know I'm not your mama, Punkin. Remember what I told you, that I was taking care of you for your real mama. Well, she's here to take you home." Sookey moved to her rocker and held onto the arm of it.

Once again, Billy called out from inside the house. "You're my mama, Sookey. Please don't give me away."

Sookey put her head in her hands and wept.

"Get out here, boy," Turner growled, "or I'll take a stick to you. We've got to go."

The screen door cracked open. Turner looked at Cora Mae and grinned. His grin dissolved when the twin barrels of a shotgun poked through the opening.

Turner grabbed for his gun, shouting, "I knew he'd be trouble! I'll kill the little bastard!"

Sookey leaped to her feet. "No!" she shouted, placing her body between Billy and the sheriff's pistol.

Cora Mae screamed, "For God's sake, Myron. Don't! That's your son!"

CHAPTER 10

▼

Nestled in the bosom of the mountains, Shanks Cove was sheltered from the noise of human existence. Solitude had always been a hallmark of the place Sookey called home, a characteristic that set it apart from countless other homesteads. The cove's peacefulness was a quality of life to be desired—even coveted—and certainly defended.

When the early snow came that year, everything in the cove disappeared beneath its soft whiteness. The normally raucous crows quieted and walked stiff legged through the drifts. The rooster forsook the dawn and slept late in the warmth of the coop. An occasional limb bent under its white load, gently deposited it on the ground, and silently returned to receive more. Leaves surrendered their rustle and twigs their snap, as nature walked by on frigid tiptoes.

Sookey stood on her front porch, watching the pink glow on the eastern horizon become mirrored in the snow-covered ridge. She wanted to share so many things with Billy. Winter's transformation of Shanks Cove was one of them. His being pulled so rudely away left an unimaginable void, as if a chunk of her soul had been ripped away without warning. For years, he was the center of her universe, central to her every action, to her every thought.

His absence left her empty, without purpose. She wandered from chore to chore, not caring if she finished or how well she did. She shed what she felt was her life's allotment of tears, and used up even more from another lifetime. Worst of all, the dry sobbing made her head ache and kept her awake to dwell on her loss.

The previous night had been tearless and sob-wracked, drawing her out onto the porch well before daylight. She waited for daybreak, watching a steady snow engulf her beloved cove. "Oh, Billy," she murmured.

Sunlight struggled over the top of the ridge and crept down into the cove, revealing the tops of the dry cornstalks out in the field. Brown and brittle, they waited to be chopped down and plowed under to make way for a new crop in the spring. She smiled. Just because the land was lying fallow didn't mean that it had surrendered to winter's harshness. It simply endured the inevitable test of its fertility. When winter finally tired and went home, the land would stir in the warmth of the same sun that was rising over it now. The earth would yield its bountiful harvest to those who stayed to nurture it.

The countless snowflakes falling around her might as well have been dogwood blossoms, spreading their eternal promise to mankind. She knew what she had to do. She had to get ready for Billy's return. She had to prepare for the rest of his life. She would do so by finishing the job she started: raising him to manhood. That is what any mother would do, and no question existed in her mind who that was. They were joined by more than the mere bond of birth and blood. They were joined at the heart.

She was certain Billy would find his way back to her, as sure as the dove returned to the cove it left as a fledgling. She had to be ready. Simply working the farm until he returned was not enough. Life had more in store for her Billy than a hundred acres and a mule. She would help make it happen.

Raising cash was foremost. Under the circumstances, the only way to start doing that was to get to Dahlonega to sell her goods. The long mountain trail was too dangerous for Maude. She might flounder in a snowdrift. Or poor visibility could cause them to lose the trail. The roads were Sookey's only choice, but they would take her through Millersville, and she had that irritation to contend with. She could pass through Millersville at night to reduce her exposure to the folks of Fortune County. She hoped most of them went to bed with the chickens.

Because of the snow, she planned to take enough food for a weeklong trip. By late afternoon, she had loaded the wagon with hams, bacon, and jars of honey and canned vegetables to sell in Dahlonega. She packed everything in wood shavings to keep it from freezing and covered the wagon bed with a large canvas tarp.

Maude seemed eager to get out of the barn, and started out with a spirited gait.

"Whoa, now, Maude," Sookey said. "We got a long way to go. You're going to be tuckered out before we get to the top of the ridge."

Night fell by the time Sookey and Maude reached the main road. The snow-fall lessened. Patchy clouds drifted overhead, and every now and then a sliver of moon shone low in the western sky. It reflected just enough light to turn the main road into a white ribbon that streamed out of sight in both directions.

The night was cold and still. Even the normal crunch of the steel-rimmed wagon wheels was muffled by the snow. A reverent silence had fallen over the land, as if the world had bowed in prayer.

Maude returned to her slow, steady gait, and they moved silently through the night. They met no one on the road and passed through Millersville without incident. When they reached the Cleveland-to-Blairsville road around midnight, Sookey guided the wagon into a level clearing in the woods.

She unhitched Maude and used the canvas tarp to make a shelter large enough to cover the bed of the wagon with Maude tied up alongside. Too late for a fire, Sookey snuggled down in the warmth of the wood shavings and soon fell asleep.

Up before the sun, Sookey and Maude made their way up the Blairsville road toward Turner's Corner. Later in the morning, they encountered a few wagons and an occasional automobile chugging along the snow-covered road, but Sookey had left Fortune County far behind and was not concerned. She simply smiled and traded friendly nods and waves.

Even fewer people traveled the Dahlonega road. She passed some men on horseback near the bridge over Waters Creek and later sighted a truck coming down the mountain from Woody Gap. The men in the cab looked like the Baxley brothers, but what would they be doing so far from home on a day fit only for a mule? She shrugged and drove on, arriving in Dahlonega by early afternoon.

Sookey went straight to the general store and traded two hams for all the salt, sugar, flour, and cornmeal she would need for the coming year. She even talked the proprietor into throwing in a tin of peaches to boot. While in the store, she nonchalantly inquired where she could purchase ginseng. No one knew. A clerk said that if anyone in town would know, it would be the cook at the hotel across the square.

Sookey loaded up her staples and drove over to the hotel. She hitched Maude to a post out front and hawked her wares right out of the wagon. The hams and honey sold fast. The jars of canned vegetables were not as popular. Seems that most folks already had plenty of their own, and a number of her jars remained.

Sookey moved the wagon to the back of the hotel and took a sack full of vegetable jars to the kitchen door. She knocked twice and opened the door.

A young woman in a white apron stood at a wood stove, stirring a pot of what smelled like beef stew. She looked up and smiled when Sookey poked her head through the doorway. "Come in out of the cold."

"I got more vegetables than I can sell out front," Sookey said. "I'll trade you for a bowl of that delicious-smelling stew."

"You like stew?" the slender woman said.

"Love it." Sookey placed the contents of her sack on a sideboard in the spacious kitchen.

Sookey introduced herself while the woman inspected the vegetable jars.

"They call me Monnie", the woman said. "Don't rightly know that I've ever seen a person your color before." She reached out and placed her hand gently on Sookey's cheek.

Sookey laughed. "I haven't seen any in a long while myself."

"You must be from over in Fortune County. I heard what they done over there." Monnie motioned for Sookey to sit at a table in the center of the room, while she dipped a large bowl of stew from the pot on the stove.

"Do you think the trade can include a slice of that cornbread and a cup of that good coffee I smell?"

Monnie agreed, and Sookey soon filled herself with a warm meal, something she had not done all day. As she drank her coffee, Monnie joined her at the table with a cup of her own, and they chatted as if they had known each other for years. From time to time, Monnie got up to tend to something in the oven or on the stovetop. Sookey guided the conversation to the subject of ginseng and inquired if the woman knew where she could buy some.

Monnie said she had gathered some on a few occasions in the past, but it was quite scarce and almost gone out of the mountains. What few times she had found any, she said she had given it to her husband to sell in Atlanta when he took his crop of vegetables to market.

"I'm going to be in Atlanta soon," Sookey said. "Do you know who he sold it to? Maybe I can buy some from him when I'm there."

"I don't know the man's name, but he's a Chinese fella who does the laundry at a hotel called the Dinkler. There wasn't much to sell, but my husband got a nice price for what he had, as I recall." She laughed. "Those Chinese people are fond of that old root. It may cost you more than you want to pay to get it away from them. If you can find someone up here in the mountains who's got some, it'd be a lot cheaper."

Monnie lit several lamps when they finished talking and excused herself to serve the food.

Sookey accepted her offer to use the hotel barn to bed down for the night. She placed Maude in an empty stall and snuggled down nearby on a pile of loose hay. She fell asleep content in the knowledge that she was welcome somewhere, even if it was just in a barn.

Snow stopped falling sometime during the night. When Sookey started back the next day, the sky was clear, not a speck of white anywhere, as if she had a bright blue bowl upside down over her. Refreshed from a warm night of rest, Maude was spry and alert, and Sookey detected a spring in her gait, as if Maude knew she was headed home.

When the two reached the Cleveland road, Sookey turned east and drove a few miles before pulling off the road. She guided the wagon into the trees far enough to be hidden from passersby. She would have to leave it there a short time, while she and Maude moved north along the ridge to the wild ginseng patch she and Billy had discovered on their first trip to Dahlonega.

Sookey threw the tarp and a bedroll onto Maude's back. She loaded her food and camping gear in two sacks around Maude's neck and headed out. Deep snow on the trail slowed them down. Maude's movement was steady but labored. After traveling several miles through the forest, Sookey located the sheltered cove where she and Billy had spent the night once before. She dismounted and guided Maude to the bottom of the slope. With her skillet, she dug out a clearing in the snow and set up camp.

It was a poor time of year to gather ginseng. She couldn't replant. Whatever she dug would be taken without leaving any offspring behind, but she needed enough samples to take to Atlanta to strike a deal for more to be delivered later. One or two roots would not be persuasive.

She tied Maude to a tree and climbed back up the slope on foot in search of the plants. The snow had drifted. Quite a few plants had died back to the ground. She used her skillet to remove snow from around each plant, then a knife to dig up the roots. The ground was hard. She stopped from time to time to catch her breath.

By late afternoon, Sookey had filled a small bag with ginseng roots. She had what she thought would be a gracious plenty and returned to her camp to spend the night.

The temperature dropped with the sun. When she finished with her small cooking fire, she built it into a roaring blaze and let it burn itself down. When nothing but a large bed of coals glowed where the fire had been, Sookey covered it with a thick layer of dirt. She erected her tarp over the spot and laid her bedroll on the warm ground. The buried bed of coals kept her and Maude warm throughout the night.

Sookey took her own sweet time getting started the next day and plodded down the ridge toward the Cleveland road. She had what she wanted and was in no hurry. Besides, she didn't want to get to Millersville until well after dark.

Being able to talk to the cook at the hotel was a welcome relief from her loneliness. She lost Billy almost two months before and had not seen her friends in over six months. Living in the country with a small child was lonely enough, but when one's only companion was a mule, the pangs of such solitude were hardly bearable. Maude was someone to talk to when she wasn't in the barn. She was a good listener, too, but that was about it. Sookey needed more. For the time being, though, the mule would have to do.

"What's your take on the hard times, Maude?" she asked. "You think President Roosevelt is going to work us out of it?"

Maude's long ears went up.

"You do? Well, that makes two of us, then. Yes, it does." She patted Maude on the neck.

Maude snorted.

"That soon? Naw. He's good, but he's not that good."

Maude stopped, almost throwing Sookey to the ground.

"What's the matter with you, mule?" Sookey said. She straightened herself on Maude's back. "Does talking politics upset you?"

When she looked up, two large men had stepped from behind trees and were blocking Maude's path.

"We saw your wagon in the woods down by the road," the one in the cap said. "And decided to follow the mule tracks to see if you needed any help." He paused and looked over his shoulder, then back at Sookey. "Do you?"

Sookey knew from the movement of the man's flat eyes and the tone of his voice that he wasn't interested in helping a stranger. He was more than likely up to no good and following someone who appeared to be alone in the woods. She thought of the money she had hidden and the valuable roots she had gathered. The idea of losing them again was unacceptable.

Sookey flashed a broad grin. "Oh, no. We're just fine. Been gathering some acorns for our hogs."

The man cocked his head. "In this snow?"

Sookey nodded. "They are hard to find. I grant you that."

The man returned a crooked smile and shifted his weight from one foot to the other.

The long-haired one tapped a stout oak stick in his gloved hands, his gaze focused on the two sacks around Maude's neck. "What you got in them sacks?" he said. A scowl covered his ruddy face.

Sookey continued to show her teeth and patted the sack on her right. "What, these? Oh, just some extra shells for this," she said. She pulled Billy's short-barreled shotgun from the sack and laid it over Maude's neck, pointing it in the direction of the men.

The men's mouths flew open. Both stepped backwards. The one with the scowl dropped his stick in the snow and showed his palms to Sookey. The other grinned sheepishly and put his empty hands out in the open.

Sookey continued to smile as she thumbed each hammer back. "I'd be awful careful wandering through these woods alone, if I was you," she said. "You don't know what manner of evil stranger you might run into."

The men nodded, their mouths still hanging open.

"Y'all take care now, you hear?" Sookey clicked her tongue. "Come on, Maude. Let's get these acorns home," she said, as she left the two men standing speechless in the snow.

CHAPTER 11

▼

On a clear morning in early spring, Sookey stood apart from small groups of people talking on the steps of the Fortune County courthouse. She had been summoned to appear in Magistrate's Court that day to answer a complaint filed by Zed Rudeseal. A dark green CCC truck with Jimmy Mack Jones at the wheel screeched to a stop in front. Zeb climbed out of the cab, slammed the door, and waved. Jimmy Mack nodded, repositioned his cap on his unruly red hair, and sped off in the direction of Atlanta.

Zed climbed the stairs, speaking and shaking hands with those nearby, and waving to others. He ignored Sookey, who followed him into the courthouse.

Zed took a seat down front near the magistrate's bench next to Sheriff Turner. He smiled at the magistrate and exchanged pleasantries with the sheriff.

Sookey took a seat on a bench in the last row. She ended up alone, as folks already there moved to a new location when she sat down.

Magistrate's Court handled all small claims, and the cases on the docket that day moved quickly, because no jury was involved. Many folks stayed in the courtroom after their case was over. She presumed they stayed out of curiosity to see what was going on between her and Zed.

The low rumble of muted conversation in the room ceased when the clerk called her case.

"Zedidiah Rudeseal versus Sookey Shanks, a person of color," the clerk intoned. "An action in replevin and trover for the return of one snuff tin and its contents, or their value, estimated to be in excess of forty dollars, all of which were wrongfully converted to her own use by the defendant. The parties will approach the bar of the court."

Zed, already in place, simply stood. A grin covered his face. He nodded and winked at several people. Sookey trudged down the aisle as heads turned to follow her progress. A hush remained over the room. The silver-haired magistrate watched her. On reaching the front, she took a position in front of the magistrate, a respectful distance from him and Zed Rudeseal.

The magistrate adjusted his wire-rimmed glasses and read from the complaint in front of him: "Sookey Shanks, the plaintiff Zedidiah Rudeseal contends that on a certain date last year, while he was in a condition of extremis, you removed from his person a snuff tin containing forty dollars. He has brought this action against you to recover the tin and its contents, or their value. You will need to admit or deny the truth of the following statements: Were you in his presence on September the seventh, 1935, near Dahlonega, Georgia?" The magistrate looked over the top of his glasses.

"I don't keep up with exact dates," Sookey said. "But to my best recollection I saw him near there about the first week or so in September. Yes, Sir."

The magistrate referred once again to the complaint. "At the time that you saw him, was he in a condition of extremis?"

Sookey scratched her cocked head and looked up sideways at the magistrate. "I don't rightly know what 'extremis' is, but if you're asking me if he was drunk, yes, Sir, he was as drunk as a coot."

The audience roared with laughter. Zed's face flushed, and he looked to the floor.

The magistrate banged the gavel. "That is not what I asked you. Was his physical condition otherwise such that he was not in control of his faculties and was unable to care for himself?"

Sookey looked toward the ceiling, placed her hand to her temple, then looked back toward the magistrate. "He wasn't in control of nothing. And aside from being drunk like I said, he was wringing wet and freezing cold. I had just pulled him out of Waters Creek, and his whole body was quivering worse than a rabbit's nose. If that's what you mean by being in extremis, he was all that and more."

Zed raised his head and looked cautiously around the room. Spectators chuckled and whispered in animated fashion. He returned his gaze to the floor.

The magistrate rapped his gavel several more times. Even then, an undercurrent of hushed voices flowed through the room.

"Do you deny taking a snuff tin from the person of Mr. Rudeseal?" the magistrate asked. He arched his bushy eyebrows.

Sookey nodded vigorously. "I do."

"Do you deny going through his pockets once you saw that he was incapacitated?"

Sookey cocked her head. "Is that the same as being, as you say, in extremis?"

The courtroom became uncomfortably still. Zed looked over at Sheriff Turner, who avoided his gaze.

"Yes," the magistrate said.

"I never went through his pockets. I just left his pockets and whatever was in them on the ground and headed for Dahlonega as fast as my old mule Maude would take us."

Deep wrinkles creased the magistrate's forehead. "You say you left his pockets on the ground. I don't understand."

Sookey stepped as close as she could to the magistrate's bench and spoke in a hushed voice. People throughout the room strained to hear her.

He sighed and shook his curly head. "Step back, woman, and speak up. This is an open courtroom, and if you have something to say, say it so all can hear."

She backed away and shrugged. "If you say so. The man was going to catch his death if I didn't get him out of those wet clothes, so I stripped him buck naked, wrapped him in a blanket, and hauled him to the nearest doctor. I don't know what happened to his clothes. Last time I saw them, they were in a pile on the ground near the bridge at Turner's Corner. They were the least of my concern at the time."

The room fell quiet. Some of the men shook their heads, and a few women put their hands to their mouths. Sheriff Turner touched his temple and looked to the floor.

The magistrate cleared his throat and spoke in a subdued tone. "From what I've heard, you were negligent and responsible for the loss of Mr. Rudeseal's clothes and his personal belongings, which are the subject of this suit. I find against you and in his favor in the sum of forty dollars and fifty cents, plus court costs of four dollars. If you need to pay it over time, you may work out the details between you." He banged his gavel.

Sookey pulled a fifty-dollar bill from the pocket of her dress and laid it on the desk in front of the clerk. "No, I'll just pay it off all at once, since he seems strapped for cash." She looked directly at Zed. "Just keep the change. It was worth it, telling my story in front of all your friends."

No one moved as Sookey walked back up the aisle and out the door.

Carter Baxley sat slurping coffee from a saucer in Thelma's Cafe when Zed walked in.

"You mind?" Zed pointed to a chair.

"Sit down," Carter said.

A wisp of a woman approached them. "You want lunch, Zed?"

"Try the special," Carter said. "That's what I'm having."

"That'll be fine, Thelma. But I'll have ice tea."

After Thelma left, Carter asked, "Where do you think Sookey Shanks came up with the kind of money she paid out in court today?"

"Were you there?"

"Naw. Heard about it, though. Everybody has. Folks say she had a fifty-dollar bill. You know that's not saved-up money, don't you?"

"Hadn't thought about it," Zed replied.

"No, Sir," Carter said. "That money was paid to her for something. I wonder what it was."

The two sat in silence for a while. "You know," Carter said, "on my way back from the CCC camp this past winter, I thought I saw her headed to Dahlonega. Your run in with her was in the fall before that, and she was on her way to Dahlonega then. What do you think is taking her over there so much?"

Zed shook his head. "I have no idea."

Thelma appeared with Zed's tea. As Zed took his first sip, Carter slammed the table with the palm of his hand. "Damn. You don't think she's found a vein on her property, or maybe somewhere in the mountains?"

Zed lowered his thick eyebrows and wrinkled his nose. "You don't mean gold, do you?"

"That's exactly what I mean. All of the veins around Dahlonega played out a long time ago, but prospectors still find dust and occasional small nuggets all the time. The only assayers left around are over there. If she's stumbled on anything, she'd take it to Dahlonega to have it assayed, and then sell it there."

"Naw," Zed said. "That can't be it."

"Then you tell me where a black woman is going to come up with a fifty-dollar bill during The Depression, and from what I hear, not concerned about the change, either."

Zed shrugged.

"Anyone who knows about Lumpkin County gold knows the main vein ran northeast and southwest through Dahlonega. You strike a line northeast from Dahlonega, and you'll run smack dab through Shanks Cove. By golly, that's it." Carter slammed the table again.

Their food arrived, and the two ate in silence. When he finished, Carter left whistling.

Sheriff Turner's Model A chugged past Clyde Truett's store just as Zed Rudeseal emerged, a brown paper package clamped under his arm. Turner pulled over and stopped. "A little late for you to still be in town, isn't it?"

"Yep, and if you're headed up the north road, I'd be much obliged for a ride."

"Sure. Hop in."

Zed climbed in, and the car jerked away from the curb.

"Where's your driver?"

"I sent him to Atlanta to pick up Nadine. She's finished with her boarding school down there. That's what this is for." He held up the package.

"What?" Turner said.

"A new dress for her homecoming."

When they arrived at Zed's place, Zed invited Turner in for cookies and cold cider. Turner could not resist. Once inside, he was greeted by an apron-clad Flossie and the sweet aroma of fresh-baked pastry. The two men took chairs in the parlor, were served by Flossie, and spent the afternoon nibbling, sipping, and chatting. Zed avoided any reference to the events of that day, and Turner did not mention them.

The sun sat low on the horizon, when the brakes squealed on Jimmy Mack's truck.

"Flossie," Zed called out. "Nadine's here."

Flossie, flour smudged on her round cheek, hurried out of the kitchen, wiping her hands on a white dishtowel. "Good. Her welcome-home cake is just about ready. Come on."

She headed for the front door. Zed and Turner fell in behind. The three of them stood on the porch and watched Jimmy Mack walk around the front of the truck and open the door for Nadine.

Flossie straightened her hair. "Isn't he sweet?"

Zed just grunted. "What's she carrying?" he asked, when Nadine stepped out of the truck.

Flossie stood still, bunching her apron in front of her.

Nadine held a small blanket in her arms as she moved toward the house with Jimmy Mack on her heels.

Blood rushed to Zed's face. "No!" he shouted. "Not in my home, you're not." He whirled around and moved back into the house, slamming the door behind him. He yelled for Flossie to come inside.

Turner stepped to one side. Flossie remained frozen in place as her daughter approached. When Nadine climbed the porch steps, Flossie moved to meet her. She peered into the top of the blanket, then hugged Nadine.

"Flossie!" Zed yelled. "Get in here. And tell Jimmy Mack to take her back to Atlanta. I don't want that little black bastard in my house. After all I did for her. I can't believe she's doing this to me."

Flossie took the blanket from Nadine and started into the house.

"For God's sake, Flossie, don't!" Zed exclaimed.

Flossie kept coming, followed timidly by Nadine and then by Turner. Jimmy Mack stayed on the porch. Once inside, Flossie walked directly to where Zed was standing.

"Say hello to your grandson," she said. She pulled back the top of the baby's blanket, revealing its pink face and flaming red hair. "Well?" Flossie said. "Say something." She held up the baby.

Nadine stood just out of sight behind her mother, gazing at the floor, kicking at the living room rug.

Zed moved his lips, but no words came.

"Here," Flossie said. She handed the baby to Zed.

Zed reached for the bundle in Flossie's hands. He held it awkwardly, away from his body. It began to cry.

"Have you forgotten how?" Flossie chided. "Make it feel secure. Pull it close."

Zed complied. The baby quieted.

Turner stared at the infant. It was a miniature Jimmy Mack Jones. He drew a deep breath and shook his head.

"What's its name?" Zed asked.

Nadine stepped from behind her mother. "The same as his father. James Macklin."

"And his last name?"

"The same as mine." Nadine held up her left hand, revealing a thin gold band. "We got married in Atlanta this afternoon."

Flossie put her liver-spotted hands to her face. "Isn't it wonderful?" She retrieved the baby from Zed.

Zed moved across the room toward his easy chair. "I need to sit down. Get that boy in here."

When Jimmy Mack appeared, he stood in front of Zed, hat in hand, shifting his weight from one foot to the other.

Zed cleared his throat. "I don't have to ask you if it's true. What I need to know is this: Was that you who ran off when Flossie went out to the barn and found Nadine half-naked back when all this mess started?"

Jimmy Mack nodded, then hung his head.

Zed looked at Turner, clenched his teeth, and shook his head. He said, voice much stronger, "Come over here, Nadine."

Nadine obeyed and stood by her new husband's side. The two of them avoided Zed's gaze.

Zed stared at Jimmy Mack. "I had no idea you were sneaking over here to see Nadine when I sent you through the mountains on CCC business. If you'd wanted to court her, you should've spoken up."

"You wouldn't have let him, Daddy," Nadine said, looking Zed in the eyes. "You got all upset when any boy noticed me."

"Now, Nadine," Zed protested.

"It's true," she said. "And you know it." She took Jimmy Mack's hand.

Zed rose and walked to the living room window. He pulled the curtains aside, but didn't look out. "Why in heaven's name did you say you'd been raped by a black man? Why did you let me believe that?"

"Mama almost caught us. Most of my clothes were off. If it wasn't a rape, I knew you'd find out who was seeing me. I was afraid you'd hurt Jimmy Mack if you knew the truth. Honest, Daddy. I did."

Zed shook his head and sighed. "I took up for you, Nadine. I dragged that poor Bailey boy's body around the square like an animal for you. I ran all the colored folks out of this county for you." He flattened his hand against his temple.

Nadine eased herself toward him and touched his arm. "I've never heard you say a kind word about any black person in my whole life, Daddy. You didn't do all that for me. You did it for you. And that's the truth of it."

Flossie retreated to the kitchen with the baby and motioned for Nadine and Jimmy Mack to follow.

Zed grabbed his head with his hands and sobbed. Turner slipped away.

CHAPTER 12

▼

Prison could not have been worse than the cramped, backstreet flat Beaulah Jackson occupied for more than a year. Her banishment to Atlanta left her longing for the simple life she left behind. Her mountain views had been replaced by rooftops, the laughter of children in the dirt streets of Turnip Town by the honking of traffic. Her carefree, happy world surrounded by blue-topped mountains had been snatched away in the snap of a finger. Her well-chinked little cabin, though crooked and unpainted, had warmed and cuddled her in winter, cooled her in summer. Its walls echoed the life-sounds of her family's generations and absorbed the aroma of their countless meals. It was home. It was gone.

After taking in washing and ironing and doing odd jobs each day to get by, her only joy came on Sundays. She dressed in her finest, took her granddaughter by the hand, and joined others on their way to an imposing red-brick church a few blocks distant. That church was the only thing she liked about Atlanta. It was grand, a far cry from the dilapidated A.M.E. church of Fortune County. She found friends. She found respite from the week's drudgery. She found peace.

Her small group always passed a dingy apartment building along the way. Each time it was the same. A blond-headed child peered at them through the curtains of a second-story window, his hands pressed to the glass. But one warm, June Sunday morning, the boy was not there. The sidewalk in front of the apartment was cordoned off, and two police cars and a coroner's van were parked in the street. Beaulah's group passed by on the other side just as two men emerged, wheeling a sheet-draped gurney.

Beaulah's granddaughter tugged her arm. "What's happening, Grandma?"

Beaulah strained to see. "Look's like someone's passed, Honey."

"Is Sunday a good day to pass?"

"Well, child," Beaulah said, "if you're going to pass, it's as good a day as any."

In just a few blocks, Beaulah and her group mounted steep stone steps and entered the sanctuary through large double doors. They were early, and Beaulah took a seat near the front.

The choir, dressed in purple and white robes, entered the loft, and the gray-haired minister took a seat behind the pulpit. Music from the gold-colored pipes of the great organ signaled the opening of the service, and the congregation rose as one to sing.

The tempo of the music and hands clapping in unison stirred her. She loved the rhythm and the ear-splitting joy of happy people. But most of all she was mesmerized by the hypnotic cadence of the minister's words:

"The book of Daniel tells us about how old King Nebuchadnezzar couldn't believe his eyes when he looked into that fiery furnace. He saw God's children, Shadrach, Meshach, and Abednego walking around inside like they was on a Sunday stroll. And they were not alone. No, Sir. There was someone else in there with them. Someone the king did not recognize. And old Nebuchadnezzar pointed to that glowing oven and said in astonishment…how'd that white boy get in here?"

The crowd remained still, all eyes fixed on the minister. Jaws dropped. A few people whispered to each other in the strained silence.

"How'd that white boy get in here, I asked." The elderly minister pointed toward the front door.

People turned in their seats. No one spoke. Beaulah craned her neck. A small blond-headed boy stood in the center aisle near the front doors. Is that the boy from the window?

Finally, the black-robed minister broke the silence. "What can we do for you, Boy?"

"I'm looking for my mama," the boy said.

The man stepped away from the pulpit and wiped his brow with a handkerchief. "One quick look around should tell you she's not here." He smiled, and a few in the congregation chuckled.

The child drew himself up and took a deep breath. "I know she's not here, but I thought some of you might know where she is."

The preacher's tone softened. "What makes you think any of us will know where your mama is?"

"Because I thought you looked after each other, like a bunch of crows would do."

"I'm going to forget your crow remark, Son, because I can see you're still young. But, why do you think we would keep up with some white woman who ain't got the sense to keep up with her own?"

The boy planted his feet, raised his head, and squared his shoulders. "My mama's not white. She has a black face like you. I thought you might know where I could find her. I haven't seen her in a long time, and I want to go home. I just don't know which way to go." He hung his head. "And, besides that, I'm hungry."

The crowd stirred. Spontaneous conversations broke out. The minister called for quiet, stepped down from the altar, and sauntered up the crimson carpet toward the youngster. He cocked his head. "What's your mama's name, Son?"

"Sookey. Sookey Shanks."

"Praise the Lord!" Beaulah shouted from across the room. "It's Billy Briggs."

All eyes turned toward her as she rose and hurried up the aisle.

"I'm Beaulah Jackson, Billy. I used to live in Millersville. I don't know where Sookey is, but I know where Sookey's mama is, and I'll take you to her. Praise the Lord."

CHAPTER 13

▼

Sookey's first trip to Atlanta had taken almost four days of steady walking. Not knowing what to expect, she left Maude behind, carrying everything she needed on her back. More than once she imagined what her friends had faced as they were forced down that same road a year earlier. At least she was prepared and took food and water.

On that trip, she first saw the sign at the county line south of Millersville. Too large to be missed by even the most inattentive traveler, its message was simple and clear: "Attention All Coloreds. Don't let the sun set on you in Fortune County." Sookey made two vows that day. One was to enjoy a lifetime of sunsets at Shanks Cove. The other was to live long enough to see the sign come down.

Sookey had located Chiang Lee right where the cook at the hotel in Dahlonega said he would be—in the laundry room of the Dinkler Hotel in downtown Atlanta. She had taken enough dried ginseng root with her to get Chiang Lee's attention, but she refused to sell to him. Sookey had already decided to avoid any sang buyers in the mountains and increase her profit by cutting out as many middlemen as possible. She had seen her father and grandfather shorted for their crops by not being able to get them to market in Atlanta. She knew that the best market for ginseng in Georgia was among the Chinese in Augusta, and she held out for a buyer there.

Her refusal to sell and her representation of a steady supply earned her an introduction to Chiang Lee's uncle, Wo Fat, the venerable leader of a large Chinese community in Augusta. Her grandfather had told her of Chinamen who migrated there near the turn of the century to construct a system of canals and levees along the Savannah River. The Chinese had a deeper appreciation of the virtues of ginseng than the mountain folk of North Georgia. Sookey intended to sell it in the place of highest demand. Ginseng was sought after by traditional Chinese herbalists, not only in Augusta, but also in China. Wo Fat was her key to opening both markets to absorb whatever volume she could produce.

Sookey left Atlanta on the train to Augusta and struck her deal with Wo Fat. Chiang Lee would thereafter receive the ginseng from Sookey in Atlanta and pay her the price she and his uncle had settled upon. She and Wo Fat agreed to renegotiate the price once a year.

The quality and number of roots in Sookey's later batches of ginseng far outstripped that of her first. She worked hard throughout the spring and early summer, making countless trips to gather roots from her secret sang patch and taking them back to Shanks Cove to dry. Sang buyers did not want fresh roots, only dry ones, and their dry weight was considerably less. She quit spending the night at the patch, lest she create a camping site there that might give it away. She made a point to stay elsewhere in the mountains and approach the patch from different directions, to avoid making a trail. She even quit moving along the ridgeline within five miles of the patch in either direction. The changes made her trip exceedingly difficult, but they kept the approaches wild and undisturbed. Any evidence of human existence in the mountains was an invitation to the curious.

Sookey resisted the urge to gather as much as she could and harvested only a small amount each time. She had to preserve the integrity of the patch, and at the same time keep an even balance between Wo Fat's demand and her supply. Removing seeds from mature stalks and planting them in the most ideal locations along the northwestern slope of the ridge ensured the longevity of her patch.

She also carried a large number of seeds back home and planted them in various locations throughout the woods in the cove to grow wild and unattended. Only a small percentage of the seeds she planted would sprout, and not all of them would mature. Years would pass before any of them could be harvested. Her plan required patience and a slow hand.

Raising cash crops on her farm was out of the question for a woman living alone. Sookey focused on crops for home and farm use and foraged deeper into the mountains in search of the illusive sang. To find it, she had to explore the wildest parts of the mountain forest, places devoid of human presence. That meant no trails to follow and trips alone that lasted a week or more at a time.

Her solitary ventures paid off. While she found no patch to equal the first one, she found several smaller patches and many isolated plants. No chance existed of finding ginseng near any place where there had been human habitation. The plants had been picked away years before. She was relegated to the most isolated areas of the North Georgia Mountains, places where bear, mountain lions, and other wild creatures roamed at will.

The sides of some mountain coves where Sookey found sang were so steep, she descended holding a rope tied to Maude up on the ridge. On command, Maude moved forward and helped pull Sookey and her root bag back up the slope. Wherever she found ginseng growing, she removed seeds and planted them in suitable areas nearby. By midsummer, she had planted at least four seeds for each plant she harvested. She scattered the remaining seeds across the forest floor to let nature take its course. Even though the roots were smaller, Sookey favored the yearling plants for harvesting and left the more mature ones to go to seed.

On her regular trips to Dahlonega to trade for supplies, she invariably stopped by the hotel kitchen and traded honey or canned vegetables for a hot meal and some conversation, then spent the night in the barn with Maude. Her solitary life left her starved for human interaction. She relished her trips to Dahlonega and the small amount of time she spent jawing with the hotel cook, Monnie.

She bypassed Millersville on her way to Dahlonega by riding Maude over the mountain trail, but her business in Atlanta had become frequent. She could not avoid passing through town on those trips. When traveling on the road to Atlanta, she felt safer in the wagon than riding Maude bareback. It was also more comfortable. Propping her long-barreled shotgun in plain view next to the seat tended to discourage trouble, but if threatened, she would reach for Billy's sawed-off shotgun hidden in the sack at her feet. Having to use it someday was her greatest fear.

Whenever Sookey drove the wagon to Atlanta, she left it and Maude in the barn of an old drover north of the city and walked to the end of the nearest trolley line. From there, the trolley took her downtown and right past the Dinkler, where she sold her goods.

By the middle of summer, Sookey had made well over nineteen hundred dollars selling ginseng to Wo Fat and had spent only sixty dollars of it. She was aware of what banks were for, though she'd never been inside of one. She knew that the Bank of Millersville had failed about six years before, and that many white folks were leery of them. So, she placed all her cash in a fruit jar and buried it under a rock in the springhouse.

During all the time that she was gathering and selling ginseng, Sookey never lost sight of her purpose for the money—to provide a future for her Billy. But all the money in the world would do him no good, if he wasn't around to benefit from it. She had no idea where he was or how much she would need to find him.

Perhaps she had enough. Finding him would be the best use for the money, and she was willing to spend it all.

On her next trip to Atlanta, Sookey removed the money from the jar and took it with her. Her movement throughout the city was never impeded. She went about her business unnoticed and unmolested. Only in the countryside did she run the risk of being accosted when traveling alone. She feared not for her personal safety, but for the safety of Billy's savings.

Before leaving the cove, she removed some stuffing through a slit in Maude's collar and inserted all the bills from the fruit jar. A few rawhide bindings held the collar flap in place, and no one would ever know. As usual, people stared at them along the Atlanta road, especially in Fortune County, but by the time they reached the small village of Roswell, no one noticed.

Sookey crossed the Chattahoochee River south of Roswell on the same wooden bridge her grandfather had crossed, headed in the opposite direction following the Civil War. Sadly, she felt no more welcome in those distant mountains than he had sixty-five years earlier. Despite his inhospitable reception, he had hacked farmland out of mountain wilderness and built a home for his family with sweat and bare hands. She was as determined to preserve it as he was to build it. That determination kept her going, that and her devotion to the child of those who wanted to drive her away.

When she got to the drover's red barn in the farming community of Dunwoody, she removed the money from Maude's collar, wrapped it in cheesecloth, and placed it in the bottom of a feed sack containing her food. It would be safe there for her trip into town. She spent the night in the barn and got an early start the next day. Leaving Maude and the wagon behind, she traveled on foot to the end of the trolley line at Buckhead, a suburb north of the city.

She always enjoyed the trolley ride. She could sit back, relax, and enjoy the huge homes, the great number of stores, and a variety of automobiles as they passed her open window. The soft click of the tracks below mesmerized her with its regularity. How excited Billy would be to ride with her, the wind through the window blowing his fine, blond hair. She smiled and closed her eyes.

Sookey stopped briefly at the Dinkler to sell her latest gathering of roots. When she asked Chiang Lee how she should go about locating the whereabouts of an Atlanta woman named Cora Mae Briggs, he suggested she contact an attorney who had helped his family with some immigration matters. When Sookey left the hotel, she held firmly in her grasp a blank laundry ticket with the attorney's name and address scribbled on it. He worked only a few blocks away.

The second-floor office of Abe Waxman was in an old brick building on Whitehall Street, not far from the Fulton County Courthouse. She had never seen a lawyer before, much less met one. She had heard that the only two lawyers in Millersville made a living suing each other's clients. Rumor had it they took turns winning. Her only image of a lawyer was that of a young Abraham Lincoln, tall and imposing, in a faded photograph that hung in the main room of her cabin in Shanks Cove. She imagined someone equally as imposing as she waited to see Attorney Waxman.

She was impressed when the secretary spoke into a small wooden box on her desk. "Sookey Shanks, *swartz*, to see you, Mr. Waxman," and delighted when, after a slight pause, he answered through the box, "Send her in."

To Sookey's surprise, she found not a tall man in a black waistcoat, but a short balding man in his shirtsleeves, peering over a pair of half-glasses from behind a cluttered table. He remained seated in a swivel chair when she entered. Behind him was an open roll-top desk, all neat and orderly, unlike the table that separated them.

"I don't do criminal work," he said without emotion.

"And I'm no criminal," Sookey replied.

He sat with his elbows on the table, rotating a pencil slowly between the thumb and forefinger of both hands. "I do mostly real estate, then a little of this and a little of that."

"I guess I need a little of that, then," Sookey said. She placed her feed sack on the table in front of her. "I'm Sookey Shanks, and I can pay."

He dropped the pencil and rose from his chair. "I'm Abe Waxman, and I'll be glad to take your money." He smiled. "But not if I can't help you. Have a seat."

Sookey sat down across the table from him. Abe returned to his chair.

"What can I do for you, Miss Shanks?"

"Sookey will be just fine. I don't know a Miss Shanks."

"All right, Sookey. How can I help you?"

Sookey leaned back in her chair, and fixed her gaze directly on his. She talked for the next thirty minutes without stopping, recounting her life with Billy to an astonished Abe Waxman. The only break in her story was when Abe crossed the room to a water cooler near the window. He got them both a cone of water.

When she finished, Abe sat staring at her. Large wrinkles appeared in his forehead as he squinted. "I'm not sure why you need my services."

Sookey sat up straight. "I want you to find Cora Mae and Billy for me. I know they're here in Atlanta."

Abe shook his head. "Now, Sookey," he said. "There's no way on this green earth that I can get that boy back for you. Even if she's not a fit mother, no court's going to—"

Sookey waved her hand. "I'm no fool, Mr. Waxman. I know I have no right to him. I just want to know where he is and that he's all right and doesn't need anything. I need to watch out for him, even if it's from a distance."

Abe's face relaxed. Wrinkles and lines disappeared. A few returned and played around the corners of his mouth when he smiled. "Okay, Sookey. If all you want is for me to try to find them, I can do that. If, as you say, she's a prostitute, she more than likely has a record. She should be easy to find."

Abe swung around in his chair facing the desk. He pulled a clean pad from a cubbyhole and wrote and spoke at the same time. "Cora Mae Briggs, you say? Is it M-a-y or M-a-e?"

"M-a-e," Sookey said.

"And Briggs, does it have one *g* or two?"

"Two."

"Is the boy's name William, or is it really Billy?"

"It's really Billy," Sookey replied.

Abe spun around. "Do you know her date of birth?"

Sookey shook her head.

"Does she have any kin hereabouts?"

"Not that I know of. She's really from Millersville. Been here since Billy was born."

Abe rose. "Okay, then. It'll take a few days. How can I reach you?"

Sookey got to her feet. She scratched the back of her head. "Don't have a phone. Can't count on getting mail through Millersville. The postmaster runs the general store, and he won't let me buy, sell, or trade there. I doubt he'd hold mail for me. Why don't you write me care of general delivery in Dahlonega. I get over there about every other week. I can pick it up there. I come to Atlanta about once a month. I can stop by here when I'm in town."

Abe nodded. "About payment…"

Before he could finish, Sookey lifted the feed sack from the table and dumped the contents in front of him. Out rolled two hard biscuits, a tin of peaches, and a wad of fifty-dollar bills.

Abe stared blankly at the cash, then gaped at Sookey. His mouth opened and closed several times before any sound emerged. When he spoke, his voice wavered. "I only need twenty-five dollars. You have enough money there to choke a mule."

Sookey laughed. "Never heard it put quite like that. Old Maude would probably agree with you." Her smile vanished, and her face grew somber. She set her jaw. "You need to know I'm willing to spend all I have, if that's what it takes to find that boy."

Abe's round head moved slowly side to side. He pulled at his ear lobe with his right hand, then scratched his smooth chin. "I guess you would," he said. "But that won't be necessary." He thought for a moment, then motioned toward Sookey's chair. "Sit down. We need to talk."

The order issued by the diminutive lawyer didn't make Sookey return to her seat, but the sense of trust that had grown within her during her short time in his presence did. He was a no-nonsense person, seemingly interested in her plight and in her need to know that Billy was safe and being cared for. Here was a white man who hadn't reacted to her blackness or judged her because of it. She sat down and waited for him to speak.

"Where you came up with all that money in these hard times is not my concern. But I'd be remiss if I let a client of mine walk around with it in a sack. Aside from having someone slit your throat over it, it's doing you absolutely no good being cooped up in a bag with a brace of biscuits. Have you ever thought of investing it?"

Sookey smiled. Billy was going to be real proud of her. She had gone from being an obscure black woman with a feed sack slung over her shoulder to a "client," all in one day. She liked the sound of "client." When she found Billy, she would give him enough money to become a "client," too. It didn't take much— only twenty-five dollars.

"What are you grinning about?" Abe asked.

"Oh, nothing. I was just thinking about something."

Abe cleared the table in front of him and placed a blank pad in the space. "Investing is serious business," he said. "You obviously have a source of income. If that's the case, you should consider investing as much as you can." He pointed to the wad of bills on the table. "How much do you have there?"

"Close to two thousand dollars," Sookey said. "And, there's more where that came from."

Abe's jaw dropped. "I'm not going to ask," he muttered. He was quiet for a moment, all the while looking into Sookey's eyes. "How much of this do you need to live on?"

"None. This money's for finding Billy."

"I've already told you I'll find him for twenty-five dollars. That's settled. Do you have any idea what you can do with this much money in these hard times?"

Sookey shook her head.

"I thought not," Abe said. "There's a lot of real estate out there that you can pick up for a song."

Sookey laughed. "I've got more of those than I do money. And I have a strong voice, too."

Abe's blue eyes sparkled. "I don't doubt that."

Sookey wanted desperately to understand what the attorney was telling her. She had never had enough money to spit on and had no sense of its uses. She spent most of her life bartering to get by. "Even if I could buy real estate, I've heard of a lot of folks, both black and white, who lost their land in the last few years. Why did that happen, if it was such a good investment?"

Abe reached behind him and pulled a long document from a drawer in his desk. "Because they didn't really own their land, and the people who owned this piece of paper took it away from them. It's called a mortgage." He handed the document to Sookey.

She took it and scanned one side and then the next.

Abe continued, "Most of the people who've been hurt by our poor financial times are those who owed money to folks who held those documents."

Sookey returned the document to Abe. "That's a powerful little piece of paper, isn't it?"

Abe placed the mortgage back in the drawer and locked it. "It is indeed. And the people who own them are powerful people. They get paid on a regular basis with good interest. If the payments don't come in, they can take the property for their own. Sometimes they take the property and rent it right back to the people they just took it away from, and they keep right on getting paid."

"And that's what's called investing?" Sookey said.

"That's one aspect of it," Abe replied. "There are certain parcels of property one ought to buy outright, because of the likelihood that it will increase in value. Not soon, mind you, but over time, especially if you choose the right location."

Sookey listened intently as Abe Waxman tried to explain to her some of the ways to invest her money. When he finished, she cocked her head to one side. "And what do you get out of all this?"

"I get paid for my advice and for drawing up the papers. The more successful you are, the more work I get to do."

She sat in silence for a moment. So many doors had been closed to her since her childhood. How was investing going to be any different? "Even if I had enough sense to know what to buy," she said. "Who's going to sell their property to a black woman?"

Abe folded his short arms and leaned back in his chair. "That's where I fit in. I'll form a company for you, and the company will buy in its name. I'll pick the property and the mortgages and do the negotiating. No one will ever know you're involved." He sat up. His words came louder and faster. "Sookey, there's raw land out there selling for a dollar an acre. One thing about land; they're not making any more of it."

"I don't know," Sookey said slowly.

Abe continued, undeterred. "There are commercial buildings and lots mortgaged at half or a third their value that'll be given up in foreclosure within a year or so. The banks hold so many shaky mortgages now, they'd be delighted to sell some at a discount." He slapped the table with the palm of his hand. "You are standing at the door of a buyer's paradise with a wad of cash. What do you say?"

Sookey stood up. "Mr. Waxman, what you say sounds all well and good, but I'm not going to spend any of Billy's finding money until he's found. After that, you and I are in business."

Abe rose to face her. He extended his hand. "Fair enough."

They shook hands, and Sookey turned to leave.

"Just a minute," Abe said. "You forgot your money."

Sookey kept walking. "No, Sir. I didn't forget. Clients don't walk around with their money in a feed sack." She stopped at the door and turned around. "You keep it safe with your other clients' money until we find Billy. Then you go buy whatever needs buying and foreclose whatever needs foreclosing."

CHAPTER 14

▼

Nothing had ignited Carter Baxley's imagination as much as the expectation of finding gold hidden on the Shanks place. Ever since he figured it out, he had counted the hours until he could go get it. He and Caleb monitored the movement of Sookey Shanks for several days. He hoped to catch her gone and have the farm to themselves. They could search it at their leisure.

When he spotted her passing through Millersville in her wagon, he knew they had the time needed. He and Caleb raced out to Shanks Cove in their old truck to have a look around.

When they stopped in the deserted yard, Caleb asked, "What if she comes back before we finish?"

"We'll do what we have to do to make her tell us where it's at," Carter said. He stopped the engine. "Then we'll put the black bitch away." He jerked on the emergency brake. "On second thought, if we can't get her to show us where it's hid, we'll put her down, anyway. We'll find it on our own." He climbed down.

The thought of finding hidden gold, coupled with killing another Negro, made Carter's scalp tingle. Little shivers started at the top of his head and ran down his spine every time he thought about it. How excited he was when he killed Bailey Turnage and the nosey ranger, and what a great time they had dragging the Turnage boy's body around the square. Gold or no gold, he could hardly wait.

Carter let nothing deter them as they swept through the old cabin. They dumped the contents of drawers on the floor. They emptied flour, sugar, and salt sacks into one huge pile. They smashed jars of canned food against the walls. Their intemperate soiree seemed more a vendetta than a search. Carter laughed aloud at the thought of accomplishing on his own what the entire county had failed to do—getting rid of Sookey Shanks. He would get paid handsomely, to boot.

After wrecking the downstairs, they climbed to the second floor, where they did more of the same. They moved methodically from room to room, emptying, pulling, smashing, and tearing. Nothing escaped them.

Carter opened a large chest in one of the upstairs bedrooms and removed an enormous bearskin, with a head the size of a watermelon. "Lord, Lord," he exclaimed. "Look at the size of that sucker. Wait till I tell Myron. Monster bears must really roam this cove after all." He emptied the contents of the chest on the floor.

Finding no gold upstairs, they returned to the first floor and went out onto the porch. Carter stood and surveyed the many outbuildings. He stretched and rubbed the back of his neck. Searching for gold was not what it was cracked up to be. After looking for only two hours, he was already sore. He sighed and headed for the barn. "You take the other buildings."

Carter quit searching in late afternoon and returned to the truck. Caleb was nowhere in sight. Carter honked the horn several times and waited. Still no Caleb. When Carter laid on the horn and kept it blasting for several seconds, Caleb emerged from the springhouse. He shook water from his hands and wiped them on the legs of his pants.

"Whew, that was cold," he said. "I felt like a raccoon groping around in there for crayfish."

"Where the hell you been?" Carter's lips curled into a scowl.

Caleb climbed into the passenger seat.

The scowl remained. "I hope you looked real good."

Caleb nodded. "I went through my half with a nit comb. It ain't there, I tell you. She's either buried it in the yard somewhere or hid it out in the woods. It'd take an army and then some to find it." He stretched and leaned back in his seat.

The huge eight-cylinder engine coughed, then came alive with an ear-tingling rumble. "Not if we're smart," Carter said, as he wrestled the long floor-shift lever out of neutral and into a grinding first gear.

The solid old truck inched away from the cabin and up the wooded lane. Carter moved through all the gears, and the whining of the transmission stopped before Caleb spoke.

"How's that?"

"Either she's got it on her," Carter replied. "Or she goes to check on it now and then. You've got to watch her from a distance and find out where her bank is."

When Carter reached the grade that would take them up to the ridge road, he dropped the truck into low gear and started the gear sequence all over again. Conversation was difficult over the screaming transmission, so they remained quiet until the truck labored to the top of the ridge and out of the cove.

"Ain't no bank in Millersville going to let her do business," Caleb said. "Besides, if she was bringing gold into a bank in these parts, everyone and his brother would know about it, for sure." Caleb smiled.

Carter turned his expressionless face toward Caleb. His right hand flew from the steering wheel. The open palm smacked Caleb in the back of the head and returned to the wheel.

The blow propelled Caleb's head forward. "What was that for?" he cried. He straightened up and rubbed the back of his head.

"Ain't no bank in Millersville going to let her do business," Carter mimicked, wagging his head back and forth. "I'm not talking about a real bank, dummy. I'm talking about her stash, her hiding place."

Caleb's mouth dropped open. "Oh."

They remained quiet when they reached the paved road into town. The regular beat of the tires on the joints of the cement road punctuated their silence. Carter finally spoke. "There's only one way to do this. When she gets back home, I'm going to drop you off on the ridge overlooking the cove first thing of a morning. Make your way through the woods to a spot where you can watch her farm and not be seen. Keep your eyes on her. Follow her if she leaves. Sooner or later, she'll lead you right to it."

"How long do I have to stay there?"

"All day, if you have to. I'll pick you up after dark and bring you back each day, if need be."

"But—"

Carter waved his hand. "I'm telling you, it's the only way. You stay on her, and I guarantee she'll lead us to her gold."

Caleb arched his eyebrows. "Do I get to kill her?"

"Whenever you're through with her, little brother."

Warned by the tire tracks on the road through the thicket, Sookey cocked her shotgun. She stopped Maude and surveyed the farmyard, before emerging into the open. Seeing no vehicle or person, she pointed the gun toward the cabin and approached. Had the whites come again to run her off? Was someone still lurking inside to catch her offguard? She crept across the porch, focused on the door but glancing at the windows. She lifted the latch with her gun barrel and pushed.

Drawer contents and toppled furniture greeted her. A chill coursed through her. She wound her way through the mess, watching for any sign of movement. Broken glass littered the kitchen floor. A white mound stood beside the overturned table. A film of flour dust covered everything in the kitchen, and the acrid smell of canned tomatoes filled the air. Sookey moved as quietly as she could, stopping often to listen, but heard nothing. She found every room upstairs torn apart, but no one remained in the cabin.

Although nothing was missing, her home had been wrecked. Laying the shotgun aside, Sookey sat on the edge of her bed, placed her head in her hands, and wept.

She worked all night cleaning her cabin. By the time she was through, it was time for chores. The sun was just topping the ridge when she finished putting extra feed in the barn for the livestock. She gathered a basket of eggs from the henhouse, then scattered a generous portion of cracked corn across the chicken yard. The shrill cry of a sentinel crow pierced the morning stillness as Sookey headed toward the springhouse to draw water. She stopped to listen and then moved on.

Later, as she carried the eggs and water toward the house, the crow called out again. This time a second crow took up the alarm. Something was stirring in the woods near the ridge. Perhaps it was the same no-counts who had vandalized the cabin. The damage had surely been done out of pure meanness. No self-respecting robber would have stooped so low.

When the crows refused to be quiet, Sookey decided to draw out into the open whoever was hiding. A large portion of her food supply had been destroyed, so she must make another trip to Dahlonega to replenish. She was tired from the long trip back from Atlanta and got no rest when she returned, because of the condition of her home. Despite her weariness, she got ready to leave again. She gathered a ham and several sides of bacon from the smokehouse. She loaded the food, some sang-digging tools, and her bedroll on Maude. Maude would be weary as well, but she had gotten some rest the night before.

Sookey made all her preparations in plain view, so anyone watching would know she was leaving on a trip. She intended to leave, then wait in the woods for the vandals to approach the house. They could not do much more damage, other than burn it down. She couldn't stand guard all the time, if burning her out was what they were of a mind to do. At least she would know who was trying to run her off, this time. If it was that peckerwood George Zell, she knew that any damage would be superficial. He had too much to lose, if he really believed he owned the place. If it was someone else, she would have to deal with it in due time.

Sookey eased herself onto the blanket draped over Maude's back and guided the animal toward the trail that led away from the cove toward Dahlonega. The trail rose sharply. She was out of sight within a few hundred yards, high enough to view the entire farmyard, as well as the road that ran through the wooded grove to the ridge. She stayed atop Maude, waited, and watched.

Very little time elapsed before a lone figure trotted down the grove road toward the farm. She studied him as he neared. My gracious, it's that no-good Baxley boy, Caleb. "Come on, Maude," she said. "We got better things to do." She clicked her tongue and pressed her knees into Maude's sides. Maude responded, and the two of them moved up the trail toward Dahlonega.

By midafternoon, Sookey and Maude were worn out. Maude set a slow pace, and Sookey kept falling asleep. Sookey stopped and made an early camp at a place that looked familiar. A small evergreen with branches that draped to the ground formed a natural shelter from the rain and the dew. Sookey crawled inside and lay on a bed of fragrant needles. She had slept there when she and Billy were first trying to make their way to Shanks Cove. The creek was nearby for water in the morning. It was still light out when Sookey fell asleep, smiling.

In the realistic dream, the man held a gun to her temple and yelled at her. She tried to move her head away, but the barrel pushed hard against her skin. She wanted to wake up, so she could roll over and start a new dream—a better one. She heard her name called several times. She opened her eyes. The gun was still there. This was no dream.

"Get up, bitch," a man said. She sat up. Kneeling in front of her within the confines of her pine tent was Caleb Baxley, a gun in his hand, a snarl on his face.

Caleb backed slowly out from under the tree, and Sookey followed on her knees. Once outside, he poked the barrel of his pistol under her arm and forced her to stand. He picked up one of her digging tools and threw it at her. "Let's go get it. We still got an hour of daylight."

Sookey was still trying to clear her head, trying to understand what was happening. "Go get what?"

The barrel of the pistol glinted in the late sun as it moved in a blur toward the side of her head. The blow threw her back on her knees. Her ears rang. The ground in front of her sparkled with flashes of light.

Caleb grabbed her by the throat and jerked her head toward him. "I'm not playing games. I want your gold, and I want it now. I know it's around here somewhere, or you wouldn't have stopped so soon in the day. You even brought your digging tools with you." He pointed to a narrow hoe with a shortened handle and a small shovel lying by her food sack.

Sookey said, voice raspy and weak, "Those are for digging sang."

"They're for digging gold!" Caleb screamed. "You lying black bitch." He lashed out at her again with his pistol barrel.

Still dizzy from the first blow, Sookey never felt the second. She fell forward on her face in the dirt. She had no idea how long she laid there. Several boot blows smashed into her ribs, and she heard Caleb talking to himself as he tried to rouse her.

"Gold or no gold, I'm going to kill her," he said. "I can hardly wait."

Sookey kept her eyes closed as she came around, trying not to react to any of Caleb's kicks. She needed time to collect her wits. She felt his breath in her ear.

"Should I put a bullet in your brain or just tie you to a tree and let the bears have you?"

Sookey groaned and rolled over on her back. "Okay. Okay. I'll take you to my glory hole."

"Hallelujah!" he cried. "We're going to her glory hole." He helped her to her feet. "I'll even carry the tools."

With Caleb on her heels, Sookey started down a nearby slope in a direction that would intersect the creek she recalled from her first visit. "Keep your eyes open for two towering rocks split by a creek," she said.

"Okay." Caleb sounded out of breath.

They walked through the woods about a quarter of a mile. "I see the creek," Caleb said.

"Turn downstream when we get there," Sookey said. After traveling another quarter of a mile, she spied the two rocks. "We're close. Keep your voice down in case anyone's around."

Caleb's voice came in a whisper. "Okay."

They rounded a bend in the creek, and Sookey stopped. "I'm dizzy from your hitting on me. I need to rest a spell."

Caleb growled, "You can rest when we get there."

"We're there. See that cave on the right side of the creek? That's it. That's my glory hole. Let me rest, and I'll help you carry it out. It'll take two of us."

Even in the gathering darkness, Sookey could see the gleam in Caleb's eyes. His mouth hung open as he stared at the cave entrance. She even thought he drooled. Caleb raced for the cave in a trance. When he disappeared inside, Sookey bolted back upstream.

As she raced away, the enraged bellow of a sow bear shattered the air, followed by what sounded like the scream of a dying rabbit.

CHAPTER 15

▼

Rainwater poured from the grooves of the corrugated tin roof over Sookey's front porch, leaving an even pattern of holes in the dirt under the eave. Myron Turner leaned against a porch post, waiting for the rain to stop. He had been out to Shanks Cove three times that week looking for Sookey. Nothing seemed amiss.

Mist blanketed the tops of the mountains surrounding the cove. A warm front had settled over North Georgia, subjecting the land to a drizzling rain over several days. Turner hated rain. It spotted his khakis, and the windshield wiper on his Model A was hand operated. He could steer and wipe or he could steer and sip shine. He could not do all three.

Dreary days like this were made for a snort or two. His last stop before reaching the cove had been Raven Cliffs, where he picked up a few quarts of Sam Clewiston's best juice. Maybe now was a good time to get into it. No one was around, and he had all the time in the world before he had to get back to town. Besides, he might need a good belt before he questioned Sookey Shanks on the whereabouts of Caleb Baxley.

Carter Baxley had come to his office a few days before and reported his brother's disappearance. Carter said he had dropped Caleb off on the ridge road leading down into the cove. Caleb had expressed an interest in talking to Sookey about selling her place. Carter had not seen him since and suspected foul play.

When the rain let up, Turner made a quick dash to his car. He removed a fruit jar from the front seat and hurried back to the porch. Settling into a wooden straight-backed chair, he tilted it against the front of the house. Balanced on the two back legs, he carefully unscrewed the metal ring that held the lid of the jar in place and slurped a mouthful from the brim. He held the clear liquid in his mouth, swallowing a little at a time. The whiskey seared its way to his stomach, where a slow burn started. The hot sensation awakened in him the unpleasant recollection of a long-forgotten ulcer. North Georgia white lightning was not a prohibited item in Turner's diet, but Doc Whitley had uncharacteristically urged moderation.

With the top ounce or so gone, the jar was easier to handle. Turner kept it on the porch floor within easy reach, taking occasional sips as he watched the rain saturate the farmland around him. He had no place to be and was beginning to enjoy the peace and solitude of Shanks Cove. No wonder Sookey was so protective of it. He would be, too.

As the day wore on and the contents of the fruit jar dwindled, Turner dozed in the chair. He woke with a start from time to time, noticed that it was still raining, and closed his eyes again. Once, with his eyes still closed, he thought he heard the faint sound of singing off in the distance. Was it part of a dream? As the sound grew louder, he opened his eyes and turned his good ear toward the source. He recognized the melody long before he heard the words. It was an old gospel song. As the sound neared, not only could he hear the words, he also recognized the singer, Sookey Shanks. Her throaty voice echoed across the cove through the pouring rain:

> "Oh, they tell me of a home far beyond the sky.
> Oh, they tell me of a home far away.
> Oh, they tell me of a home where no storm clouds rise.
> Oh, they tell me of an unclouded day.
> Oh, the land of cloudless days.
> Oh, the land of an unclouded sky.
> Oh, they tell me of a home where no storm clouds rise.
> Oh, they tell me of an unclouded day."

A large brown mule slowly emerged from the mist on the other side of the cove. It plodded toward him down a sloped trail that fed into the cove from the south. Sookey sat astride the mule, singing at the top of her voice. A canvas tarp the size of a human body was slung across the shoulders of the mule in front of her. She stopped singing when she noticed Turner in the porch chair. The mule continued forward and carried her right to the edge of the porch.

Turner took another sip without taking his gaze off of Sookey. "Whose body you got draped over that mule?"

Sookey stared at him. "That jar in your hand sure has put queer thoughts in your head, but again, that's what it's supposed to do. Isn't it?"

Turner put down the jar and rocked forward in his chair. He studied the tarp. "Fruit jar or no, that still looks like a body under that canvas. You want to tell me about it?"

Sookey slid off the mule, onto the porch. A puddle formed on the floor planks under her, as water dripped from her saturated clothes. "I haven't time to worry about you right now, Sheriff. I've got to get into something dry before I catch my death." She brushed past him and entered the house.

The mule stood in the rain, flicking its ears from time to time, followed by an occasional headshake. Turner continued to focus on the deathly still form under the tarp. His stop by Raven Cliffs had been a good idea. He needed the contents of that jar right now. He took another sip and rose on unsteady legs.

How was he going to deal with Carter and avoid the lynching Carter would likely instigate? Whatever happened, one thing was for certain: Fortune County could now rid itself of Sookey Shanks.

The crows in the thicket below the ridge exploded into black specks when Carter Baxley's truck roared past. Their raucous calls mixed with the laughter of men and the barking of dogs riding on the truck bed.

Turner stood on the porch alongside the mule. He spied Carter at the wheel and Ezra Stynchecombe sitting beside him. As soon as the truck stopped, Carter jumped from the cab and hurried toward Turner. He stopped when he noticed the canvas tarp draped on the back of the mule.

"That better not be what I think it is," Carter snarled.

In one smooth movement, Turner removed his hat, wiped his forehead with the back of his hand, and replaced his hat. "Afraid it may be," he drawled.

Carter whirled around and returned to the truck. He fumbled under the seat and retrieved a long-barreled revolver.

"Hold on, now," Turner said. "Put that hog leg away. I've got this situation under control."

Before he could say another word, the screen door opened, and Sookey stepped onto the porch.

Carter sprang toward her. "What'd you do to my brother?" he shouted, pointing the pistol at the canvas.

Unperturbed, Sookey crossed the porch and stopped beside the mule. "I never touched him."

Carter ignored the steps and leaped onto the porch. He pointed the pistol at Sookey. "So help me, Myron, if she's harmed him, I'll kill her where she stands."

"Now, Carter," Turner said, easing toward him. He positioned himself between Sookey and the approaching Carter.

Sookey began to unlash the rope around the canvas.

Carter pushed his way past Turner and shoved her out of the way. "Don't you touch him." Carter untied the last two knots with the pistol still in one hand and yanked the canvas away. "My poor—" He froze. Instead of Caleb, two full feed sacks hung across the back of the mule.

Sookey pushed Carter aside. "It's been raining the better part of a week. I didn't go all the way to Dahlonega just to have the rain ruin my supplies. Now, if you men will excuse me, I'll just get them inside." She released the rope holding the two sacks together at the top and stepped toward the door with them.

"Well, where's my brother?" Carter stammered. He held the pistol at his side, pointed toward the porch floor. "I brought him out here five days ago and haven't seen him since."

Sookey held the screen door open with one foot. "If he's been missing that long, I dare say he's been eat up by the bears. We got some big'uns in these mountains, you know. You didn't happen to leave him out in these woods after dark, did you?" She disappeared into the house.

Carter turned toward Turner. "Myron, you don't believe all that talk about a giant bear, do you?"

Turner cocked his head. "Well, personally I don't. But, half the men on the back of your truck claim to have seen it." He looked over at Carter's truck. "Don't you, boys?"

They nodded.

Ezra Stynchcombe moved to the edge of the truck bed. "If Caleb's out there, my dogs'll find him. If there's a big old bear out there, they'll find it, too, and tear it up. I say we turn them loose."

The men on the truck shouted their agreement and were soon drowned out by the throaty barking of the hounds.

"Hear that, Sheriff?" Ezra yelled. "They're ready to have at it."

Turner raised his arms for quiet. "The way I hear it, the only time that big bear's been seen around here has been at night. It'll be dark in less than two hours. It'll take that long for them to pick up the scent on this wet ground. Then they'll have to follow it." He took off his hat and held it in both hands, while continuing to address the men. "If there's really a big bear out there somewhere, it behooves you all to wait till morning. Then I won't be having to tell your widows and children that you had more guts than good sense."

A murmur ran through the men. They avoided Carter's gaze. The dogs grew silent.

Carter sighed heavily and slid the pistol into his belt. "She sure has y'all bamboozled with her bear talk. More than likely, she blew poor Caleb away with that short-barrel she's known to carry in a feed sack, and he's lying dead out there somewhere. But I can wait till morning. There's probably nothing we can do for him now." He looked at Turner. "Are you going to join us?"

Turner nodded and put on his hat.

Carter climbed into the truck cab. "Good. We'll see you back out here at first light." He started the engine. "And Sheriff, I want her to come along." He pointed toward the house.

"I'll see to it," Turner said.

Barks and shouts echoed throughout the cove as the impromptu search party commenced its grim business. The bad weather had cleared out during the night. Both men and dogs seemed in good spirits. Sookey knew that some of Caleb's scent would linger for a few days. She hoped that the earlier rain had taken care of what time had not. The longer the dogs circled and barked, the more comfortable she became.

She sat in a rocker on the porch with Turner. Carter waited on the truck bed. They all listened for the same thing—a signal from one of the dogs that it was on scent. Mountain folk had heard it all their lives. To some who never owned a dog, just sitting on the porch and listening to them hunt was a pastime.

Turner rolled and lit a cigarette. He tossed the spent match out into the yard. "Carter must think you buried Caleb out there somewhere."

"Why do you say that?" Sookey asked.

"Because he brought a pick and shovel. I saw them in the truck when he went to get one of Caleb's shirts for the dogs."

Sookey rocked her chair several times. "Or else he's going digging for gold."

They both laughed, Sookey the loudest.

From a wooded trail across the cove came the melodious baying of a distinct hound.

"It's old Traveler!" Ezra Stynchcombe cried out across the field. "She's on scent and tracking up the ridge."

In an instant, the collective vocal cords of the pack began emulating the eerie call of Traveler. They came from all over the cove, headed straight for the sound of their successful pack-mate, dragging their hapless handlers behind them, as if each one needed to be next in line behind Traveler, or even to move ahead if the occasion arose.

The baying of the hounds sent a shiver through Sookey.

Carter leaped from the bed of the truck and sprinted across the cove. "Come on," he called to Turner and Sookey.

"Aren't you going to take your pick and shovel?" Turner called back.

"I'll get them when I need them!" Carter yelled as he started up the trail.

Turner jumped off the porch and trotted toward the spot where the others had disappeared into the forest. Sookey followed close behind. Turner slowed to a walk when the trail ascended the ridge.

After he had walked about a mile along the trail, Turner glanced over his shoulder at Sookey. "I still hear them up ahead. Maybe we should try to catch up."

"What for?" Sookey said. "They'll keep."

"Well, we might get lost out here, for one thing."

Sookey laughed. "We're not going to get lost, Sheriff. This is where I live. You wouldn't be worried about us sharing these woods with a few bears, now would you?"

Turner grunted and picked up the pace.

The day passed tediously as they moved deeper into the mountain forest. Turner and Sookey could not catch up with the dogs, which were obviously getting just enough of the scent to maintain their enthusiasm.

When the baying took on a deeper and more soulful tone, Sookey knew the scent was stronger. The sound of the dogs became static. What had been moving away from her and Turner most of the day was getting louder, as she and the sheriff moved up the trail. The dogs had stopped.

Sookey recognized the place as soon as she rounded a bend in the trail. The yelping dogs circled the droopy-limbed evergreen where Caleb had rousted her from sleep. The tree's full branches touched the ground, sheltering its bed of pine needles and the scent of Caleb Baxley.

When she arrived, several of the dogs crowded around her and sniffed the hem of her dress. Oh Lord. The tree had preserved her scent, too. She held her breath.

"Get them off of her," Carter yelled. "It'll ruin their scent."

Two of the handlers jerked on the long leather leashes. Sookey breathed again.

Ezra Stynchcombe pulled Traveler away from the tree. "He must've spent the night here. There doesn't seem to be any more of his scent on the trail. Let's fan out and start circling the tree and see where we pick it up again."

The men had difficulty removing their dogs from the strong scent, but they soon perceived they had not treed their quarry. They ran eagerly in ever-increasing circles around the evergreen. Sooner or later they would cross Caleb's and her trail once more. A feeling of dread came over her. The dogs were good, no question about it.

The baying started again, and the dogs dragged their handlers in the direction of the creek. Sookey kept them in sight this time, and Turner struggled to keep up. They plunged down the slope of the ridge. They did not hesitate, when they reached the creek. They turned and headed downstream.

Because of a bend in the creek, Sookey did not see the dogs reach the cave, but she heard them. Their baying turned to howling, punctuated by frenzied barking. They smelled bear. When she reached the mouth of the cave, the pack of snarling dogs blocked the entrance. The men, their guns at the ready, stood nervously back. The dog handlers wrestled with the long leashes, trying to keep the excited animals out of the cave. Unlike the dogs, the men seemed reluctant to enter.

"Turn 'em loose!" Carter shouted. "Whatever it is, we need to find out right now."

"No!" Ezra screamed. "Them's my dogs, and they don't need to be taking on whatever it is on its own ground. I get a fair price for tracking down escapees for the state. I can't afford to lose—"

Traveler broke free and streaked into the cave.

"Let them all go!" Ezra shouted. "She can't handle it alone."

As one, the rest of the dogs charged forward. Sookey cringed at the thought of the expected encounter. Within seconds, all the growling and snarling ceased. One by one, the dogs reappeared and milled around the cave entrance, whining and sniffing the ground.

Carter checked his gun and peered cautiously into the darkness.

"There ain't nothing to be afraid of in there," Ezra said. "Old Traveler would've had a piece of it by now."

Turner stepped in front of Carter. "Let me go." He slipped into the cave alone.

Everyone waited outside, glancing at one another and then at the cave entrance. Turner emerged after several tense minutes. He carried a saddle, a wadded piece of cloth, and a revolver. The men gathered around him.

"There's bear sign all over that cave," he said. He looked at Sookey. "And from what I saw inside, it's got to be bigger than anything I've ever seen in my life." He held up the saddle. "It ate a whole horse, except the bones, and it gnawed on most of them. This here's probably Ranger Bentley's saddle. It's got his initials burned in it."

"What about Caleb?" Carter cried.

Turner offered the pistol and what looked like a shirt to Carter. The shirt was covered with almost-black stains of dried blood. "There's only one set of human bones in there. They're fresh. Are these things Caleb's?"

Carter stepped closer and took the items, examining them briefly. "Yes." His voice was barely audible. His shoulders drooped as he turned and walked away. After just a few steps, he stopped. Without turning around, he said, "Is there enough of him to bury?"

"Nothing you'd recognize," Turner said. "But the boys can gather up enough to say words over." He looked at the men. "Can't you, boys?"

The men nodded.

Carter glared at Sookey. "According to the dogs, Caleb made a beeline for that cave, like he knew right where he was going, and he wasn't paying any mind to what might be in there."

Carter's eyes narrowed to mere slits. Sookey swallowed. Cunning and more dangerous than Caleb, he wasn't mourning. He was plotting.

Without another word, Carter climbed back upstream toward the trail along the ridge. Ezra gathered up his dogs and followed. Turner and Sookey waited outside the cave while the last of the men gathered Caleb's remains. They came out carrying a sack and started the long trek back to Shanks Cove.

Turner threw the saddle over his shoulder, holding it by one stirrup. "Come on," he said to Sookey. "I don't want to be left behind out here."

"Yeah," Sookey replied. "I don't want to be here when that old bear returns and finds his saddle gone."

Turner shook his head at her. "If I was you, I'd be more concerned about not stepping in that pile of bear scat in front of you."

Sookey looked down and spied a fresh pile of bear dung near her feet. Stepping over it, she said, "You don't think that could be—"

"Could be," Turner said.

Sookey laughed as she walked away. "Well, what do you know? One of the Baxley boys finally made something of himself."

CHAPTER 16

▼

Sheriff Turner knew that Carter Baxley was not going to let the death of his brother go unavenged. Even though he had stopped complaining about the presence of Sookey Shanks in the county, Carter's anger was still simmering just below the surface. Carter's fight with Sookey was far from over.

While Turner would have rather stayed away from Raven Cliffs for appearance's sake, he made a special trip to see how the loss of Caleb had affected moonshine distribution. Unless Carter had enlisted someone else, Carter was going to be hauling and selling the shine by himself. Working alone was uncharacteristic of him, and Turner was curious to see if there was a new hand in the fruit jar.

Turner gave the usual honks on the horn and was soon riding uneasily in the bosun's chair up the cliff's sheer rock face. God, he hated it. The worst part was knowing that he had to make the return trip as well.

Sam Clewiston met Turner at the top. About a dozen jar-filled boxes were stacked around the lift.

"Y'all making a run today?" Turner asked.

Sam nodded.

"Who's going with Carter?"

Sam pointed to his scrawny son, who was struggling toward them carrying a cardboard box.

Turner snorted. "Seems hardly big enough, if you ask me."

Sam pulled at one of the straps of his overalls. "He's toted every one of them boxes over here," he said. "He's a strong'un, Sheriff. Just turned thirteen."

"What does Carter say?"

Before Sam could answer, the boy spoke. "This here's the last one, Daddy. Mr. Baxley said we should start lowering them down."

Turner took the box from the boy. It was heavy, no question about that. "What's your name, Boy?"

The boy stuck a bare, big toe into the dirt and moved it around to form a depression. "Hoyt," he said without looking up.

"Hoyt, what does Mr. Baxley say about you going along on this trip?" Turner asked.

The boy continued to gaze at his feet. "He ain't said nothing about a trip. Just that he don't intend to carry any of them boxes, so I started carrying them down here. After the sixth one, he said, 'You'll do.'"

Turner gritted his teeth and pursed his lips. He stacked the box and walked toward the cave where he expected to find Carter. After taking only a few steps, he glanced back. "Don't lower any of those boxes until I get out of here. I don't want someone to come along and think I'm doing it."

As Turner passed the smoking cookers, Carter appeared at the cave entrance, his shotgun slung under one arm.

"What brings you up here?" Carter said.

"Just wanted to see how your delivery was getting on without Caleb. Met your new helper back there."

"Oh, Hoyt. Yeah, he'll do just fine."

"Kinda young, don't you think?"

Carter moved to meet Turner as he approached. "He's strong and will keep his mouth shut. His daddy'll see to that."

"If you say so," Turner said.

The two of them headed back toward the lift, walking in silence.

When they arrived, Turner said, "Any problems?"

Carter gazed at Sam and the boy, then back toward Turner. "Let's go down first," he said. "Then we can talk about it."

One at a time the two men climbed into the bosun's chair and were lowered to the base of the cliff.

Carter spoke as they walked toward Turner's car. "It's Zed Rudeseal."

"What about Zed?"

"He wants out."

"So let him."

"Myron, with the coloreds gone, the Friday-night business at the camp is the best single stop we make. We have more sales there in one night than we make in a week for the whole rest of the county. We fired up that extra cooker just for the CCC boys."

Turner climbed into his car and started it. "If the man wants out, we should let him out. Besides, he can hurt us."

Carter shook his bushy head. "The way I see it, the Feds would be more interested in us giving him up, than in him giving us up. All you need do is remind him. He's your friend." A crooked smile appeared.

"Won't do any such thing," Turner said. "If you want to lay that on him, you do it." He put the coupe in gear and drove away.

CHAPTER 17

▼

It was only the second letter Sookey had ever received. The first had been a note on her sixteenth birthday from her mother's sister down in Albany. She knew who this one was from even before she read the return address of Abraham Waxman, Esquire. She hurried out to the sidewalk in front of the Dahlonega general store that also served as the Lumpkin County Post Office. Her hands trembled as she tore at the glued flap. She could not suppress a smile. More than a year had passed since she'd seen Billy, and she was on the verge of reading about where he was and what he was doing. She could hardly wait.

The neatly typed news of Cora Mae's death did not register at first. When it did, she felt as if she had been punched in the stomach. She became strangely cold when she read the part that said no one in Atlanta who knew anything about Cora Mae had ever heard of Billy, including her landlady. The last line of the letter summoned Sookey to meet with Abe Waxman—a superfluous request. Nothing could keep her away. She unhitched Maude from a post in front of the store and headed to Atlanta by way of Millersville.

Sookey created a stir whenever she passed through Millersville, but she caused even more this time, because she stopped. Her entry into the county courthouse brought additional attention to her presence in town. Folks gawked. She ignored them.

She intercepted Myron Turner as he came out of his office on the first floor. "Where's Billy?" she said.

Even though he did not flinch, a slight widening of his blue eyes gave him away.

"I don't have time for you right now," he said. He turned to close the door.

"You'd better make time," Sookey said. "Or else I'm going to ask you again in a very loud voice, only this time I'm going to say 'your son, Billy.'"

Turner gritted his teeth and shook his head. He expelled a deep breath, pushed open the door, and surveyed the courthouse hallway. "Get inside." He stood in the doorway, his hand on the knob, until Sookey had entered the room, then closed the door.

He stood in the middle of his office, glaring at her. "You know good and well he's with Cora Mae. That was all settled last year. Now, what's this all about?"

"Cora Mae's dead." She put her hands on her hips. "Are you telling me you didn't know that?"

Turner's mouth flew open. "What? How'd you—dead, you say? What happened?"

"Was an overdose, I hear. Problem is, no one knows where Billy is. Worst part is her landlady never heard of him. You sure he was living with her?"

Turner had trouble speaking. "When, uh, when did this, uh, happen?"

"I'm not sure, but I'll know more when I get to Atlanta. I'm on my way now. You sure he was living with Cora Mae?"

Turner nodded. "I took him there myself. She planned to start him in school. I'm sure I'd have heard if she changed her mind."

Sookey moved to the door. "Well, I'll let you know, because I'm not coming back until I find him." She left Turner standing in his office, scratching his head.

Her trip to Atlanta was the fastest ever. She pushed Maude to keep moving, and the old mule understood. Abe Waxman was expecting her.

He spoke after Sookey was seated in his office. "I got Cora Mae's address from the police, but when I went to her apartment on a pretense, someone else was living there. The landlady told me about her death from an overdose."

"And she didn't know where Billy was?"

Abe cleared his throat. "Said she didn't know a child lived with Cora Mae. She doubted that one could've lived there, because of what Cora Mae did for a living. Anyway, she claims she never saw Billy."

Sookey got to her feet. "Will you take me there?"

"Yes, but it won't do any good."

"It'll make me feel better."

"Okay," Abe said, and led her to his car.

Though she had seen many, Sookey had never ridden in an auto. The cough of the cranking engine startled her. Engine noise wasn't new to her, but never this close. As they pulled away from Abe's office, she grasped the edge of the window frame and held on, white-knuckled. Abe drove a short distance to a tired, old building close to the downtown business district and parked in front.

"Is this it?"

"This is it."

Considerable pedestrian and vehicle traffic filled the area. Her head turned with each passing vehicle. Her eyes searched among the people on the sidewalk.

"I want to go inside," Sookey said.

"The apartment has been rented for several weeks. I really don't see—"

Sookey opened the car door. "Mr. Waxman, if I was a bloodhound, this is where I'd start sniffing."

Abe grinned. "Second-floor studio, facing the street."

Sookey knocked on the studio door. An elderly gentleman appeared.

"I have some ironing to deliver to Miss Cora Mae Briggs," Sookey said. "Is she in?"

The man laughed. "I hope it don't take you that long to do ironing. Otherwise a body would run plum out of clothes." He paused and studied Sookey. "There ain't no one here by that name, and I've been here two weeks. You best go talk to the landlady about where you can deliver your ironing."

Sookey looked past him into the apartment. It contained only one large room hosting a bed, a table and chairs, a kitchenette, and a small sofa facing the window. Oh, how confined Billy had lived during the past year.

"You need any ironing done?" she said.

"Not on the schedule you keep," he said. He shut the door.

When Sookey returned to the street, she told Abe to go. She wanted to look around the neighborhood. He refused and stayed to search with her. They left the car parked in front of the apartment building and took to the sidewalk, walking away from downtown. The farther they went, the deeper they moved into a predominantly black neighborhood, where small stores and shops intermingled with living quarters.

"He was here," Sookey said, as she surveyed the buildings around her.

Abe struggled to keep up with her rapid pace. "How could you know that?" He leaned over to catch his breath.

"I can feel it," she said. "Just like I feel a summer rain before it falls, or know a deer is watching me from its hiding place in the forest. It's something you know, but don't know why you know it."

"Maybe we should ask some of these shopkeepers if they've seen him." Abe gestured toward the closest set of store fronts.

Sookey stopped. "Before we do that, there's someone else I should ask first." She turned and mounted the steps of a red-brick church facing the street. She pushed on the large double doors and went inside. Abe followed and caught the doors before they banged shut.

Sookey stopped when she saw Abe behind her. "Your God don't mind you coming in here?"

Abe laughed. "Not if it helps me collect my twenty-five dollars."

Sookey smiled at him and then sat in a nearby pew. Abe sat down beside her. In the empty sanctuary, rows of pews were lined up like soldiers on parade. A dark wooden pulpit stood on a raised platform that stretched across the entire front of the room. A deep red carpet split the assembled pews and ran from the front door to the altar.

Although the room was still, Sookey could imagine the sound of exuberant singing and clapping filling the air and overflowing out onto the street. The golden pipes of the organ covered the back wall, glowing softly in reflected light. She had never heard the sound of an organ live, only on the radio when she and Billy lived on Pea Ridge.

"How magnificent that big organ must sound in this room," Sookey said. "I'll bet it struggles some not to be drowned out by the pure joy of the folks who sing and worship here."

Sookey sat in awe. Such a grand church! The abandoned clapboard building with a crooked cross on top and cardboard replacements for broken window-panes had been the only church she had ever known. A nudge from Abe brought her out of her wonderment.

"We should go soon," he said. "I need to be home before sundown."

"Go on," Sookey said. "I think I'll find a place around here to stay the night. I've got some more looking to do. Besides, I think I'd like to come back here for the Sunday service. I want to hear that organ get cranked up."

Abe rose. "Will you be all right?"

"I'll be just fine," she said. "Thank you for everything. I'll talk to you later."

When Abe was gone, Sookey bowed her head and whispered a prayer, first of thanks, and then for Billy's safe return. When she opened her eyes, light was dancing softly against the stained-glass window on the far side of the room, brightening the faces of angels and lambs. She smiled and said, "Amen."

A local black merchant helped Sookey get a room in a nearby boarding house. It was clean, the rates were reasonable, and the plentiful family-styled meals reminded her of her mother's table. She decided to remain a few days and to make it her hanging-out place whenever she needed to stay over in Atlanta.

Her search of the neighborhood had turned up only one possible sighting of Billy. A kindly shop owner said he occasionally gave fruit and sweets to a hungry-looking white boy about Billy's age, but had not seen him in several weeks. A pain sliced through Sookey's chest, when she thought Billy might be hungry. Even though she and Billy had been penniless back at Shanks Cove, they ate well. A considerable portion of her time on the farm had been devoted to making sure of that. She was angry with Myron Turner for taking Billy away. She was angry with Cora Mae for neglecting him. She was angry with herself for waiting so long before trying to reconnect. Her only consolation was that Billy had apparently begun to forage for himself in this concrete forest.

Sunday provided a respite. She climbed the granite steps of the red-brick church with a handful of other worshipers. She took a seat near the front. The organist took her place and shuffled through her sheet music. When she began to play, the notes flowed softly through her feet and fingers into the pipes of that great organ. From there, the pipes took the music, molded it into a vast array of stately tones, and delivered them into the spacious room around her.

Sookey closed her eyes. She could hear the shrill cry of the hawk on the wing, the bark of the squirrels in the hickory trees. She detected the chirp of the raccoons feeding on persimmons and the deep bellow of the mother bear calling for her young. She heard the whisper of wind in the tops of the pines and the rumble of thunder echoing across the valley. Sookey could see clearly in her mind the greatest cathedral of all, her beloved North Georgia Mountains. Surely, God was as much there as here.

As she stood on the top of the world, the warmth of the sun on her face, she heard her name being carried on the wind. She gazed across the blue-crested ridges, searching for whoever was calling. She saw no one, but heard it again as plain as day. "Sookey. Sookey Shanks." A hand touched Sookey's shoulder. Her eyes popped open. The church was full. The minister and choir were in their seats. Someone in the pew behind was touching her.

"Sookey, it's me. Beaulah Jackson."

Sookey whirled around, nearly speechless at the sight of her old friend. The two whispered their hellos and traded information as best they could in the hushed confines of the sanctuary. When the congregation rose, Sookey rose with them, armed with the knowledge of Billy's whereabouts.

Rather than sing with the rest, Sookey shouted, "Thank you, Lord," and hurried to the door, en route to Albany.

Only one southbound passenger train went out of Atlanta on Sunday that would pass through Albany, and Sookey had missed it. The next one left before dawn Monday morning. She got a seat, because the car was empty. The conductor instructed her to move to the cooks' quarters in the kitchen of the dining car, should any whites board her car along the way. She didn't have to move until the train reached Macon. Once relegated to the kitchen, however, she preferred the company of the service staff to sitting in a coach car alone. She even made a few cooking suggestions and pitched in enough to earn free meals for the rest of the trip.

When nothing was left to do, she sat and watched the gently rolling fields of cotton, corn, and sorghum interspersed among thick woodlands. Peaches were beginning to ripen on trees that stooped under their weight like old men. Stately pecan trees held hands in ordered rows on a fresh carpet of grass. Oh, if she could just run barefoot among the trees and then lie in the green coolness of their collective shade.

As the slender rails sliced through the heart of Georgia, she saw firsthand the farms and fields that were its lifeblood. Lone figures struggled behind mule-drawn plows in shimmering heat. Men pitched lines of raked hay into a faded red bailer. Cattle gathered near the edges of ponds or clustered in the meager shade of the only tree in the pasture. Solitary farmhouses sat stark and white in the sun, with moss-covered cisterns and rusting silos standing guard. Wisps of smoke rose from around black wash pots, and sheets billowed on backyard lines. An occasional shotgun shack squatted alone in a field, cotton planted almost to the share cropper's door.

The train moved without stopping through small look-alike towns, each with cotton gins, feed stores, and dilapidated barns bragging about Clabber Girl baking powder and Red Rooster snuff. They crossed groaning trestles over cypress-filled black-water creeks. She saw for miles between the ruler-straight rows of pines on tree farms masquerading as woods. Always close at hand were the steam-powered sawmills, each with its own sawdust Matterhorn surrounded by stacks of graded lumber drying in the sun.

The rhythm of steel on steel hypnotized her, and the passing countryside became a blur of ever-changing shapes and colors. She could hardly contain her anticipation. Would he be taller? Would he be gaunt from hunger? Would he recognize her? Those and myriad other questions ricocheted through her mind until the monotony of peanut fields made her doze in the late-day sun.

When she awoke, six dusty miles separated her and the Albany depot from her Aunt Phoebe's place—six miles that seemed like a hundred. As she trudged up the unpaved road leading to her aunt's farm, she smiled at the thought of walking in on her surprised parents, her brother and sister, and, of course, her Billy.

When the tree-shaded yellow farmhouse finally came into view, the ever-so-slight movement of a tire swing suspended from a poplar in the side yard of the house caught her eye. Even in the dwindling light, she could tell that a child occupied the swing. Her heart pounded. She picked up the pace. As she neared, the movement of the swing stopped. A small figure shot from the circular seat and bolted down the road toward her. She halted just short of a collision, had barely enough time to exclaim, "Praise the Lord," and scooped Billy into her out-stretched arms.

Amid squeals of "Sookey, Sookey," he buried his face between her neck and shoulder and sobbed.

Tears traced crooked lines down his dusty cheeks as she held him tightly to her, reluctant to release her grip, lest someone take him away again. She stood, clinging to him, rocking from side to side in the middle of the dirt road, as darkness fell around them.

"I knew you'd come," Billy finally said. "I've been watching this road from the swing every day. I just knew you'd come for me."

Sookey relaxed her embrace and looked him in the face. "The devil himself couldn't have kept me away." She kissed him on the cheek.

He hugged her again. "You're my mama. Yes, you are."

CHAPTER 18

▼

Carter Baxley sat on the rear of his rundown truck, parked off the road leading through the gate of the CCC Camp. He watched a long line of men pass the pay-master's table on the porch of the camp office. They're a good lot, he thought, hard working and doing all they could to provide for their kin during trying times. Mostly mountain men, their faces and forearms dark as leather, the rest of their bodies hid ghastly white under their shirts and overalls. Although all sported hats or caps, they still had squint lines etched around the corners of their eyes from long hours in the sun.

Eager to get their pay, some lit out for home and for fields in need of tending. A few gathered on the back of someone's truck for a ride to the nearest town. Others counted their money several times, then put it in their pockets and wandered back to their bunks or came in search of Carter's Speedwagon.

Glad to relieve them of some of their cash, he whistled as he dispensed jar after jar to the liquor-thirsty men.

When the line behind Carter's truck thinned, Zed Rudeseal walked through the gate and stood out of the way until the last man had made his purchase and left. Carter covered his load with a canvas tarp and grabbed a coil of rope.

Zed cleared his throat. "I want this to be your last time here," he said.

Carter stopped and scowled. "I've been paying you good money. More than I've ever paid anyone. I didn't do that for no short run."

Zed reached into his pocket and removed two twenty-dollar bills. "Here. Take this month's payment back, then." He held them out to Carter.

Carter stared at the money and shook his head. "No." He tied one end of the rope to the side of the bed and threw the coil across the top of the canvas. "We have a deal."

"We had a deal, and I carried out my end of it. Now the deal is over. Don't come back out here."

Carter tied the last knot, walked to the cab of the truck, and mounted the steel running board. He turned back toward Zed. "I don't need to come right up to your gate to sell my goods to these boys. This is still a free country, you know."

Zed swept his arm in front of him. "This is all Forest Service land. You can't get within three miles of here without being on it. My boys are not going to walk that far and back just for a quart of shine."

"What're you gonna do if I sell on their land? Call the feds? You're in this as deep as I am. Deeper, I'd say. Every man in camp knows what you've been up to."

"You may be right, Carter, but none of them know what you've been doing up on Raven Cliffs, which is also Forest Service land. So if the feds have to come out here, I may lose my job, but you're going to jail."

The Speedwagon roared to life and almost hit Zed as it backed out of the underbrush and onto the road. It drove off in its own dust storm.

Sookey and Billy stood hand-in-hand in Abe Waxman's reception room.

Abe came out of his office and stopped when he saw the two. He straightened his bow tie and grinned. "I see you found him."

"Sure did," Sookey said. She looked down at Billy. "Take off your cap, Punkin. It's not polite."

Billy snatched the cap from his head.

Sookey smoothed his hair. "I just bought him some school clothes, and he's not used to the cap." She motioned toward Abe. "This here's our lawyer, Mr. Waxman."

Abe stepped forward and extended his hand. "Sookey's told me nice things about you, Son."

Billy glanced at Abe's hand and then at Sookey.

She let go of Billy and nudged him. "Go ahead," she whispered.

Abe and Billy shook hands.

Abe placed his hand on Billy's shoulder. "Seeing as how I didn't find him, I want to return my fee."

Sookey shook her head. "No, I got my twenty-five dollars worth, but it's time for you to do whatever it is you do best. I'll do the same, but first I'm going to take Billy home."

Sookey and Billy took the trolley to the end of the line and walked from there to Dunwoody. They spent the night in the drover's barn and set out for home on Maude the next day. They traveled until dark, then slept in the woods. In the late afternoon of the following day, Sookey, Billy, and Maude walked slowly into Millersville from the south road. To discourage trouble before it started, Sookey retrieved the short-barrel when they reached the edge of town and laid it across Maude's neck. She guided Maude to the county courthouse and stopped beside Myron Turner's Model A, parked in front.

She could not see into his office windows, but sensed he was watching. He didn't miss much. Sooner or later he would appear. Within five minutes, the front doors of the courthouse swung open, and Turner emerged. He stood on the front steps while he calmly rolled and lit a cigarette, glancing from time to time in her direction. He must see Billy sitting behind her. How did he feel, knowing that Billy was okay and back in her care? Something told her Turner was struggling with the notion that Billy was his own flesh and blood. He must be in a quandary, trying to pull the thoughts in his head in line with the feelings in his heart.

Before Sookey saw him, Turner had approached and was holding Maude by the halter. "I see you found him."

"I did."

"Have any trouble?"

"None to mention."

Billy peered around Sookey.

"You all right, boy?" Turner asked.

Billy nodded.

"Speak up, Punkin," Sookey chided, "or else the high sheriff'll think the cat got your tongue."

"Yes, Sir," he said softly.

Turner looked up at Sookey. "Where was he?"

"Down in Albany. It's a long story, but everything's fine now. We should be getting on home. It'll be dark by the time we get there."

Turner released the halter and stepped back. "Is Cora Mae really gone?"

"Yep. Just like I said."

Turner shook his head. "That's really a shame." He sucked on his cigarette and held the smoke for several seconds. When he exhaled, puffs of smoke accompanied his first few words. "I been thinking hard about the boy, Sookey. Lord knows I want to do right by him, but it's just not possible, me being married and all."

"What are you saying, Sheriff?"

Turner tossed his spent cigarette into the street. "I'm saying I'd love to have a son to carry on my name, and if things in my life were different, I'd be proud for Billy to be the one. But I can't survive a scandal. You understand, don't you?"

Sookey simply nudged Maude out into the street.

As she moved away, Turner called out to her, "You expecting trouble?"

Sookey glanced down at her shotgun and replied over her shoulder, "No, but even a rattlesnake will give a warning."

CHAPTER 19

▼

The incessant sound of a truck horn fractured the midmorning stillness on the streets of Millersville. Turner listened as it grew louder. The noise wasn't the boisterous exuberance of young men announcing a victory or simply raising cain. An urgency peppered the sound, urgency bordering on panic.

Turner went to the window. The street was clear. Only his car and that of the clerk of court were parked out front. The insistent cry of the truck remained in the air, much closer. He detected movement out of the corner of his eye before he saw the vehicle. It sped into view and slid to a frantic stop parallel to the curb, still partially in the street. It was a CCC flatbed with a lone driver. Turner recognized the hair before the face. Jimmy Mack Jones.

Turner intercepted Jimmy Mack before he could get through the courthouse doors. His eyes were wild, his speech incoherent. His skin looked like biscuit dough, rolled out and floured. The young man's knees buckled. Turner caught him before he could fall face first onto the granite steps and sat him against one of the nearest pillars.

The blasting horn had attracted a number of people who followed the truck and gathered around it out on the street.

"Come down here, Sheriff," Clyde Truett shouted.

Turner moved quickly down the steps and over to the back of the truck where the crowd had assembled. After Turner pushed people aside, a glance revealed the reason for Jimmy Mack's incapacitation. The bloated body of Zed Rudeseal, his chest like a smashed watermelon, lay on the truck bed. The crowd talked in hushed tones.

Turner climbed up on the flatbed and gingerly rolled Zed onto his side. The back of his shirt and overalls were peppered with small holes in a wide pattern. The front and back pockets of his overalls were pulled inside out and hung limply around him like white tongues. Turner patted them out of habit. Empty. The blast had destroyed one of Zed's overall galluses, and the front of his overalls flopped over diagonally. A snuff tin showed through the ripped fabric of the bib. Turner pulled it free, wiped the blood from it on Zed's shirt, and placed it in his own shirt pocket.

"Take him over to Doc Whitley," Turner said and jumped from the truck bed.

A few onlookers stood near the doors to the courthouse. Jimmy Mack was trying to gain his feet as Turner ascended the front steps. "Give him a few minutes to steady himself, then help him inside," Turner commanded. He moved through the doors toward his office.

With Jimmy Mack in his office, Turner gave him a whiff of ammonia and then began to question him about Zed's obvious murder. He learned that even though Zed had not returned from work several days before, the family was not alarmed. He had been acting strange of late, and was spending a lot of time away from home. When he didn't come home all day the next day, Jimmy Mack went in search of him. No one notified the sheriff, for fear that Zed might be off on another binge. Jimmy Mack searched the mountain roads between their home and the camp over in Union County, but found nothing.

"I was on my way here to report him missing, and then I remembered him talking a lot at home about that Shanks woman and how ill she'd been treated. Wondering if he could ever make up for what he'd done." He caught his breath. "So, I decided to drive by Shanks Cove. I spotted his car in the woods on the ridge. Some crows were circling the thicket below me, so I went down to the valley floor to take a look. That's where I found Zed in the underbrush." Jimmy Mack rose unsteadily to his feet. "Give me a gun, Sheriff, and I'll kill her myself."

"Sit back down," Turner said, pressing on Jimmy Mack's shoulder. "Before you fall on your face. And don't be jumping to any hasty conclusions, either."

Jimmy Mack returned to his chair. "What conclusion can I make? Sookey Shanks had bones to pick with Zed. She carries a shotgun most everywhere she goes—has even threatened folks with it. You're no exception, Sheriff. And I found him laying dead on her farm, with only the crows watching over him. What conclusion can anyone make?"

Turner pulled his chair away from his desk and sat down. He picked up a thin letter opener made of horn and began twisting it between the fingers of both hands as he spoke. "Zed was done in with a shotgun, all right. Shot in the back from a safe distance, I'd say, as if someone sneaked up on him."

Jimmy Mack's freckled face lit up. "That's right. That's what I'm saying. That gutless coward."

"Listen to yourself. You're upset and not thinking straight. Of all the things Sookey Shanks is, she's not gutless, and she's no coward. I dare say, if she ever shoots anyone, it'll be straight on, and the last thing they'll ever see will be both barrels of her shotgun right in their face."

"But, Sheriff—"

Tuner dropped the letter opener to the desk. His eyes bore in on Jimmy Mack. "Shut up and listen to me, before you start a riot I can't control."

Jimmy Mack clenched his teeth. He hung his head and stared at the floor. Color had returned to his face, and he seemed to be regaining his strength. He glanced up. "But he was found on her place, and she had every reason in the world to get even with him, including getting her money back."

"Did Zed carry a wallet?"

"Yes."

"Was he known to carry money in his pockets?"

"Not enough to mention. He didn't have much to start with."

"Well, his wallet is missing, and his pockets are empty." Turner reached into his shirt pocket and pulled out the snuff tin. He raised it to his ear and shook it, then held it toward Jimmy Mack. "I took this out of Zed's overalls. Do you know what he carries in it?"

Jimmy Mack shrugged. "Snuff?"

Turner smiled. "I'll bet it's full of money."

Jimmy Mack stared at the tin. Turner slowly opened it, turned it upside down, and shook it. A wad of currency fell out onto the desk. Jimmy Mack's red head snapped back and his mouth flew open. Turner unfolded the money and laid two twenty-dollar bills in front of Jimmy Mack.

"You weren't in court the day Zed recovered forty dollars from Sookey, were you?" Turner said.

Jimmy Mack shook his head.

"Had you been," Turner continued, "you would have heard him accuse her of taking a snuff tin containing forty dollars from his overalls while he was incapacitated." Turner set the tin on the desk in front of Jimmy Mack. "If Sookey was trying to get her money back, she would have known right where to look and would not have left that tin behind. Only someone who wasn't in court that day wouldn't know where Zed kept his real money. Besides, she passed through here yesterday on her way home from Atlanta. That body I saw on your truck is over two days old."

Jimmy Mack squinted and tightened his mouth. "If she didn't do it, who did?"

Turner rose and walked around his desk to stand by Jimmy Mack. "I don't rightly know who would have wanted him dead," he said. "Could have been a drifter looking for some quick money. There're quite a few of them about, these days. Go on home and tell the family. I'll see to it that he gets fixed up presentable, before they come to get him. In the meantime, I'll go out and talk to Sookey Shanks and look over the place where he was shot. Maybe I'll come up with something."

Turner escorted Jimmy Mack to the door and watched from the window as a few men gathered around him out on the street. He stayed at the window until Jimmy Mack drove away. Then Turner jumped in his car and headed to Raven Cliffs. All the way there, he fretted about Carter's hotheaded volatility. He was out of control. Turner loathed the killing, and Carter's attempt to frame Sookey was transparent. It would cause more problems than Turner could possibly handle. Better not to have a suspect than to inflame the county once more against Sookey. What would happen to Billy, if anyone took action against her? For now, Turner knew his secret was safe. A threat to Billy, though, would draw him out into the open. Damn you Carter, you've gone too far.

Carter's truck was not at the base of the cliffs. A few taps on his horn brought Sam Clewiston peering over the edge. He informed Turner that Carter and Hoyt had just left to take a load of shine up to Blue Ridge. Turner was livid. With the exception of the CCC camp, they never sold shine outside their home county. Being exposed to arrest in some other police jurisdiction was unwise. Turner could do little to influence law enforcement outside Fortune County. Apparently, Carter was trying to make up for not being able to sell at the camp, now that Zed was no longer around to protect them. Carter was running the risk of a revenue-tax conviction for himself and young Hoyt. Turner needed to have a tough conversation with Carter before things got totally out of hand.

Turner sped away from the cliffs, taking the most logical route to Blue Ridge. He careened along the mountain roads as fast as his courage would allow. He used his siren until he crossed the Fortune County line. He did not use it after that, fearing that he would call too much attention to the loaded Speedwagon if he caught up with it. Turner crossed a small portion of White County and moved deep into Union County, thinking every minute that he would spot Carter around the next bend. Turner finally stopped and turned around. Either

Carter's truck had sprouted wings, or else he had gone a different way. Maybe he was not going to Blue Ridge after all. He could have been on his way to Tennessee to try to sell shine to the copper miners across the border and didn't want Sam to know where he had taken Hoyt.

The trip back to Shanks Cove was long, but he needed to see the scene of Zed's death and talk to Sookey before filling out a report. Perhaps it was just as well he had not talked to Carter. At least, he could write the report with a clean conscience and not have to tiptoe around facts as he did with the reports of Bailey Turnage and Ranger Bentley.

Something was amiss. Dust still settled on the bushes beside the road, and fresh tire tracks marred the road surface. He spotted smoke, possibly from a torch, and a number of vehicles parked haphazardly in front of Sookey's place, before he broke through the thicket. Armed men stood in front of the vehicles. Sookey and Billy stood close to one another on the front porch, each holding a shotgun. The men turned as Turner screeched to a halt behind their parked vehicles.

Clyde Truett stepped forward and spoke for the group as Turner approached. "Zed Rudeseal was our friend, Sheriff. We want to know what you aim to do to his murderer."

The men around him nodded.

Turner stopped. "And who might that be?"

Truett's gaunt face went blank. He gazed around at the men, then back at Turner. "Why, Sookey Shanks, of course. Who else?"

"Who put that fool notion in your head?" Turner said as he started forward.

The men moved aside to let him pass, and Truett turned to keep him in sight. "No one," Truett said to Turner's back. "We heard Zed was found dead out here. There sure wasn't any love lost between those two. What else were we to think?"

Turner stopped at the steps and spun around. He set his jaw and looked them each in the eyes before speaking. All the crowd needed was any sign of encouragement to fan already inflamed passions, and a lynching would occur for sure. "You folks have been itching to get rid of Sookey Shanks since before I can remember. This is just another concocted excuse and a damn poor one, at that. I suggest you go on home and let me do my job." Turner mounted the porch and stood between Sookey and Billy, facing the men.

Clyde Truett stepped out in front of the crowd. "Well, we aim to do something about Zed's killing, since you don't, and there are more of us than you can stop."

The men behind him voiced their agreement.

Turner unsnapped the leather strap that held his pistol secure and pulled it slowly from its holster. He held it at his side, pointed toward the porch floor. "You're right, Clyde. So, we've got to decide right now which ones of you we're going to kill." Without taking his gaze off the men, he spoke aloud to Sookey and Billy. "Billy, you put your first barrel into Mr. Truett there, then scatter the second one into the crowd. While he's reloading, Sookey, you put one barrel into Ben over there with the torch, and the other one into George standing next to him with the rope. I'll take Curtis and Garrison, since they're the best shots, then anyone else I can. If either of you are still on your feet after that and can get off another shot, take out anyone who's still standing."

Truett's thin lips curled and a crooked smile crossed his pale face. "I'm not afraid of that little runt—" The metallic sound of the hammers being cocked on Billy's shotgun filled the air. His sneer disappeared. He stepped back. The men close to Truett inched backward.

"One thing I've learned about this boy, Clyde. He'll do exactly as he's told. I wouldn't test him."

The eerie silence was broken once more by the click of Sookey's hammers moving back as well. Truett raised his hands. "We got no fight with you, Sheriff. We just want to see justice done."

"Sookey Shanks was nowhere near Fortune County when Zed was killed," he said. "I know that for a fact. He was my friend, too. You wouldn't be helping his memory any, if you took out your revenge on Sookey and let his real killer go free. Now, get on home."

Turner's hard gaze moved from man to man, looking for their resolve and for any rash movement. He watched their shoulders, their hands, but mostly their eyes. His pistol grew hot in his hand. The men glanced at one another and shrugged. They broke into small knots, conversed sullenly, and slowly drifted away to their vehicles, glancing his way every now and then. Turner secured his pistol in its holster, then stayed, watching, until the yard was empty.

When it was safe, he drove back to the thicket and examined the trampled place where Zed had fallen. Blood dotted the ground in coagulated black gobs. Bits of flesh still clinging to fragments of colored cloth and blue denim adorned low-lying bushes with a macabre montage. He located two spent shotgun-shell casings nearby and sniffed the acrid odor that signified how dangerous Fortune County had become. At least Sookey and Billy would be safe that night.

CHAPTER 20

▼

Sookey's strong, brown legs pressed into Maude's sides, guiding her through the trees and tangled undergrowth of the mountainside. Maude needed little direction on a trail. Only when a trail split or she wanted to scratch her hide on a tree did Sookey need to guide her. When they were moving off trail between ridgelines, Sookey constantly communicated instructions to Maude with her knees. One of the reasons for Sookey's phenomenal success locating ginseng was her willingness to bear the hardship of travel in the thick forest between ridges where others refused to go. The natural trail atop a ridge was well suited for rapid movement of people and animals through the mountains. The space in between was best for gathering.

Sookey had sorely missed Billy's company during her long mountain treks. She smiled at the thought of his riding along behind her once more. She was comforted by the press of his small body against hers whenever Maude moved down a slope and by the grip of his slender arms around her waist when they started uphill. Having someone to talk to, other than her one-way conversations with a mule, was also a pleasure. Billy, too, seemed starved for company. He had been a little chatterbox ever since she found him. Their first trip into the mountains since his return was no different. He asked more questions than she had answers for, all about their surroundings and the wild things that filled their bellies, cured their ills, and healed their wounds. Sookey was pleased that he was so eager to learn and absorb her knowledge. She delighted in telling and pointing, allowing him to sniff and taste. That which he touched, smelled, and tasted would be a part of him for life. He would be able to spot it in an instant or find it in the dark.

"Take me to the top of the world, Sookey," he said, when they reached the top of one ridge.

"I will, Punkin, but only if you can point the way. It's time I found out if you remember anything I taught you." Sookey turned sideways to look back at him.

He squinted up at the sun, then took a quick look around. Without hesitating, he pointed off to the southwest toward a distant ridge. "It's down that way."

Sookey grinned. Not getting lost was key to mountain survival. If Billy had learned that much, he had won half the battle.

"And where's Shanks Cove from here?" she said.

He pointed in a different direction.

"Good boy." She turned Maude southwesterly along the trail. "We'll have to cross over to the next ridge before we get there. I know a good place."

They followed the ridgeline for several hours before crossing over. On the second ridge, the trail ascended, gently at first. As it grew steeper, Maude kept to her steady pace, slowly conquering the height. They emerged onto a solid rock bald that looked down on the mountains around them. A mosaic of gray and white cloud columns bordered in pale blue towered above them. The bluish peaks in the distance melted and disappeared into the matching hue of the horizon. The sun hid mischievously behind a towering cloud formation, peeking out occasionally to poke yellow spokes through holes in the cloud base, while its rays turned the top a coppery gold. The cry of a distant hawk floated on the wind, answered only by its lonely echo among the peaks. The wind blew hard and steady into their faces from out of the west. Thunder rumbled across the land.

"Here you are, Punkin. The top of the world. Isn't it grand?" She slid off Maude's back and helped Billy to the ground.

The two of them stood quietly, hand in hand, breathing air saturated by all the ingredients of the green expanse that lay before them. Sookey released Billy's hand and smoothed his windblown hair. "You like it up here?" she asked.

Billy nodded. "Yes, Ma'am. I feel free up here."

"I know how you feel, Punkin, but freedom is a funny thing. You can't be free up on a mountain, if you're not free down in the valley, too."

Billy rubbed his near-white eyebrows. "We're not free down there," he said. "Are we?"

Sookey did not answer. She gazed toward a distant peak. After a while, she closed her eyes and hummed softly. The cool breeze kissed her face, and the warmth of the smooth, stone parapet caressed her bare feet. Her heart smiled as she stood on that high place, gently rocking back and forth, humming. She was in church once again.

"We'll spend the night up here," she finally said. "We needn't be trying to get home in the dark." She unpacked Maude and turned her loose to graze in a stand of trees at the far end of the bald. Her root bag was full, and she had a flour sack filled with chamomile for herb tea, pennyroyal for coughs and colds, yellowroot and wild peppermint for an upset stomach, and red sassafras for a tonic against fever and to purify the blood. She sent Billy off to gather firewood, while she set up camp on the summit. "We're going to sleep right next to the stars," she called out to him.

After they had eaten and their fire had dwindled to pink and gray coals, they stretched out on their blankets with nothing between them and the night sky. The cloud cover had moved on, and the black bowl above was alive with specks and streaks of light. As they lay watching and occasionally talking, Billy inched his way under her arm, snuggling close. Sookey held him against her body, feeling his heartbeat.

"What are stars?" he said.

Sookey laughed. "How'd I know you were going to ask me that?"

"I don't know."

"I don't rightly know what they are, Punkin, but I like to believe they're tiny holes in heaven for God's light to shine through."

"Really?"

"Really. And, do you hear them singing up there?"

"Who?"

"All our ancestors. They're singing to us through those tiny holes."

"I don't hear anything."

"Listen close," she whispered.

The two lay quietly for a moment, before Billy spoke again. "I still don't hear them."

"Okay," she said. "I'll sing along, so you can hear what they're saying."

Sookey's strong, clear voice wafted into the darkness around them.

> "There's a land that is fairer than day,
>
> And by faith we can see it afar.
>
> For our Father waits over the way,
>
> To prepare us a dwelling place there.
>
> In the sweet by-and-by,
>
> We shall meet on that beautiful shore.

In the sweet by-and-by,
We shall meet on that beautiful shore."

In the remaining months of warm weather, Sookey and Billy made several more trips into the mountains to forage, then on to Atlanta to sell and deliver the proceeds to Abe Waxman. Her ginseng sales had remained constant, but she had interested Wo Fat in purchasing a variety of other herbs and spices, too. She welcomed the additional income, but the gathering took time. Not only was Billy good company on the long rides, he was a steady and uncomplaining worker, as well.

When summer finally passed the baton to its colder cousin, the shorter, cooler days signaled the approaching school term. Billy would be in the second grade. She dreaded turning him over to a stranger for most of the day. He had not been out of her sight since his return. But Billy's excitement was infectious. His anticipation and her deep-rooted desire that he make something of his life overcame her reluctance. Besides, what good would all their hard work and sacrifice do if he never left Shanks Cove?

School started when the fall harvest was in and the farm children came in from the fields. On the first day, Sookey and Billy set out for Millersville before light and arrived with time to spare. Sookey left him standing—lunch pail in hand— in front of the one-story, wooden schoolhouse. She was on her way home before the first child arrived. She hoped her absence would make Billy's day go easier.

When she and Maude returned at day's end to retrieve him, a few children ran laughing after each other in the schoolyard. But Billy stood alone at the edge of some nearby woods. He was bareheaded. His shirt was dirty and torn, and a speck of dried blood marked the corner of his mouth. A red welt showed under one eye. He lowered his head as Sookey approached.

"You all right, Punkin?" Sookey climbed down off of Maude.

Billy nodded and fell into her embrace, burying his face in her dress.

She patted him on the head. "Where's your cap?" He pulled away and pointed out across the schoolyard toward a knot of older children running after each other. A cap was being thrown from one to the other as part of their game.

"And your lunch pail?"

Billy shrugged. "One of those big boys took my cap and my lunch before school started."

"Did you tell your teacher?"

"I told the lady in the office."

"And what did she do about it?"

"Nothing. She told me to go home."

Heat rushed to Sookey's face. She knelt in front of Billy. "She what?"

"She said I didn't belong there, and I should go home. I've been waiting out here for you."

Sookey's eyebrows raised. "You been standing out here all day?"

Billy nodded again.

"Poor baby." Sookey put her arm around his shoulder and walked him over to Maude.

Together they rode across the spacious schoolyard to the front of the faded-red school, where Sookey dismounted onto the steps. "I'll be right back," she said.

The school had only four classrooms, two on each side of a wide hallway. The office door was open, but Sookey stopped at the doorway and tapped on the frame. All she could see was a desk, two chairs, and a wooden file cabinet. A severe-looking woman sat at the desk, engrossed in papers in front of her.

Sookey tapped once more. "Excuse me."

The woman looked up. Her graying hair was knotted into a tight bun. Her dark blue, long-sleeved dress with a high lace collar accentuated the length of her neck. The woman's expression did not change when she saw Sookey at the door.

"Excuse me," Sookey repeated, as she stepped into the room. "I'm Sookey Shanks, and I was wanting to know why Billy Briggs was sent home today. Did he misbehave or something?"

The woman's tight lips cracked open just wide enough for words to escape. "We don't allow coloreds in this school." Her gaze returned to the papers in front of her.

The muscles rippled in Sookey's jaw as she gritted her teeth, then relaxed them into a sugary smile. "I'll be glad to go outside and yell back at you, but my question's going to be the same. Why did you send Billy Briggs home today? Was he misbehaving?"

The woman's head snapped up. "I'm not talking about you," the woman said. "I'm talking about your boy."

A warm glow filled Sookey. That was the first time anyone had referred to Billy as being hers. It had a nice ring to it. She smiled. "But he's not colored."

The woman slammed her pencil to the desk. "Might as well be. Been raised his whole life as one. His being here just spells trouble. It's best for us and for him if he doesn't return."

"But—"

"Please go. I'll not discuss this further." She returned to the work on her desk.

As Sookey turned to leave, she spied the woman's petite blue straw hat hanging on a coat rack behind the door. A white ribbon encircled it, ending in the back with a swallow-tailed bow. She lifted the hat without the woman noticing and left. Slipping the hat onto her head, she led Maude, with Billy astride, across the schoolyard to where the children were playing. She called out to the large boy who held Billy's cap. He seemed older than the rest.

"What do you want, old woman?" he said, hitching up his britches.

"I'd like for you to give me this child's cap." She pointed at Billy.

"You do, huh?" the boy said. He sauntered over to Sookey. The other children followed, whispering and giggling. "I guess I can do that," the boy said. He handed the cap to Sookey.

Sookey took it, thanked the boy, and turned her back to him to hand the cap to Billy. As she did, the boy grabbed the ribbons dangling behind the blue straw hat and snatched it off of her head. The children erupted in laughter and ran off. Their laughter turned to howls when the boy threw the straw into the dirt and stomped it.

Sookey called out to him as she mounted, "Be sure and tell your teacher in there how you bested this old colored woman."

"Don't worry," he said, laughing. "I will."

Sookey grinned and clicked her tongue. "Come on, Maude. Take us home."

CHAPTER 21

▼

Sookey was chopping weeds around her cabbage plants when the crows started making a fuss in the thicket. She listened long enough to hear the whine of a vehicle descending the ridge road, before she returned to the security of her porch and her ever-present shotgun. She focused on the road through the thicket, waiting. She did not recognize the small truck when it appeared. Not until it screeched to a stop in front of her did she recognize the driver, Clyde Truett. She picked up her shotgun.

Clyde got out of the truck, waving both hands. "Hold on there. Put that thing down. I've got something for you." He reached back into the truck and held up an over-sized envelope.

Sookey laid the gun within reach and waited for Clyde to climb the porch steps.

He handed her the envelope. "It's Special Delivery."

Sookey's shook her head. She could not imagine the Millersville postmaster driving all the way out to Shanks Cove to deliver mail to her personally, when she could not get her mail through general delivery in town. She took the envelope and held it as if it were a dozen eggs. She examined it, turning it over to read everything printed on it, including the cost of the postage. It was addressed to her in care of Postmaster, Millersville, Georgia, from Postal Inspector, U.S. Post Office, Atlanta, Georgia. "Special Delivery" was stamped across the front of the envelope in bold, red letters.

Clyde stood close by, shifting his weight from one foot to the other, all the while eyeing the envelope. "Well," he said, "aren't you going to..." He hesitated, then gestured toward the envelope. "You know...open it?"

Sookey laid the envelope on the seat of a nearby rocker. "Yes, but right now I've got to finish weeding my cabbages before it gets too dark." She brushed past him, headed back to the garden.

"But, but…" Clyde sputtered. "Aren't you…"

Sookey could hear the frustration in his voice as she resumed weeding. She kept her back to him as she worked and listened as his truck doors creaked open, slammed shut, and the truck started up and drove away. When he was out of sight, she threw her hoe to the ground and raced for the porch, yelling for Billy.

Billy came out of the woods near the beehives. They sat on the porch in adjoining rockers as Sookey opened the strange envelope. She found a typewritten letter and another envelope inside. The letter was from Assistant Postal Inspector Bernard Shapiro.

Dear Miss Shanks,

My Uncle Abe Waxman advises that you may have experienced difficulty getting your mail at the Millersville Post Office. He has asked me to make sure you get his letter to you, which I have enclosed. I have corresponded with the Millersville postmaster and asked that he specially deliver this envelope to you, as it contains important documents, and to assure me that you receive your other mail on a regular basis.

Sookey smiled. She had sure chosen the right lawyer. She ripped into Abe's letter, having no idea what to expect, but heart racing to have gotten it, especially at the unwitting hands of Clyde Truett.

Dear Sookey,

I've finally located a teacher for Billy. I think she's a fallen angel, but she'll be perfect. I'll explain when I see you. I plan to bring her up to Shanks Cove on Friday next. Your letter said you had an empty cabin she could use. Please make sure it is ready. She has an infant. Hope that doesn't present a problem.

Sincerely,

Abe Waxman

With food and a place to live supplied, finding a teacher was easy in those hard times. What would be difficult was ending up with someone sufficiently educated who would also be willing to live in isolation on a colored person's farm in the mountains. Sookey hoped the teacher understood and would accept the rejection of the community, which made the position available in the first place. Whoever lived with her and Billy, irrespective of the reason, would be lumped into their pot and stirred in the same stew. Life at Shanks Cove was not going to be easy.

Sookey was sweeping leaves from the steps of the small, hewn-log cabin she had cleaned for the teacher, when Abe's four-door sedan pulled into the farmyard. She motioned for him to come to her.

Abe crossed in front of the car and helped from the passenger's seat a slender woman carrying a blanketed child. The woman was a head taller than the beaming Abe Waxman. As she approached, the early sun played halo tricks around her upswept strawberry-blond hair. Before the two arrived, Billy appeared from around the side of the little cabin with a handful of wild flowers.

"Put them inside, Punkin, then come meet your teacher." Sookey turned toward Abe. "Have any trouble finding me?"

"Nope. Seems like everyone in Fortune County knows where you live. Sookey, meet Nicolette Fortier, Billy's new teacher. Nicolette, this is Sookey Shanks."

Nicolette smiled. "How do you do. Mr. Waxman has told me many nice things about you."

Sookey nodded. "Certainly nice to meet you, Mrs. Fortier."

"Miss," she replied.

She was soft spoken, and her accent stirred Sookey's curiosity. Sookey's gaze darted to the fingers of the woman's left hand. Even with Nicolette's peach complexion, Sookey could discern a thin band of lighter-colored skin circling her ring finger. "I'm sorry," Sookey said.

Billy came out of the cabin. Putting her arm on his shoulder, Sookey said, "This is Billy. Billy, say hello to Miss Fortier."

"Please call me Nicolette."

"Hello," he said. But his gaze got no further than the blanket in her arms.

Nicolette laughed. "I see we have left someone out. Billy, meet Christine." She kneeled and opened the blanket, revealing a miniature of herself.

A broad grin covered Billy's face.

"If we can sit, I'll let you hold her."

Billy raced to the steps and held out his arms for the infant. The others sat in porch chairs nearby.

"The boy's been wanting a puppy," Sookey said. "Guess I can forget worrying about that, now."

"Tell her about yourself, Nicolette," Abe said. My letter didn't go into any details."

Nicolette turned toward Sookey and put her hand on the arm of Sookey's chair. "I was born in Rheims, France and attended a convent school there from the time I was twelve, being trained as a teacher in the humanities as well as in the sciences. I came to Canada when I was twenty-four and lived with an order in Quebec for a year, then left to teach at the St. Ignatius School in Washington, D.C."

Sookey studied her while she spoke. Nicolette was lithe and willowy, with delicate features that seemed more chiseled from pink marble than covered with fair skin. She struggled not to stare, never having seen anyone so striking. "How long did you teach there?"

"Two years."

"Why did you leave?"

Nicolette cleared her throat and swallowed. "To have a child."

Despite her approval of Nicolette as a teacher for Billy, Sookey viewed her as a delicate flower likely to be blown over by the storm of hatred that had settled over Shanks Cove. How would such a sensitive woman with nothing to gain or prove handle the inevitable rejection that would come with the job?

Sookey looked at Abe. "She'll do just fine."

So began the private education of Billy Briggs in a tiny cabin at the feet of Nicolette Fortier. What Sookey had purchased for Billy was better than anything he ever could have received in the county school—a personal and intense education tailored to Billy's needs. Abe Waxman had brought Nicolette to the farm and filled her wish list of books and supplies. She had more than she needed for Billy's early education. As the weather grew colder, "Miss Nicolette" began to teach him what he needed to know to live in a world outside of Shanks Cove. Sookey continued to teach him how to survive in a world surrounded by mountains and rejection.

CHAPTER 22

▼

Preparation for winter at Shanks Cove neared completion. The shelves of Sookey's kitchen overflowed with jars of vegetables canned during the summer. The dirt floor of her root cellar bulged with buried potatoes and cabbages. Onions dangled in pungent bunches from the low cellar ceiling, restricting movement in the cramped space. Although cured hams and bacon slabs hung in abundance from the storage room rafters, the advent of colder weather signaled the time to butcher and cure the next year's supply. With no schedule to keep, Sookey slaughtered and dressed the hogs, while Billy loosened the hair on the carcasses with boiling water and scraped the skin smooth. Sookey handled the butchering, and Billy applied the curing mixture of salt and brown sugar to the hams and wrapped them in clean burlap. Sookey hung the sides of bacon in the smokehouse where a green hickory fire smoldered. Nicolette, who had first watched from a distance, asked if she could help. Sookey put her to work tending the lard-rendering pots and the fires beneath them. After the mincemeat was canned and the sausage made, Nicolette asked with amazement, "Is there any part of a pig you don't use?"

"Yep," Sookey replied. "The squeal."

During happier times, hog killing at Shanks Cove was a celebration. Sookey's father invited pigless neighbors to participate and take home cuts of meat not readily susceptible to preserving. Like her father, those neighbors had been driven out of the county. The closest living persons were the Clewistons up on Raven Cliffs. Sookey decided to share her bounty with them, or at least make the offer. It would be a good outing for Nicolette and baby Christine before the first snow.

They set out in the wagon early on a Sunday morning. Sookey knew what occupied the Clewistons' time up on the cliffs, but presumed that they, like all good mountain folk, would rest on the sabbath. Besides, she had no intention of going to the top. She intended to call at the base and send her gifts up in the basket, if the Clewistons would have them.

When the group from Shanks Cove arrived, Sam Clewiston was leery and stayed back out of sight, forcing Sookey to shout whatever she had to say. After much shouting back and forth, Sam peeked over the edge and studied the wagonload of visitors below. The presence of Nicolette and the baby in the wagon seemed to placate his concern. He finally agreed to accept Sookey's offerings, and she filled the lowered basket with fresh pork, several jars of honey, and some new-crop apples Billy had picked the day before.

As the creaking wagon followed Maude back down the winding road leading from the base of the cliffs, the laughter of excited children rang out high above.

They took a different route home. Sookey wanted to visit the abandoned A.M.E. church on the way. "This is a good place to have lunch," she said as she guided Maude into a stand of hardwoods beside the church.

Billy leaped from the wagon to explore the churchyard. Nicolette prepared to change Christine's diaper. Sookey climbed down and stretched while studying the tired, old building. Its dark windows stared back at her with the hollow-eyed look of the aged. Flecks of chipped paint littered the ground under the eaves. A makeshift wooden cross struck a comic pose on the roof. Birds fluttered through broken panes when Sookey opened the front door. The pews wore gray shawls of dust. Memories of voices raised in praise filled her mind, and she recalled the hellfire and brimstone sermons that always raised the temperature of already sweltering, summer nights.

"Lunch is ready," Nicolette cried out, breaking Sookey's momentary reverie.

"Coming," she called back.

After they ate, and while Billy played with Christine, Sookey took Nicolette on a trip through the overgrown graveyard. She stepped over sunken gravesites, while poking through the weeds to locate the stone markers. "I really ought to come back over here and clean this place up," Sookey said as they walked back toward the wagon.

Nicolette nodded. "I'll help. Do you mind if I look inside?"

"It's dusty."

"That's okay."

Sookey shrugged and opened the front door. She followed Nicolette into the dim sanctuary. Nicolette hesitated and looked to her right on entering. Quickly crossing herself, she moved down the center aisle, heading straight for the upright piano sitting to one side down front. Wiping the piano seat clean with a handkerchief, she sat down and stared at the key cover for a moment before raising it. After rubbing her hands and flexing her fingers, she played. As out of tune as it was, Nicolette was able to coax a delicate melody from the old piano. Stopping in mid-chord, she stood and lifted the hinged top of the upright and peered inside. "Come see," she said.

Sookey moved toward her. "What is it?"

"There's dead grass in the highest octave."

Sookey looked down among the piano strings. "Don't know nothing about octaves, but I know a field mouse's nest when I see one. I guess she thought church was out for good." Sookey laughed, reached in, and removed a handful of leaves and dry grass. She picked up a tattered hymn book. "Can you play this?" She handed the open book to Nicolette.

Nicolette studied the music for a moment, nodded, and played once more.

Sookey beamed and sat down beside Nicolette. "That's my favorite, Sookey said, then sang,

> "This world is not my home. I'm just a passing through.
> My treasures are laid up somewhere beyond the blue.
> The angels beckon me from Heaven's open door,
> And I don't feel at home in this world anymore."

The vermillion and yellow swaths etched for a while across the mountainsides had faded to a somber brown. In many places, limbs stood nude and shivering in the wind, awaiting the inevitable snows of a mountain winter. Carter Baxley sat hidden on the ridge watching the cove. The chimney of the main cabin emitted no smoke, and only a wisp rose above a small cabin in the rear. It had been that way for hours. No one must be home.

Carter left his truck and crept toward the farm, staying close to the underbrush beside the road. Crows stirred and took wing as he passed through a thicket, but the woods and farmyard were otherwise quiet.

Once inside Sookey's cabin, he renewed his search for her gold, but did not waste time destroying her belongings. Finding nothing on the ground floor, he trotted up the stairs. As he searched a back bedroom, he heard a door slam in the distance. Running to the window, he saw a slender woman with reddish hair descending the steps of the small cabin in the rearyard, a basket in each hand. She headed in his direction.

Carter slipped to the top of the stairs and listened. The backdoor of Sookey's cabin opened and banged shut. Light footsteps echoed in the kitchen.

"Hello!" a woman cried. "It's Nicolette. The crows gave you away. I have a surprise for Billy."

The sweet aroma of hot apples wafted upstairs. Was that pie? Carter stepped back, when the woman entered the main room carrying a handful of fat lighter.

"It's awfully cold in here. I'll start a fire. You two must be half frozen." Nicolette struck a match and held it to a resin-gorged piece of kindling. When black smoke curled from the flaming end, she turned her back to the stairs and placed the burning stick under wood stacked in the fireplace. Carter rushed down the stairs, the thud of his boots resounding in the room.

Nicolettte looked over her shoulder. "Is that you Soo…" A cry of fear and surprise escaped her as she stood and whirled to face Carter. She broke for the kitchen. His arm snaked out. He grabbed her hair and pulled her hard against his chest. Her head jerked around, her eyes only inches from his mouth.

Even though the cabin was cold enough for breath-puffs, beads of sweat covered Carter's face. He stared at her through thin slits. "Where is it?" he said, his voice flat and emotionless.

"Who are you? What do you want?"

"Where is it?" he repeated. His saliva sprinkled Nicolette's face.

"Where is what?" She tried to wipe away his spit.

The knuckles of his fist slammed against her temple. Her eyes glazed over.

"Where is it? I'm not going to ask you again." Carter released his grip on her hair, and she crumpled face down on the rough-hewn planks like a bag of rags. As she lay there unconscious, Carter went back upstairs to resume his poking and prying into one thing and then another. When she began to stir, he returned.

"Are you going to help me, or do I have to wring your pretty little neck?"

Nicolette struggled to stand, but could get only to her knees. "Oh, please, no."

Carter grasped her hair once again and snatched her to her feet. He held her head back as far as it would go, exposing her throat to his free hand. He applied pressure to her windpipe. Her breathing became labored and almost convulsive.

Nicolette struggled to speak. "What are you looking for? I'll give you anything you want."

"I want Sookey's gold!" Carter screamed. "Tell me where it is, and I'm out of here. Screw with me, and I'll kill you where you stand."

Nicolette raised her hands, palms up, all the while gasping for air. Carter released enough pressure for her to breathe.

"I know nothing of gold or of anything of value. Holy Mary, Mother of God as my witness. I work here as a teacher. Please don't hurt me. I'll tell you anything I know."

A yellow-toothed grin split his face. "Damn, if I don't believe you. Spoken like a true teacher. You'd tell me if you knew, now wouldn't you?"

Nicolette nodded.

"Did I hear you say you was Nicolette?"

She nodded again.

"Well, I got other plans for you anyway, Nicolette. Plans that call for you being nice and warm, not stiff and stone-cold." Carter released his grip on her hair and throat. She slipped to the floor. As she lay gulping air, he ripped away the bodice of her dress. "Them's nice," he snickered. "But what you got guarding 'em?"

A crucifix dangled on a fragile chain between Nicolette's exposed breasts. Her hands flew upward to cover herself, but he slapped them away. Grabbing the crucifix in his large hand, he snatched it from her body and flung it across the room. "You didn't think a tiny-little statue of Jesus was going to stop me, did you?"

He pulled on her undergarments. His rough hands clawed at her softness. She screamed and struggled, but his shoulder pressed hard against her. The weight of his body pinned her to the floor. Her arms flailed against his back. As he fought to get into position, her teeth gripped both shirt and flesh of his left shoulder.

Carter howled and tried to break free. Nicolette hung on like a pit bull. He struggled to rise. She kept her teeth clamped to his shoulder as he tried to lift her dead weight. Halfway up, he collapsed. Nicolette crashed to the floor under him. Her head thumped against the thick floor timbers. She lay still.

Carter reached for his stinging shoulder. He could feel teeth marks through the fabric. "Damn!" he exclaimed. "I'll show you." He grabbed Nicolette's skirt and tore it free, discarding it in a tattered heap beside her.

The piercing cry of a baby rose from the kitchen. Carter leaped to his feet, shaking. He dashed to the doorway. Two baskets sat on the table, one filled with pies and applesauce, the other with a pink-blanketed infant. In disbelief, Carter lifted the crying baby and cradled it in his huge hands. His massive finger brushed the tears from its red, tear-stained face. He held it close to his chest and rocked. "There, now, little one," he cooed. "No one's going to hurt you." He looked back to where Nicolette lay unconscious and exposed. "Or the one who's supposed to be watching out for you."

When the baby quieted, Carter rummaged around the cabin for a blanket. He nestled the child against Nicolette and covered them. He stoked the fire and left.

CHAPTER 23

▼

Nicolette recovered from the assault by Thanksgiving, suffering only from an occasional headache. She had been unable to describe her assailant enough for Sheriff Turner to identify a suspect. The man's stated search for gold gave Sookey a suspicion, but better to keep to herself. She nursed Nicolette back to health, while Billy cared for Christine. Before long, all returned to normal at the cove, and they settled in for the winter, the harshest one Sookey could remember.

Since the first snow in mid-December, several new layers had fallen each month. The unpaved mountain roads became impassable to vehicles after the second heavy snowfall. They remained that way for the rest of the winter. The county stopped trying to clear the unpaved roads by the end of January, and snow was still falling during the first week in March. The only movement through the mountains was on foot or horseback.

Sookey's preparation throughout the year had made them self-sufficient and avoided the necessity of having to venture beyond the confines of the farm. Whenever new snow fell, Sookey used Maude to open paths through the drifts, connecting the house to all the outbuildings. Maude seemed to enjoy the brisk excursions into the snow but was eager to return to the warmth of the animal-filled barn.

The quiet time of winter was best used repairing and refurbishing harnesses, tools, and farm implements. Nicolette concentrated on Billy's education. In the evenings, they all gathered by the fireplace in the main cabin, and Nicolette entertained them by reading aloud from a selection of books Abe Waxman had provided.

In the middle of one of those readings, as the wind moaned and spit snow at the windows, a dull thump on the front porch startled everyone. Thinking that the intruder had returned, Sookey sprang for the shotgun by the door. She cocked it in a heartbeat. Nicolette lowered her book to her lap and stared at the door.

"Who's out there?" Sookey yelled. Only the wind answered. Sookey moved to a window and peered out, shotgun at the ready. She could barely penetrate the blackness, and there was not enough light from the windows to see clearly. A dark, shapeless lump lay near the top of the steps. "Who is it?" she yelled.

A faint, muffled cry rose for an instant but was borne away in the storm. Sookey turned to instruct Billy to get his shotgun and back her up and saw him already standing behind her, gun in hand. She raised the latch and pulled open the heavy door a few inches. Placing the barrel of her shotgun in the crack, she eased the door open the rest of the way. A rush of cold air and snow swirled into the cabin. Sookey stood in the opening, her eyes smarting from the cold, straining to see.

The motionless lump on the porch was a slightly built man. He lay curled up as if asleep. Sookey poked him with the gun barrel. No movement. Snow and ice covered his clothing. "Billy," Sookey cried. "Come help me. Someone's near froze out here."

The two of them dragged the man to the fire, where Sookey removed his hat and gloves. "Why, it's Sam Clewiston," Sookey said. "Nicolette, make something hot to drink. Billy, run up and get a blanket." Sookey removed Sam's coat and held him between her and the fire as she rubbed his hands and arms. When Sam began to respond, she forced hot coffee into him and made him sit near the fireplace, draped in a blanket.

"It's the wife," he managed to say. "It's her time, but she's in trouble. Been trying to drop that baby all day, but can't. She's in a lot of pain. I'm afraid I'm going to lose them both. I'd heard you was a midwife and all."

"Did you walk all the way here through that blizzard?"

Sam nodded.

"It must be five miles or more," Sookey said.

"Can you help her?" His voice was calm, but his eyes reddened under flickering lids. They searched Sookey's face for an answer and got none. "I know you have every right not to heed a white man's call for help, the way you and your kind have been treated and all. I wouldn't blame you if you turned me away. I do thank you for your recent kindness. We ain't got no life up on the cliffs, but my wife and young 'uns is all I got. Please."

Sookey shook her head. "I don't know how you made it here through this snow, and I don't rightly see how I can get there, either. I'll help you, but we best wait till it breaks."

Sam rose from his place at the fire. He removed the blanket and reached for his coat. "I don't know when that'll be, and I can't leave her up there like that. I've got to get back."

"You won't make it back. And you won't be any help to her or your family froze out there on the trail."

"Thank you, anyway," Sam said. He looked over at Nicolette and nodded. "Ma'am." He started for the door.

"Wait a minute," Sookey said. "I'll get my things. I've got a mule that can break a trail. Maybe the three of us can make it." She turned to Billy. "You keep Miss Nicolette and the baby here with you till I get back, and watch out for them."

Bundled up against the bitter cold, Sookey plunged into the night on the back of Maude, with Sam Clewiston right behind, holding to Maude's tail.

Without anyone to operate the bosun's chair, Sookey and Sam had to take the long way around to get to the top of Raven Cliffs. Sam and his family lived in a makeshift structure on the cliffs. The living room and kitchen were in a shed built flush against the side of a towering rock outcropping. Opening off the living room into the face of the rock were several large natural caves that were connected and served as bedrooms and storage areas for the family.

Sam's wife lay in the largest of these chambers atop a straw-filled tick mattress on a rough-hewn four-poster bed with ropes for springs. She was incoherent. Sam's two children, their faces tear-streaked, rushed to his arms when he entered.

Sookey went right to the foot of the bed and examined the sweat-drenched woman. "It's a breech," Sookey said, stepping back. "Get me a quart of shine," she barked, as she removed her hat and coat.

"But..." Sam stammered, his lamp-black pupils pushing color from his eyes.

"I have no time to tell you what I'm doing or why. Just do as I say."

Sam bolted for a stack of cardboard boxes in the storeroom and returned with a jar of clear whiskey. Sookey rolled up her sleeves and held her cupped hands toward Sam. "Now, pour." Sam removed the cap and poured some into Sookey's hands. "More," she said, as she bathed her hands and then her arms to the elbows. She shook the excess to the floor where it joined the rest of the puddle.

Sookey reached into the groaning woman in an attempt to reposition the emerging infant. She glanced at the two wide-eyed children standing nearby.

"Get some cool cloths for your mama's head and face. Sam, see if you can get her to relax and stop pushing."

Sam stood frozen, his mouth fixed open, eyes staring hard at portions of the infant's hands and feet protruding from his wife. Sookey repeated her instructions to him. He did not respond.

"Sam!" Sookey yelled. "Get her to relax and stop trying to push this baby out. I've got to turn it, or we'll lose both of them."

Sam's head snapped around as if slapped. He stared first a Sookey, and then at the jar in his hand. He took a long swig of moonshine and wiped his mouth on his sleeve.

"Sam!" Sookey shouted again. "Do it."

Sam went to the head of the bed and talked to his wife in soothing tones. The children returned with wet cloths. He bathed her face with one and placed another on her forehead. Sookey worked rapidly without speaking, when the pressure subsided.

"Now," Sookey said. "Tell her to push."

When the woman did, a blood-soaked infant girl popped into Sookey's hands. "Be praised!" Sookey sighed.

CHAPTER 24

▼

Even after the snow had disappeared, weeks would pass before the back roads were dry enough to support Carter Baxley's Speedwagon. The last thing he needed was to leave rutted tracks to his mountain hideaway, or worse, to be mired up to his axles on government land with a load of illicit whiskey. When he could finally drive the mountain roads, he'd been out of business for months. Not only had the still fires been out for the winter, his small surplus of moonshine had been snowbound on the cliffs. He resolved to keep his surplus more accessible the next year.

Shortly after Carter reached the top of the lift, Hoyt Clewiston made a casual reference to his new sister, thanks to that colored woman. Carter grabbed Sam by the bib of his overalls and knocked him to the ground. Hoyt ran to his father's prone body, kneeling between him and Carter.

"*Nobody* comes up here but me and Myron Turner!" Carter screamed. "*Nobody.*"

"You leave my daddy be," Hoyt said, glaring at Carter. "My mama would've died, if Daddy hadn't gone after that woman."

Carter spit on the ground in front of Hoyt. "You'll wish she had died dropping that young 'un if Sookey Shanks ever comes back up here. I'll feed the lot of you to the turkey buzzards." He walked toward the opening of the large storage cave where his extra shine was stored. "Now get off the ground and load up my truck with all those boxes of shine in here."

Hoyt hesitated and then rose. He shuffled toward the cave, head down.

"Start mixing mash!" Carter barked at Sam, who was still on his back rubbing the side of his face. "We got a lot of ground to make up."

When the truck was loaded and ready to make the first run of the season, Hoyt refused to go. An already incensed Carter was livid. "You won't amount to nothin', just like your old man!" At least you could learn something useful going with me. Tell him, Sam."

Sam, pouring cornmeal in a barrel, glanced toward Hoyt, but not at him, and then cast his gaze to the ground. "Go with him, son. Your mama and the baby need the money."

"But, Daddy—"

"Go on, now. It'll be all right. You'll see."

Carter left the cliffs headed north toward the Tennessee line, a sullen Hoyt riding beside him. The miners at Copperhill would be pleased to see him coming. If this time was anything like the last, he could get rid of his entire load in one stop. Maybe losing the CCC business wasn't so bad after all.

Sheriff Turner could hear his phone ringing as he inserted the key in his office door. Refusing to start doing business until he drank his morning coffee, he took his time entering and putting away his things. Maybe the caller would give up. For reasons he never understood, many so-called emergencies simply went away if no one responded.

Turner left the jangling phone as he sauntered down to the clerk's office for a cup of fresh coffee. The ringing started again when he returned. He answered after a couple of sips and spoke to the sheriff of Polk County, Tennessee.

"The feds made a liquor arrest last night out at the mine," the Tennessee sheriff said. "Picked up a boy they turned over to me. Can't be more than thirteen. Says he's from Fortune County. Name's Clewiston. Hoyt Clewiston. Know him?"

A chill coursed Turner's spine. *Carter's gone and done it.* "Know the family. Good folks. They recently reported him a runaway. Don't tell me a thirteen-year-old is the best the feds can do on a liquor bust up there."

"Oh, no, they got the shiner, but figured the boy for no more than a toter. I'll turn him over to you, if you'll come get him. You folks down there can deal with him as you please. Tennessee don't need to be housing and feeding no Georgia runaways."

Turner exhaled. Hoyt's true involvement had apparently escaped detection, and the authorities were not interested in questioning the boy's parents. "Who's the shiner, by the way?" Turner asked. "Wouldn't be one of those Smokey Mountain Rickett boys we hear so much about down here, would it?"

"No. I hear he's from your area. That's probably how the runaway got hitched up with him. Goes by the name of Baxley."

"I know a Carter Baxley," Turner said.

"That's him."

"Well, I'll be. There's been rumors that he's running shine, but we haven't had any problem down here, and I've been unable to come up with anything on him. It may be because he's selling it out of state."

"May be," the Tennessee sheriff agreed. "When you think you can pick up the boy?"

"Can't do it today," Turner said. "Would first thing tomorrow work for you?"

"That'll be fine. I'll see you then."

"Good." Turner dropped the ear piece of the phone into its cradle. He slammed his fist on the desk. "Damn."

When Turner arrived in Copperhill the next day to retrieve Hoyt, Carter Baxley had already been moved and was being held in federal custody in Knoxville. His money and unsold shine were being held as evidence. His truck and shotgun had been confiscated as contraband. Hoyt was being held in the Copperhill jail, separated from the other prisoners.

As Turner approached Hoyt's cell, Hoyt began wiggling like a puppy. To prevent Hoyt from blurting out something incriminating, Turner began a steady stream of chatter as soon as he reached the cell door. "So, you're the young 'un your mama told me so much about. She's been worried sick over you." As the jailer opened the cell, Turner continued to talk and kept it up as he led the quizzical boy toward the jailhouse door. "Now, don't you try to explain or give me some dumb excuse about why you ran off like you did, and for God's sake, don't tell me you didn't run off, because I'll never be able to explain to these good folks of Copperhill why I drove all the way up here to get you."

The boy's lips gasped for words like a fish struggling for oxygen, and Turner interrupted each time with one-way conversation. Turner and Hoyt were almost to Turner's Model A, before the boy finally caught on. When they were safely in Turner's car and it no longer mattered, Hoyt had nothing to say all the way back to Millersville.

The feds had Carter Baxley dead to rights selling non-tax-paid liquor, and they refused to plea bargain. Turner wired Carter's lawyer a small amount of money to help with his defense, but otherwise refused to get involved, reminding Carter of his admonition to sell only in Fortune County. Carter threatened to implicate Turner in the moonshine operation if he didn't do more. Turner informed Carter for the first time that he had retrieved two spent shotgun shells from beside the bodies of Bailey Turnage and Ranger Bentley, and one from beside the body of Zed Rudeseal. "They all have the same hammer mark on the brass casings. The feds would be mighty interested in knowing, especially since they have your shotgun for comparison, and more so because two of the men worked for them, and the one who didn't, died on federal land."

Carter Baxley hung up the phone.

Turner clasped his hands behind his head and leaned back. Losing the shine business was a heavy blow, but if the killing stopped, it was worth it.

CHAPTER 25

▼

Sookey Shanks viewed the greening of the mountain forest as a promise kept. To her, spring was but a reminder of a greater promise awaiting fulfillment. Its methodical arrival each year, and the rebirth it kindled, provided all the assurance she needed that her faith was well placed. Generations would pass, wars would start, stop, and be forgotten, presidents and kings would rise and fall, and still the greening would come, year after year.

Sookey swore she could smell it before it arrived, said she could hear the sap rise, could see the branches enlarge before new leaves crawled out into the light. She loved the greening. It meant that she could soon mount Maude and head out in search of the forest's bounty; that the warm earth would soon crumble between her bare toes as she walked the fields, dropping seeds into well-spaced holes left by her planting stick. Her bee hives would swell with new honey and her sows with piglets. In spring, biddies flowed across the chicken yard like the yellow-and-brown wake of a passing hen, pecking for craw pebbles. Sookey's world would be fresh and new again.

Word of Carter's arrest and conviction arrived quickly at Shanks Cove, through the mouth of Sam Clewiston. "Six years," he said it was. "All to be served in the federal pen in Atlanta."

Sam came to thank Sookey for giving him his wife and child. He brought meager gifts. "It ain't much, I know, but it's all we got," he said, laying two tanned deer hides and several raccoon pelts on Sookey's porch. With that, Sam and Hoyt left the cove.

As the full blossom of spring unfolded throughout the mountains, Shanks Cove came alive. The pigs returned to their wallows, and Maude left the barn.

Sookey plowed under the previous year's withered crop remains and smoothed the soil with a log float. Nicolette, a quick and willing learner, was able to relieve Sookey occasionally and guide Maude across the vast cornfield with delicately accented "gees" and "haws." She would later confess with some chagrin that the experience afforded her an intimate rear view of the huge animal she would otherwise have missed. Even after the fields and the garden were cultivated into orderly rows, the time to plant had not arrived. Tradition dictated that seeds should not enter the earth before Good Friday.

As Easter neared, Sookey's thoughts turned to her church. Perhaps Nicolette would accompany her to the old building and they could hold a worship service of their own. The God Nicolette occasionally referred to sounded so much like her own, and Easter seemed to hold the same significance for each of them. Nicolette agreed without hesitation. Sookey did not think it fitting to attend an Easter service in old clothes, even if no one else attended. Besides, Nicolette had never been to Millersville. Abe Waxman had whizzed her right through, stopping only for directions. A trip to town to shop for new clothes was in order.

They left on a Saturday, all piled into the wagon, their songs drowning out the crunch of the wagon wheels. Sookey handled the reins. Nicolette sat by her side, trying to sing louder, and then breaking into laughter when she could not. Billy sat on a pile of quilts and pillows in the back watching over Christine. The little girl stood, peering over the sideboards, her fingers clutching them tightly for balance against the gentle sway. The salt-and-peppery aroma of chicken rolled in flour and fried in hot bacon grease wafted out of a packed basket and teased them well before time to stop for lunch.

A breeze blew some loose strands of Nicolette's strawberry-blond hair into her face. She smoothed it with a brush of her hand. She looked at Sookey. "There is something about the way you cook the...how do you say...the chicken...that would make a Frenchman forget his woman."

"Only for a minute," Sookey said with a smile.

"Yes, you are right. For just a minute."

The two women leaned against each other in laughter.

"What are you two laughing about up there?" Billy asked.

Sookey stopped laughing and glanced over her shoulder. "In due time, Punkin. In due time."

Sookey turned back toward Nicolette. They both started laughing anew.

Nicolette stretched her back and shoulders and stifled a yawn. "You have never spoken of a man. Did you ever have one?" She cocked her head toward Sookey.

Sookey rubbed her chin, and turned to see if Billy was listening. "Was a time before Billy that I took up with a fella. Daddy always told me a man would not go rushing to buy a cow so long as he could get milk through the fence. But I paid him no mind."

A wheel sank into a depression, jostling Sookey. She repositioned herself on the creaking seat. "Things was real good between my man and me for a while. He treated me right and brought me wild flowers and such. Then he changed." She scratched the side of her head and gazed away.

"How so?" Nicolette said

"Well," Sookey said in a lowered voice, "he would call me sweet names when he was wanting something, but he called me 'woman' the whole rest of the time. Then I noticed him turning his head when other girls was around. You know, a man don't have to be strapping or even handsome. Just so he holds you higher than all other women *and* lets you know it every once in a while."

Nicolette smiled and nodded. "Where is he now?"

"He lit out for Chicago, when I told him about a baby coming."

"Baby? You had a baby?"

"Sookey shook her head. "Lost it. Just before I helped birth Billy.

Nicolette patted Sookey's arm. "Sorry."

"Maybe it was for the best," Sookey said. She sighed. "Don't know how I could've raised two with no help. One's been hard enough."

Nicolette put her arm around Sookey.

"What about you? Where's Christine's daddy?"

Nicolette clasped her hands in her lap, hunched her shoulders, and rocked. "It should never have happened, but I was young and so curious. He never knew. He was a good man, and I left so he wouldn't be ruined by our one time together. That's about all I can say."

Sookey and Nicolette rode in silence until it was time to stop for lunch. Sookey laid a sheet in the shade of a small chestnut, while Billy retrieved the food basket. After they ate, Sookey stood on the wagon and hoisted Billy high enough to pick several handfuls of leaves, which she placed in a sack under her seat.

"What are you going to do with those?" Nicolette asked, as the groaning wagon pulled back onto the road.

"Boil 'em and put up the juice that oozes out. It's good for burnt skin."

"You use everything, don't you?"

Sookey smiled. "Everything but the—"

"Squeal," Nicolette said. She shook her head and laughed.

Saturdays in Millersville were busy. Folks came to town from all over the county to shop and otherwise handle business. The advent of Easter made it even busier than usual. Mules and wagons and a few automobiles filled the streets. People moved along the sidewalks, talking and gawking. Because of the number of people and vehicles moving about, Nicolette and Sookey's entrance into town went relatively unnoticed. Sookey had warned Nicolette of the reception she and Billy had received from the townsfolk. Sookey decided that she and Christine should remain in the wagon while Nicolette and Billy did the shopping. Perhaps, things would go better this time.

Several places in Millersville offered work clothes, but Clyde Truett's store had the only selection of Sunday-go-to-meetings. They stopped there.

Sookey studied the people on the sidewalk. "From the size of the crowd, looks like everybody aims to get all gussied up for Easter."

As Billy climbed down from the wagon, Sookey pressed a penny into his hand. "Get yourself some candy."

He grinned and hurried to Nicolette's side. The crowd on the sidewalk in front of Truett's parted, allowing them to pass. A few followed them into the store.

Sookey dandled Christine on her knee, and sang to her as they waited. A few passersby slowed and stared, talking in hushed tones. Some moved on down the sidewalk, occasionally looking back. Others frowned and entered Truett's.

Nicolette and Billy emerged from the store, empty-handed. Little color remained in Nicolette's face. Once back in the wagon, Billy handed Sookey the penny. Their eyes met. He hung his head.

Sookey reached for Nicolette's arm. "I'm sorry. I thought you being the one buying would somehow make it different. I was wrong. What did they say to you?"

Nicolette clamped her lips and nodded but did not speak.

"I wouldn't have you hurt, none," Sookey said. "I hope you know that."

Nicolette cleared her throat. "The man who runs the place said our money was dirty, and he didn't know what we did at the cove to earn it. But I'm all right. I was surprised, though, at the way the man in there treated Billy."

"How so?"

"When one of the women said something about Billy being in the store, the man seemed surprised. Said he didn't recognize Billy without his shotgun. Then shoved Billy's candy money back across the counter at him, and told us to leave."

Sookey tapped the reins on Maude's rump. The wagon lurched forward. "It'll be okay. We best head home, though. We're not prepared for a trip all the way to Dahlonega."

"What did the man mean about not recognizing Billy without his shotgun?" Nicolette said. "Certainly Billy hasn't shot anyone."

"Oh, no," Sookey said. "Me either. But we've scared off our share of folks with 'em." Sookey moistened her lips. "Nope. I taught Billy that next to having no other gods or idols, the most important commandment was no killing. Now, folks around here don't know that about us, cause if they did, we wouldn't last very long." She glanced at Nicolette. "None of us."

Try as she may on the road home, Sookey was unable to rekindle the festive mood. Mostly, she sang alone. Her efforts to converse with Billy and Nicolette were met with polite but short responses. A pall of disappointment hung like swamp fog over the little group. Only Maude showed a happiness of gait that a mule has on the way back to the corn crib.

"I know what's wrong with us," Sookey announced. "We've been too concerned about dressing up our outsides without giving a thought to dressing up on the inside."

"What do you mean?" Nicolette asked.

Billy looked up from where Christine lay sleeping.

"Take those folks back in Millersville," Sookey continued. "They're getting all prettied up for the best of the Lord's days without one thought of how ugly they must be on the inside. Just look at the way they treated you and little Billy. They had no call to do that."

"What are you suggesting?" Nicolette asked.

"Well, I'm thinking that we've been so all fired set on dressing up ourselves that we forgot about more important things."

Nicolette cocked her head toward Sookey. "Like what?"

"Like, maybe, how shabby God's house is, for one thing."

Nicolette pursed her lips and nodded. "We did talk about fixing it up, didn't we?"

"Yes," Sookey added. "And what better time than just before Easter. It'll take us a good while to do it. It's a mess." She glanced at Nicolette and then over her shoulder at Billy. "Is everyone up to it?"

"I am," Billy and Nicolette answered in unison.

"Good," Sookey said. She popped the reins. "Pick it up some, Maude. We've got work to do."

"We do." Nicolette laughed. "Just like one big happy family."

Sookey nodded and smiled.

Sookey spent a full day at home gathering tools and supplies necessary to clean and fix up the old A.M.E. church. She and Nicolette worked late into the night preparing enough food for at least two days. Too much work awaited them for a one-day trip. Sookey planned to camp out on the church grounds and stay until finished. Easter was still a week away. They set out the next day at sunup, a sleepy group if ever one was.

As the wagon rolled into the churchyard, Sookey's gaze was drawn to the cross atop the building. Not only was it standing straight and tall, a new whiteness reflected the morning sun. In fact, the entire church boasted a fresh coat of gleaming white paint, trimmed in dark green.

"My Lord," Sookey whispered. "Even the broken windows have all been fixed." She stepped out of the stopped wagon and stared at her church. Her mouth hung open. She moved toward the door, heart lurching. Had some other congregation considered it abandoned and taken it as its own? "I should have come and fixed it sooner," she muttered.

The door eased open on well-oiled hinges. Sookey entered, with Nicolette right behind. The eye-watering odor of fresh paint hung heavy in the air. The wood floor had been painted a light gray. The walls and window sills were the same white and green as on the outside. The yellow pine pews glowed a soft honey gold. Sookey walked up the aisle, in a mixture of wonderment and trepidation. Sunlight flowed through a sparkling clean window of colored glass on the rear wall, turning the pulpit into a kaleidoscope of blue, green, yellow, and gold. The old upright had the sheen of ebony.

"Someone's left a note on top of the piano," Nicolette said. She handed it to Sookey.

The handwriting was decidedly feminine and neatly penned. Sookey read it aloud.

Dear God,

We thank you for sending Sookey Shanks to us in our time of need. We are sorry that the faithful of this church got run off.

We've fixed it up in case they ever come back.

The Clewistons
(Sam, Lessie, Hoyt, Sister, and Clara, who Sam calls Little Sookey)

CHAPTER 26

▼

No one preached at Sookey's homemade Easter service. They only sang. Sookey found it hard to believe that nine people and one piano made the kind of music that filled the Mt. Olive A.M.E. Church on Easter Sunday, 1937. A passerby reported that he heard enough music to convince him that either the colored congregation had returned for Easter, or else the dead had arisen from the church cemetery. He thought the latter might be the case, because he swore he saw a great light shine from on high, turning the dilapidated building into a gleaming white edifice right before his eyes. He also swore on his beloved mother's memory that he saw the face of Bailey Turnage peering at him through a church window.

When Millersville's curious drove out on Monday to see for themselves, most believed it must be so. What else could explain the sudden and miraculous transformation of the old church? People walked big-eyed around it, peering inside in awe, too timid to enter. The graveyard grass was neatly trimmed, and the stones used as markers were crowned with fresh wildflowers. From that day forward, Mt. Olive was both feared and revered as a place where God had paid a visit on his way to judgment.

With spring planting to be done, Sookey approached Sam Clewiston. "Now that Carter Baxley's in prison, I don't rightly see how you and the family's gonna make it up on Raven Cliffs."

"I've been frettin' about that myself," Sam said.

"Why don't you and Hoyt come down and lend a hand with the planting and help work the farm. That'll give me and Billy more time to forage."

Sam scratched his tousled head. "We ain't got no way to get back and forth, except walk. We do that everyday and we'll be too tired to help."

"Then I got a better idea," Sookey said. "I'll move the lot of you in with me til you can build a cabin next to Nicolette's."

The Clewistons moved to Shanks Cove. When Sam and Hoyt were not in the field or the garden, they worked at constructing a cabin with materials Sookey supplied. They completed it and moved in the following year.

With his family settled in their new home, Sam came to Sookey and Nicolette. "Seems as if Nicolette is a might crowded now that she's teaching Billy, Hoyt, and Sister in her tiny cabin. And in just a few years, both Christine and Clara are gonna need some schoolin'."

Sookey nodded. Nicolette cocked her head.

"What would you say, if I built her a little schoolhouse right here at the cove?"

"I should've thought of that myself. Let's do it," Sookey said.

Nicolette clasped her hands and squealed.

Everyone big enough to carry a board pitched in to help Sam. They worked on the schoolhouse for a year, finishing it in the summer of 1939. Sookey tied a ribbon across the door and handed her scissors to Nicolette. All cheered when she sliced her way inside.

Sookey pulled Sam aside and placed money in his hand. "I want you to take the wagon into Millersville by yourself and get some supplies for the school. Don't tell anyone there what you're up to, or they won't sell 'em to you. And while you're there, see if you can get us another mule. Maude needs some help around here."

Sam did as he was asked and returned with a new mule tied to the back of the wagon.

Sookey met him in the yard. "She looks a might scrawny, but she'll do. You have any trouble?"

Sam climbed down and stretched. "Naw. But I heard a lot of talk."

"How so?"

"Well, for one thing, looks like there's some kinda war starting up in Europe."

"And?"

"And I ran into that George Zell fella. He's boasting around that he sold his worthless title to this land to some arrogant Jew lawyer from Atlanta for seventy-five dollars."

Sookey smiled.

"Said he was gonna enjoy watching an arrogant Jew run an arrogant colored woman off her land."

Sookey began unloading the wagon. "Is that all?"

"Only that George's friend, Boyce Peacock, said it must be the same stupid Jew boy who's been purchasing the depressed stock of the Bank of Millersville and buying up worthless property and mortgages in and around town. George said some folks never learn."

Sookey pressed her hands flat together and placed them against her face. She sighed and grinned.

In the spring of 1942 when Sookey returned from her first trip of that year to Atlanta, she gathered the cove residents in her cabin. "The United States is at war. It's going on all over the world. Mr. Waxman tells me that young men are being made to go fight. Billy is only eleven, so he's not going, but Hoyt should turn eighteen before long, and they could call him."

Sam and Lessie both reached for their son.

Hoyt straightened and held up his head. "I'm ready."

Lessie put her hand over her mouth.

Because the cove had no electricity, and because no one in Millersville would speak to her, Sookey kept up with the progress of the war through her monthly trips to Atlanta.

"Bring back newspapers," Nicolette said. "I'll read them aloud at night in the main cabin."

When Hoyt turned eighteen, he left Shanks Cove to join the Marine Corps. Lessie received only one letter with a photo of him in his uniform, before a green sedan with a white star on the side arrived at the cove.

Everyone gathered on Sookey's porch when they saw it coming down the ridge road. Lessie and Sam sat holding each other as a uniformed officer mounted the steps and announced Hoyt's death on a Pacific island neither Lessie nor Sookey could pronounce.

"Please accept the condolence of a grateful nation," the officer said.

Lessie screamed.

Sam gritted his teeth and muttered, "I always made him be a man. He never had a chance to be a boy."

Lessie grieved openly for months. Sam never mentioned Hoyt's name in Sookey's presence again. She wondered why. Did it bring to mind all the hardships of Hoyt's depression-era childhood? Was it because Sam was never able to take his children to the beach, and his only son died with a rifle in his hands trying to get to one? Or maybe that was just the way some men were able to live with unimaginable grief. Whatever made Sam act that way, it was as if Hoyt had never existed.

By the summer of 1943, with war raging around the globe, the demand for ginseng and other hard-to-find herbs soared. Sookey, Billy, and Maude spent endless days in the mountains. If not for the seeds Sookey scattered throughout the woods of Shanks Cove years before, they would have had to stay on the trail twice as long to meet Wo Fat's needs. The gathering season was short—May through September—and Sookey made the most of it. Sam and New Mule did the tilling and planting. Lessie, Nicolette, and the girls handled the house chores, the cooking, the canning, and cared for the livestock. It was, as Nicolette had once said, one big happy family. It was, that is, until the last week of June of that year.

Nothing on the farm looked amiss as Sookey rode Maude down the steep trail into the cove. Their three-day trip had gone well, and she was reluctant to end it. She had promised the girls they could spend Saturday in Dahlonega. They would have to leave before light on Friday and stay the night on the road to make it. Lessie was excited and promised to prepare all the food they would need for the trip there and back.

Sookey smiled as she heard Billy singing to himself behind her. She scanned the farmyard ahead for Christine, but did not see her,

Ever since she learned to walk, Christine had been Billy's shadow, following him everywhere around the farm, babbling his name along with her request for this or that. Before the schoolhouse was built, she sat quietly beside him in Nicolette's cabin as he read aloud or recited his lessons. When classes moved to the new building, she peered from her cabin window for him to emerge. When he did, she rushed outside to join him, and then walked almost lock-stepped behind him while he went about his chores.

Christine's adoration was not wasted on Billy. He reveled in it and always delayed long enough for her to join him. He went out of his way to make sure she could keep up, and protected her from her own curiosity, as if she were a wee kitten. When Christine started to school, no one questioned her claim on the bench right next to him. Whenever Billy accompanied Sookey into the mountains, Christine watched for his return and raced to meet him well before he reached the house. If he were astride Maude, he grasped her arm and pulled her up behind him, always letting her sit on Maude's soft rump. If on foot, he ran to meet her halfway and scooped her into his arms.

Christine did not come to meet Billy that day.

Sookey eased Maude to the edge of her front porch and dismounted without touching the ground. She pulled her two sacks from around Maude's neck and placed them on the porch. "Take her to the barn and feed her, Punkin. Then wash up for supper."

Billy rode Maude away, and Sookey carried her bags into the house. "We're home," she called out as she came through the door. "Who's been here? I see tire tracks in the—"

Lessie was seated across the room in a chair facing the door, a blank stare on her face. Sam's body lay crumpled at her feet. The floor around him was stained. Two men stood in the semidarkness behind her. One had his hand on her shoulder. Sookey's gaze darted around the room. Nothing was in place. Furniture was disarrayed—some of it overturned. Books had been knocked from their shelves. Drawers stuck out like sullen lips, their contents drooled onto the floor below. As she stared at the men across the room, her hand moved ever so slightly to the edge of the door frame behind her. Her fingers brushed against the massive hand-hewn timbers that butted against the doorpost. The unmistakable click of cocking shotgun hammers destroyed the silence, as well as her hope that her long barrel was still leaning against the inside of the door.

"You looking for this?" a man's voice from the kitchen said.

She recognized it. "Carter Baxley?"

"It's me, all right," he said, stepping into view, her shotgun in hand. "It's been a while, hasn't it?"

Sookey did not answer. She looked at Lessie, then Sam. "Is he—"

"As a doornail," the thin one with his hand on Lessie said.

"That there's Elegant Feeney," Carter said, pointing with the shotgun. "Don't know his given name. Met up with him in prison. Beside him is his brother, Aldo. You may have heard of them. Everyone in Atlanta has."

The two men swelled with the recognition.

Sookey gritted her teeth. "Can't say as I have." She turned away from the men and to Carter. Her upper lip curled. A tingling singed the nape of her neck. Her muscles tightened until she thought something would snap. She estimated the distance between her and Carter. Could she make it? Neither of the two men had a weapon in view, but she knew they had them. Their kind always did. They were not the immediate threat. Carter was. He made it easier by stepping closer.

"I don't like the look I see in your eyes," he said and sneered. "I don't want to have to kill you, but I will."

Aldo spoke up for the first time. "If you do, we may never lay eyes on her gold."

"Gold?" Sookey exclaimed. "Are you going around killing folks because you think we have gold?"

"We *know* you have gold," Elegant said. "That's all Carter talked about since I've knowed him. Promised to cut me and Aldo in on it, if we helped him find it when he got out."

Her stomach churned. Caleb Baxley had been demanding gold from her before he died. His wild-eyed hunger for it made him rush headlong into the bear den years before. Carter must have sent him to ransack her cabin and then follow her on the trail. The stranger who assaulted Nicolette spoke of gold as well. What was the source of the gold rumor? Regardless of how it got started, Sookey surmised that two people were dead and one almost raped because of it. A cold chill coursed through her as she fretted over the safety of those she thought of family.

"I'll give you anything you want, but there is no gold. I swear. I've got twenty-five dollars in a fruit jar out in the springhouse. You can have it, but that's all I have."

Elegant spit on the floor. "We wouldn't walk across the street for twenty-five dollars. Would we, Aldo?"

Aldo shook his round head.

"Maybe not," Carter said. "But twenty-five dollars is twenty-five dollars, and right now we got nothing for gas to get us on down the road, once we get the gold."

"Unless they take gold!" Aldo said.

Everyone flinched when the front door sprang open and Billy bounded out of breath into the room. "Sookey, Sookey." He gasped. "There's a car hidden in the—"

Carter leveled the barrel of the shotgun at him. "Welcome to the party, Boy."

Billy melted into the side of Sookey's body. She put an arm around him and held him to her.

A twisted smile formed on Carter's face as he eyed Billy and Sookey. "Well, now. We just may have found a way to find that gold quick and easy like. Come over here, Boy."

Sookey put both arms around Billy. "This boy doesn't know anything about any gold. Leave him be."

"I'll be the judge of that," Carter said. He stepped forward and aimed the shotgun at Billy's head. "Turn him loose, or I'll kill him where he stands."

Billy said with a measured tone, "I'll be all right." He pulled away from Sookey and moved toward Carter.

Carter followed Billy with the end of his gun barrel and spoke to Aldo. "You take her out to the springhouse and get that money, while I talk to the boy in the kitchen. Elegant, you stay here and keep your eyes on the white woman."

Aldo pulled a pistol from the back waistband of his trousers, motioned with it for Sookey to go outside, and followed her through the door.

CHAPTER 27

▼

Myron Turner knew of the bulletin issued about three men being sought in Atlanta. They had obtained gasoline without providing gas ration stamps. On receiving a tip that their vehicle may have passed through Millersville, he drove out the north road for a look. He understood they occupied the same model car as his, except for the color. With gas being as scarce as it was, he had no intention of using all of his just to find a few ration-stamp scoffers. If he did not see them by the time he got halfway to the county line, he would turn back.

The road north of town was empty of traffic. His car started to run hot, so he turned off the pavement onto a dirt road before reaching a metal bridge that spanned a small creek. He parked near the bridge, with the intention of adding creek water to his radiator. In the dirt, a lone set of fresh tire tracks indicated that a vehicle had left the main road, headed in the direction of Shanks Cove. It had not returned. He climbed back in without getting water and followed the tracks.

By the time Turner reached the ridge road, his car's temperature gauge was pegged. Afraid the engine would seize if he didn't shut it down, he pulled over and stopped. After checking to be sure his revolver was fully loaded, he removed his father's lever-action Winchester from its sling in the driver's side door. The tire tracks led down into the cove. He chambered a round in the rifle and followed the tracks on foot, staying to the side of the road where the foliage gave him some cover. He sprang into the underbrush and froze when a raucous chorus of crows sounded in the thicket. He remained still until the noise subsided, then crept through the woods in a low crouch.

He stopped before the woods ended at the farmyard and waited there out of sight. He had an unimpeded view of the yard, but saw no car. The opening of the cabin door surprised him, and he ducked behind a bush. Sookey stepped out onto the porch, followed by a tall, barrel-chested man gesturing at her with a pistol, as if trying to make a point with a chicken leg. Turner recognized Aldo Feeney from the posters. He knew about him and his brother. They had served ten years on an attempted bank robbery charge. Once out, they tried it again, but a bank guard died foiling their attempt. Aldo's brother and the third person were surely nearby. Turner put the bead of his rifle sight on Aldo's head and held it there as the man walked unwittingly through the valley of the shadow of death. The only thing that kept Aldo's head from splattering into mush like an overripe watermelon was Turner's concern for what might be going on inside the cabin and for the whereabouts of Billy and the other cove residents.

The two moved across the yard and disappeared into the springhouse. Turner sighted his rifle on the springhouse door, waiting for Aldo to emerge. Sookey appeared first. Aldo came out with a fruit jar in his hand. He smashed it against the side of the springhouse and put the contents in his pocket. Turner kept the rifle sighted on him as he forced Sookey back toward the cabin. The distance between Aldo Feeney and eternity was only the thickness of Myron Turner's trigger finger.

Movement out of the corner of his eye alerted Turner as his rifle sight followed Aldo up the porch steps. He shifted his gaze to the opening of the cabin door. Before Sookey could enter, Aldo was joined on the porch by what appeared to be a younger man carrying a shotgun. He was the same height, but thinner and bore a resemblance to Aldo. Must be Elegant, the younger brother. Turner moved his rifle to cover the newcomer. A third one was still somewhere nearby. Billy stepped into the doorway. Someone's hand was on his shoulder. Turner could not see who it was, and he didn't have a shot he could risk taking.

"The kid don't know anything about the gold. Either she takes y'all to it, or I blow the kid away."

Turner gasped. Carter Baxley had returned.

Sookey's voice rose in anguish as she pleaded with Carter. "Please let him go. There *is* no gold. You'll be killing an innocent child for no reason. There's nothing I can take them to," she said, gesturing. "I'll give you anything you want. The farm. Anything, but I have no gold."

"I'll give you anything you want," Carter mocked. "The farm. Anything, but I have no gold. That is so touching." The volume of Carter's voice increased almost to a yell. "If you don't come up with gold, this kid's going to die, whether you have any or not! You're both going to die." Carter paused for a moment. "It's out there somewhere, y'all. I know it. Make her take you to it. If she gives you the runaround, kill her. If she comes up with the gold, fire two shots."

Both Aldo and Elegant nodded. Aldo motioned with the pistol for Sookey to leave the porch. The trio crossed the yard in single file, headed for the south trail with Sookey in the lead and Elegant bringing up the rear.

Carter pulled Billy back into the cabin and slammed the door. Turner lowered his rifle and melted into the woods.

"We've been walking for ten minutes, at least," Elegant complained. "How much farther is it?"

"We're about halfway there," Sookey said.

"Halfway? Hell, you're just givin' us the runaround, like Carter said."

"Yeah," Aldo said. "I've a mind to—"

"Do you want gold or not?" Sookey said. "If you do, you'd better be willing to walk to my hiding place to get it." All she could hope to do was get her citified captors lost in the mountains long enough for her to slip away and return to the cabin. After that, only God knew how she could get Billy away from Carter Baxley, but she had to get there, first.

To keep the Feeneys confused, Sookey stayed off the ridges. She plunged through the thick undergrowth of the ravines in between, making every effort to avoid the game trails. She crossed only an occasional ridge, resulting in laborious climbing up one slope and sliding almost out of control down another. Even she was beginning to tire. Heavy breathing came from the men behind her. The briars had taken their toll, as well, tearing their clothes and flesh. Sookey never missed an opportunity to let a bent branch or sapling slap Aldo in the face. Elegant got the same punishing blows from an unwitting Aldo.

When she had taken them as far as she dared, Sookey stopped and pointed ahead. "Watch your step. We're coming to the edge of a rock face. It's a straight drop a couple of hundred feet. My gold is buried under some rocks about halfway down. I'll get it." She started forward.

Aldo grabbed her arm. "Oh, no. My brother will go with you." He looked over his shoulder. "Won't you, Elegant?"

Elegant panted. "What?"

"Climb down that cliff ahead to get the gold."

Elegant scratched his curly head. "I don't know about climbing down no cliff."

"That's a good idea," Sookey said. "Four eyes are better than two for watching out for the snakes."

"Snakes?" the two brothers said together.

"Yeah. Copperheads. They live among the rocks. But they're likely to crawl off if we make enough noise as we climb down."

The Feeneys were silent. Sookey stood and waited while the two stared at each other. After a moment, Aldo walked to the edge and peered over. Elegant followed, but stood back a little way. "Come over here," Aldo said to Sookey. "Show me where it's at."

Sookey walked to the edge and pointed. "See that outcrop with the whitish-looking rock pointing off to the right? That's where it's hid. We just need to climb down there and get it. You can go first, if you like."

"Oh, no," Elegant said. "You go first." He looked at Aldo. "Why don't you follow her? I'll watch out for y'all from up here."

Aldo grimaced. "I guess she can go alone. We can both watch out for snakes a lot better, if we're not so intent on climbing."

"Suit yourself." Sookey climbed over the edge and started down toward the outcropping ledge. If she could get below the ledge, it would shield her from their guns as she continued to the bottom. Once there, she could disappear and return unnoticed to the cabin.

She inched down the steep slope, picking her way among the rocks. She kicked loose ones out of her way. After about ten yards, a shot shattered the silence above her. She ducked. How could they know what she was planning? Then Aldo's body passed close by in midair, rotating slowly while it plunged toward the base. Before her mind could interpret the sight, another shot rang out. What looked like a rag-doll version of Elegant Feeney went by her, falling from her view. Warm, red moisture sprinkled her face and arms. She stared at her arm. Feeney blood?

"You okay down there?" Myron Turner stood at the edge.

"Been following you for miles. You just about beat me to death. Never got a clear shot at them till you were out of the way and had them highlighted against the sky. Come on up. I'll give you a hand."

Sookey scrambled to the top.

Turner pulled her over the edge. "You ready to go get Billy?"

Sookey wheeled around and struck out through the woods. "Stay with me. We're not going back the way we came. I know a quicker way."

Turner struggled to keep up. Sookey glided through the forest without disturbing even the leaves underfoot. Her swift, quiet passage was more deer-like than human, causing him to lose track of her several times. "Stay up with me," she called back. "You're the one with all the guns."

They split up when they got close to Sookey's cabin. The plan was for Turner to approach from the road through the thicket, supposedly looking for water for his car back up on the ridge road. With Carter distracted, Sookey would attempt to slip into the kitchen from the rear and spirit Billy away. Once Billy was safe, Turner could deal with Carter as he saw fit.

Turner neared the porch of the cabin. He sensed a burning sensation in his stomach. A tremor coursed through his fingers. He made a fist, more from instinct than logic, to steady his hand. His uneasiness surprised him. Danger was part of the job of being a lawman. But he could not recall another instance where he had a stake in the success or failure of his encounter. Carter's threat to kill Billy had unnerved him. He had lost the detachment needed by any hunter when stalking a predator in his lair. While Turner had never acknowledged Billy as his own, he was damned if he was going to allow the evil of Carter Baxley to extinguish all that was good in Billy Briggs.

Turner knew that his plan was going sour when his knock was answered by a nervous Lessie Clewiston instead of Carter. From Sookey's account of Lessie's state when she last saw her, Turner had not expected Lessie to be able to function. He thought Carter would open the door himself or remain silent and give the appearance that no one was there.

Turner asked Lessie if Sookey was home. He explained that he needed some water for his radiator. Over his protestations, Lessie insisted that he come inside. He was afraid not to accept, lest his visit appear contrived. For appearances, he leaned his rifle against the outside wall and stepped inside.

Carter sat in a chair across the room, a pistol held loosely in his lap. Sam Clewiston lay at his feet, just as Sookey had earlier described. Billy was standing near the center of the room. Turner feigned surprise at Carter's presence, as he nonchalantly moved in Billy's direction. He explained that he came looking for water and expected to find Sookey. He professed ignorance of Carter's release from prison.

"Who's that on the floor?" Turner asked, leaning forward. "Is that Sam?"

"Sure is," Carter replied. "Do you always come calling with your revolver loose in the holster?"

Turner glanced down. The leather strap that held his pistol secure was not in place. He bit his lower lip and laughed. "Yeah. I have to draw so often these days, the darn thing won't stay put anymore." He made no effort to secure his weapon, but kept his gaze on Carter. "What's wrong with old Sam?"

"Had himself a spell and fell out. Sookey and some of my friends have gone to get him some of those herbs Sookey is always collecting. It should fix him right up, eh, Lessie?"

Lessie threw her frail hands to her ashen face and nodded, but did not speak. Her dilated eyes moved from side to side in dark sockets. She shivered. Turner took a step forward. "Looks like he's lost a lot of blood. Just what kind of spell did he have?"

Carter righted the pistol in his lap with a flick of his wrist. It remained in his lap, now pointed directly at Turner. "At the Atlanta Pen, they call it Buttinsky's Disease. It's often fatal. It's not something you want to catch, Myron, so why don't you just butt out?"

"I will, but I'd like to take Billy and Lessie with me. No questions asked."

Carter studied Turner for a moment before speaking. "Can't do that, Myron. They know too much already. And besides, I have a score to settle with Sookey when they all return. Billy here is part of it. They should be back in a few minutes, so why don't you take your water and git. Like you say, no questions asked."

Turner dropped his hand to his side. It brushed against cold gunmetal. "You know I can't do that. Let Billy and Lessie go with me, and I'll blame whatever happened here on the Feeney brothers."

Carter's mouth flew open. "I never mentioned the Feeneys. How'd you know about them?"

"They won't be coming back. I've already taken care of them."

"No! No!" Carter cried, leaping to his feet. "They found the gold. I heard the…" Carter shook his head. "No, no," he whimpered. "That can't be."

"And you won't be able to settle any score with Sookey," Turner added. "I turned her loose. So let's just drop it right here, and no one else gets hurt."

Carter's eyes narrowed to thin slits. A crooked smile appeared. The rotating cylinder clicked. His pistol swung toward Billy. Turner reached for his own revolver. He couldn't stop Carter. No one could. Carter was a man possessed, and at that distance, he couldn't miss. The forty-four caliber lead slug would hit Billy square in the chest. It would penetrate cleanly, flatten out because of its softness, and bully its way through the rest of the boy's body. No one survived a forty-four shot to the chest.

A groan sliced through the room like a scythe. It rose rapidly from the floor and tapered off as quickly as it started. The sound ended with a dull thud. Turner caught a glimpse of Sam's body rolling over. Carter's head jerked toward the man all thought was dead, then back. Turner leaped in front of Billy as Carter fired. Carter's slug hit Turner in the chest, knocking him back into Billy. Turner fired as he was being hit, then fell to the floor with Billy beneath him. His slug dug harmlessly into the cabin wall.

Carter rose and stepped over Turner's quivering body. He pressed the muzzle against Billy's forehead and thumbed the hammer back. Two more metallic clicks resounded, then a room-shaking roar, and Carter Baxley's head disappeared in a fine, red mist.

Sookey, both barrels of her shotgun smoking, stood at the door to the kitchen. She rushed into the room. Billy sat on the floor with Turner's head cradled in his lap. He pulled the pistol from Turner's hand, glanced at it, and flung it across the room. The gun skittered along the floor and banged against the log wall. Sookey threw her shotgun after it. Turner looked up at Billy, then over at Sookey. He smiled at her and nodded. As his life ebbed away on the cabin floor, Turner pulled Billy's face down to his and kissed him on the cheek.

CHAPTER 28

▼

Sookey waited with Lessie on the Clewiston's porch for Abe's car to arrive from Doc Whitley's. "That must be them, now." Sookey pointed to a dust trail at the top of the ridge road. The clatter of Abe's sedan engine reached her.

Lessie wrung her frail hands. "I hope he's all right."

"Whatever he is," Sookey said, "he's a lot better off here with us than with old Doc Whitley. Bless his poor drunken soul."

Abe's car rattled to a stop in front of them, and the two women rushed to the passenger's side. Sam, one arm in a sling and one leg in a splint, grinned at them through the open window. Lessie jammed half of her thin body through the opening and washed Sam's face with kisses.

Sookey laughed. "Whoa, woman. It would be a crying shame for him to survive the shootin' but not the homecomin'. Let's get him inside and in the bed."

"Get his crutch out of the back, Lessie," Abe said. "And Sookey and I will help him into the house."

With Sam tucked in and Lessie in a chair at his side, Abe and Sookey returned and sat on the porch.

Sookey cocked her head and grimaced. "I guess things are kinda crazy in town."

"Not as much as you'd think," Abe said. "The news of the deaths of Carter Baxley and Sheriff Turner didn't sit too well with a lot of folks. From what I heard, Clyde Truett and his cohorts wanted to come out here and finish what they started a long time ago."

Sookey pursed her lips and nodded. "What stopped them?"

"Well, it seems a special grand jury convened and found that the sheriff died a hero, attempting to capture a gang of bank robbers who'd holed up out here."

"And Carter?"

"They felt that he'd joined up with them once he got out of prison."

"Y'all want some ice tea?" Lessie called from inside.

"Not me," Abe answered over his shoulder. "I've got to start back to Atlanta in just a minute."

"Me neither, but thank you," Sookey said.

Abe stood and stepped toward his car. "The most convincing proof came from some government men who were trying to close the federal bank robbery case against the Feeneys. Their autopsy and ballistics evidence confirmed what y'all said about what happened that day." He opened the door and climbed behind the wheel.

Sookey rose and followed. "I feel sorry for Sheriff Turner's widow."

"Yeah," Abe said. "All she got was a bronze plaque of appreciation from the Bank of Millersville." He shook his head. "I hear she traded it at Clyde Truett's store for a pound of coffee. It's a good thing they didn't have any children."

"Yeah." Sookey hesitated. "It's a good thing."

Abe cranked his engine.

"By the way," Sookey said, "did you ever hear any talk about that bunch looking for gold?"

"Gold?" Abe laughed. "No. Why do you ask?"

"No reason. Just a crazy notion."

"Oh, I almost forgot. They found a complete bite-mark scar on Carter Baxley's left chest. I guess we know who it was who attacked Nicolette."

Sookey breathed easier, knowing that the rumor that apparently started with Carter Baxley died with him.

Life at Shanks Cove returned to normal and moved on after Sam healed that summer. His only residual injury was a slight limp. No one ever claimed the Feeneys' car, and Sam used it to teach everyone on the farm to drive, except Sookey.

"I prefer to ride Maude," she said, "And have no use for any kind of transportation I can't talk to." She thought for a few seconds. "Not cuss at, mind you, because you're obliged to do that to a car every now and again. But really talk to, plain and simple-like." As an afterthought she added, "Now, talking doesn't always mean answering, cause listening is as much talking as saying is, and

Maude is the best I ever saw at that. I can't imagine that old green Ford ever listening to a word I say."

After that explanation, Sam never tried to get Sookey behind the wheel again.

The car did not leave the cove, and many challenges confronted the new drivers. "Before I will agree that any of you has really learned to drive," Sam said, "I want to see you come to a complete stop on the road up the ridge, shift into first gear, and pull up the slope without rolling back."

Everyone groaned.

One laughter-filled afternoon, Sookey stood on the road through the thicket and watched Nicolette allow the motor to conk out four times on the ridge road. On the last time, the car rolled so far back into the thicket Sookey and Maude had to pull it out.

"I told you it wasn't better than my mule."

"What happened?" Sam asked Nicolette, when the car was back on the road.

She put her hands to her head. "The…how do you say…the clutch…and the brake are like Christine and me. They are very close and look so much alike."

Lessie, Nicolette, Billy, and Sister all learned on the only tank of gas. When it ran out, Sookey and Maude pulled the car to the barn, where it stayed until Christine and Clara were tall enough to reach the pedals. By then, the war had ended, and Sam could obtain a few cans of gasoline with ease and without question.

Just as she had with the Clewistons, Sookey shared the bounty of Shanks Cove during the ensuing years with many isolated mountain families. On those occasional visits, Sookey noticed that children who lived deep in the mountains far from Millersville went unschooled. One night when the Clewiston's gathered in Sookey's cabin to listen to Nicolette read, Sookey approached her.

"How do you feel about expanding the school to include children from outside the cove? Those who can't get to school in Millersville. There are so many out there who will never learn to read and write, if we don't do something."

Nicolette's green eyes sparkled. "I think it's a grand idea. All I will need is some additional books and other teaching materials. Abe can help me get them in Atlanta."

"The school will have to be enlarged and improved," Sam said to Sookey. "I can do it, if you can get the building material up here."

The group made plans around the fire over several evenings, and construction of the new school began the following spring, which was during Billy's last year of high-school studies. Sam did most of the work, but, as before, everyone on the farm joined in. It was completed by the end of that summer, just before Billy pre-pared to leave for his first year at the University of Georgia.

To celebrate the completion of the school, and to reveal the plans for the first time to the mountain folk who had unschooled children, Sookey planned a late-summer barbeque.

Billy set out with Nicolette and the girls in the wagon and ranged the back roads of the mountains, extending personal invitations. Over several days, they spread the word and returned stiff and sore, having slept on porches, in haylofts, and on one occasion under the wagon. They were unsure of the tentative recep-tion and could not assure Sookey that anyone would attend the barbeque, much less the school.

Sam built tables outside from scrap lumber, and Lessie and Sookey filled them with all manner of meats, vegetables, biscuits, cakes, and pies. Nicolette made apple and blackberry cobblers and baked fresh bread. Fresh milk and apple juice cooled in the springhouse. Sam kept a stash of hard cider, elderberry wine, and apple brandy out in the barn for the more adventuresome adults.

The festivities were set to start at noon on the last Saturday in August, but by 2 o'clock no one had arrived. A somber mood permeated the cove families. All had worked hard to make the day memorable, and all the work seemed for naught. Sookey sat alone on the porch of the main cabin, rocking. Billy sat on the steps below her. Sam and Lessie huddled near the end of one of the tables talking quietly. Nicolette gathered the girls at her feet, trying to keep them entertained and out of the food.

Just as Sookey rose to tell everyone that they should go ahead and eat by them-selves, the crows in the thicket stirred and rose on the wing. All heads swung toward the sound. A flatbed truck rumbled down the ridge road. People of all ages crammed the truck bed. Some stood and peered over the cab, others sat with their legs dangling off the sides. Its horn overpowered the complaints of the crows and resounded throughout the cove. Sookey and Nicolette laughed as the truck drew near. Abe Waxman was at the wheel.

"Thought these folks could use a lift," he said out the window, after the truck stopped in front of the cabin. "Been driving the back roads since early morning, trying to find folks who wanted to come. Sorry we're late." He stepped down and hugged Sookey and then Nicolette.

"You're not late," Sookey said. "You're just in time. We were just getting ready to eat."

The celebration continued all afternoon, with games for the children and much conversation for the adults. A tour of the school was the high point of the day. Nicolette explained her graduated teaching methods and had each of her students demonstrate some knowledge or skill they had acquired in school at the cove. She topped it off with the unveiling of a new piano, a gift from Abe Waxman.

Darkness descended on their celebration, and Sam asked everyone to pay attention while he made a trip to the tool shed. As all watched, he stepped in the door and moved something with one hand. When he did, the windows of all the cabins and the school came alive with soft light.

A new school was born the day electricity came to Shanks Cove. Their lives would never be the same.

CHAPTER 29

▼

"There it is, Billy," Abe said. "Your home for the next four years."

Billy peered through the open window of Abe Waxman's sedan. Heated air from the engine of the slow-moving car and hot air rising from the pavement surrounded Sookey's head and face. Beads of perspiration covered Billy's forehead. His shirt stuck to his back, when he leaned forward.

Sookey stirred the air in the back seat with a cardboard fan. "I still think I could've brought him over here on Maude."

"You could have," Abe said. "But he would've always been known as the boy who came to college on a mule. You wouldn't want that. Besides, Nicolette and I wanted to be a part of this, too." Abe looked into the rearview mirror. "Isn't that right?"

"Wouldn't have missed it," Nicolette said.

Abe pulled into a tree-lined side street and stopped. "Let's walk. It'll be cooler in the shade."

Billy leaped from the car and stood staring at a cluster of old red brick buildings behind an iron arch that served as the main entrance to the campus. Abe, Sookey, and Nicolette followed him to the sidewalk.

Nicolette nudged Billy's arm. "A little bigger than the cove school, huh?"

Billy's mouth hung open, but he did not respond.

"Let me show you around," Abe said. He took Sookey and Nicolette by the arm and ushered them through the entrance.

Billy ran to catch up, and the group spent several hours gawking before returning to the car.

On the way back, Abe walked beside Sookey and Billy. He put his arm around the tall teenager's shoulders. "I hope you realize how proud Sookey is of you and how hard she's worked to get you here."

"I know, Mr. Waxman. I won't let her down." He took Sookey by the hand.

Abe patted Billy and said, "Get in the car, everybody. I have a surprise for Billy."

Abe drove to a nearby area of small businesses and stopped in front of a drugstore. "This is Bivins Pharmacy. I know the owner. Let's go in."

Inside, Abe gestured toward a heavyset man behind the counter. "This is the druggist, Harold Bivins. Harold is an old friend of mine, and he has agreed to employ Billy part-time."

Harold nodded toward Nicolette and shook hands with Billy. "Welcome to the only pharmacy in town. You won't find any strange herbs or ground-up roots in here. I sell only medicine that makes people well."

Sookey grunted and opened her mouth.

Abe touched her arm before she could speak. "I'm sure you do, and we're all pleased that Billy can work here and learn from you while he goes to college." Abe glanced at Sookey. "Aren't we?"

Sookey grimaced and nodded. "It's always nice to learn about new ways to cure white folks. Sure is."

"The boy will work summers, I presume," Harold said.

Sookey stared at Abe and cocked her head.

"Because," Harold continued, "I need help year-round and don't want someone who takes three months off every year."

Abe squeezed Sookey's arm. "Oh, he intends to stay and work for you during the summer. You did mean to pay for fulltime help during those months, didn't you?"

Harold hesitated and shrugged. "Yeah."

Abe released Sookey. "It's settled, then. That right, Billy?"

Billy peeked at Sookey. She nodded.

"That's right," Billy said.

Harold walked to a coat rack near the front door, retrieved a white drugstore jacket, and handed it to Billy. "From now on this'll be your uniform."

C H A P T E R   30

▼

Sookey's routine remained the same while Billy was away at college. But now, Christine sat behind her on Maude's soft rump during her mountain treks.

"Teach me what Billy knows, Sookey. I want to surprise him when he comes home."

"You know more than you think, child. You been raised in the mountains your whole life. When I find us some ragweed, I'll show you how to ease a insect bite. But till then, we'll start with you tasting that green persimmon over there."

The reputation of the school at Shanks Cove drew children from isolated homesteads and small farms in hidden coves. No one was turned away. The swelling enrollment forced Sookey to enlarge the schoolhouse, hire additional teachers, and add dormitory cabins for them and for students residing too far away for daily travel. She tripled the size of the garden, and when not studying, children tended it and worked the farm. By the summer of 1950, the school was self-sufficient.

During Sookey's last trip to Atlanta, Abe Waxman fretted about a war going on in a place called Korea, but it meant little to her until Billy's letter came.

Dear Sookey,

I received a draft notice last week for the Army. Looks like I'm going to have to leave school because of what's going on in Korea.

I told Mr. Bivins I would work as long as I could, but I'm scheduled for a physical exam this Monday, then it's off to New Jersey. Won't be able to get home before I leave. Sorry. Love you.

Billy

The letter read, Sookey rushed to the schoolhouse. She found Nicolette at a desk in an empty room. "Show me where Korea is," Sookey said.

"What's wrong?"

"Looks like Billy may be going there." She handed Nicolette the letter.

Nicolette read it and returned it to Sookey. She lowered an oilskin map of Asia hanging over the blackboard and pointed. "Right here."

"Can't rightly tell where it is," Sookey said.

Nicolette walked over to a small globe on a shelf. She spun it around and tapped it with a finger. "Maybe this will give you a better idea."

Sookey put her hands on her hips. "Why, they're sending him halfway round the world."

"Yes, and someone will be shooting at him, too."

Sookey's shoulders stooped. She put her head in her hands and rocked. "I knew I never should have let him out of my sight."

Nicolette put an arm around Sookey and walked her to the door. "Don't worry. He's almost a grown man, now. He can take care of himself. You raised him right and taught him well. He'll be all right. You'll see."

Billy never made it back to the cove before he shipped overseas. His letters to Sookey were frequent, however, and she reduced the number of foraging trips just to be there for them. Shanks Cove was now on an RFD route, and the school had a mailbox up on the ridge road. Sookey and Maude plodded up there every-day just to check.

Sookey was pleased when she learned that Billy had been inducted into the Medical Service Corps, and was a medic rather than a fighting soldier. "Sorta like a doctor," she would say, when referring to what Billy did in the Army. Then she would add, "And that's good, 'cause that's the way he's been raised. Said he couldn't stand the thought of killing, and I know exactly what he means."

Billy's letters said he couldn't reveal where he was, but Sookey brought news-papers back from her trips to Atlanta, and had Nicolette stick colored pins in Korean cities on the large wall map, if fighting was mentioned there. Soon the pins ran the length of the small country, all the way to China.

As a winter wind slapped and bullied her cabin, and flicked snowflakes past the windows then back again, Sookey sat, letter in hand, staring at a dwindling fire.

Lessie, who had brought Sookey fresh-baked bread, put her hand on Sookey's shoulder. "Are you okay?"

"I am, but I'm not so sure he is. He says so many folks is dying on both sides, and he is covered with their blood most all the time. Why do you think a boy as tender as Billy has to go through this?"

Lessie hung her head. "I don't know. Maybe for the same reason as Hoyt."

Sookey gazed up at Lessie and patted her hand. "Forgive me, Lessie. Here I am feeling sorry for myself, all the while reading a letter from my boy." She patted Lessie's hand again.

Lessie nodded and left.

The frequency of Billy's letters slowed, and Sookey marked time between them by watching the brittle leaves that clung so tenaciously to the scraggly dogwood in the front yard reluctantly release their grip. When the last one fell free and whirled away with the wind, the letters stopped.

Sookey's useless trips to the mailbox never stopped. She goaded Maude up to the ridge with lively comments, and returned silent and reserved. Her disappointment permeated the air of Shanks Cove. No one mentioned the possible reasons. They didn't have to.

The cawing of the crows summoned Sookey to her front porch. Her legs trembled when the olive drab sedan hove into view on the road through the thicket. She grasped the back of the nearest rocker to steady herself when she saw the white insignia stenciled on its side. She sat down. The arrival was a page out of the past.

Everyone in the cove knew the car had come. Everyone knew why. Children lined the school windows. Nicolette burst through the school door only steps behind Christine. Sam raced out of breath from the field. They all reached Sookey's front porch and positioned themselves behind her before the two Army officers mounted the steps.

The tall officer on the top step looked past Sookey and spoke to Sam and Lessie. "We were told in town that we could find a Mrs. Shanks here."

Sookey hesitated, then signaled with her hand. "I'm Sookey Shanks."

The man's long face clouded. He continued to address Sam and Lessie. "There must be some mistake. We're looking for the next of kin of Corporal Billy Briggs."

"I'm his next of kin," Sookey said.

"I don't think you understand. We're looking for someone who's related to Corporal Briggs."

"I understand you," Sookey said. "And I am his only kin."

The heads of everyone on the porch nodded. The two officers looked at each other. The heavy-set one on the lower step shrugged. The first officer turned around and faced Sookey. "I'm sorry to inform you, Mrs. Bri...uhh...Mrs. Shanks, that your...your kin, Corporal Billy Briggs, is missing in action in the Republic of Korea. Please accept the heartfelt condolence of a grateful nation." He saluted and stepped back.

Sookey looked up from her rocker. "Missing, you say. Not dead? Just missing?"

"Yes. Missing in action. He is not presumed to be dead or alive. He is simply listed as missing."

"Lord be praised," Sookey said with a sigh.

The second officer stepped forward. "Corporal Briggs has also been cited for gallantry in the face of enemy action, in that during intense fighting for hill number 931 in the Republic of Korea, Corporal Briggs, with no regard for his own safety, constantly exposed himself to enemy fire to rescue and treat the wounded of his battalion. Refusing to abandon the wounded under his care, he was last seen administering aid to them as Chinese forces overran his battalion's position. It is my pleasure to present you with his Silver Star." The officer handed Sookey a thin black box, saluted, and stepped back.

Sookey didn't move from her rocker until the green sedan disappeared from view. Everyone remained in place, and no one spoke as she left the porch and headed toward the barn. After a few minutes, she returned with Maude in tow.

"Where you bound, Sookey?" Sam asked.

"I'm going to the top of the world. I've got some serious talking to do, and I need to get as close as I can to make sure I'm heard."

"You gonna be all right?" Lessie said. "Won't you need some food or something?"

"I'll be just fine," Sookey said. She straddled Maude and headed out of the cove.

Sookey reached the rock bald high in the blue mountains at dusk. The top rim of the sun was moving out of sight. Sunset in the mountains had always been a time of awe and wonderment. That day, the ever-changing reddish hues of the western sky were but reflections of the hell that had swallowed up her child.

Sookey pulled from her pocket the black box the Army officer had given her. Inside was a small, five-pointed gold star with a smaller silver star in its center, encircled by a laurel wreath. Attached to the top was a ribbon of blue and white stripes, with a single red stripe down the middle. She turned the star over and read the inscription: For Gallantry In Action.

With the sun gone, darkness descended on the mountains like a black curtain. The night sky was clear, and pinpoints of light appeared as if summoned by the switch in Sookey's tool shed. She held the medal toward the sky.

"I've come to give you back your star, Lord. A star belongs in heaven just like a child belongs at home with its mama. I loaned my Billy to someone, and instead of giving him back, all they gave me was this here star. I know stars are precious, and this one must be, too, for them to send two fancy gentlemen all gussied up and in a fine car to give it to me. But it's not near as precious to me as my Billy is."

Sookey laid the medal out on a large flat rock and knelt beside it. The solid rock scraped her bare knees. She folded her hands before her.

"Lord, Billy is as good a boy as ever came out of these mountains. He's someone you can be right proud of. You were kind enough to give him to me as a wee baby, and I've done my very best to raise him right for you and for me. He lost his mama and his daddy, and I've been all he's got for many years now. I know he's not my blood, but a child of my womb couldn't be any closer to my heart than Billy. You know I would give my life for him. Almost did once, and I would do it now, if that's what you want of me to bring him back safe. It hardly seems the time for Billy to leave this world. He's got so much good to do in it before he goes. No books will ever mention his being here, but the world you made for us will be a better one when he's finished with it. But then I guess you already knew that. If Billy is with you now, I don't want to stay down here without him, and I'm ready to come be with the both of you whenever you call my name. So I'll just stay right here until I hear from you."

Only a breath intervened between Sookey's prayer and the song in her heart:

> "When the roll is called up yonder,
> When the roll is called up yonder,
> When the roll is called up yonder,
> When the roll is called up yonder, I'll be there."

Sookey passed the night on her knees, singing all the hymns of her childhood. Her melodies drifted out into the chilly blackness and settled over the forest like a warm blanket. By the time she reached the end of her mental hymnal, she had fallen asleep, her forehead resting on the rock that held Billy's medal.

She slept through sunrise. When she awoke, clouds obscured the sky. Stiff, she had difficulty standing. She got to her feet, and blood trickled down her shins from both knees, disappearing among her bare toes. As Sookey attempted to wipe the blood from her legs, a flash of light struck her eyes. A thin ray of sunshine had escaped the cloud cover and was shining on the golden star as it lay on the makeshift rock altar. The star sparkled for a moment, and the ray was gone as quickly as it had appeared.

Sookey looked skyward. "Thank you, Lord," she said, with a smile. She left the medal where it lay and headed back to Shanks Cove.

CHAPTER 31

▼

Abe Waxman slammed the door to his car and ascended the steps to Sookey's porch. Sookey sat in a rocker, a bowl of green beans in her lap.

"I got Sam's message that you needed to see me," Abe said.

Sookey laid the bowl on the porch floor. "I'll be right back." She went inside and returned with a folded sheet of paper. "A deputy came by here two days ago and gave me this." She handed the paper to Abe.

"Sit down," Abe said. He sat beside her. He put on his half-glasses and read the paper. "It's a cease and desist order from the Fortune County Commission. Apparently they've passed an ordinance that requires all private schools to obtain a permit before they can legally operate."

"Does that apply to me?"

He removed his glasses and straightened his navy-blue bowtie. "It applies *specifically* to you. You have the only private school in the county. Since you don't have a permit, they've ordered you to shut down within the next ten days."

Sookey rocked in silence for a moment, then stopped. "Do I have to?"

"Not unless you're ready to go to jail."

"They just won't quit, will they?"

Abe rose and placed the order in the pocket of his coat. "No, they won't. Your ten days run out next Thursday. Let me see what I can do."

Abe left and returned the afternoon of the following day. He found Sookey and Nicolette on Sookey's porch and sat between them.

"I filed an application with the clerk of the county commission for a permit this morning," he said. "I learned that the regular meeting of the commission is next Wednesday evening. We'll have an opportunity to be heard before your time runs out. Under the circumstances, Sookey, you ought not be there. Nicolette and I will handle it."

Nicolette fidgeted with a small handkerchief. "It would be a shame to turn all our children away. What chance do we have?"

Abe scratched his balding head. "It's hard to say. The commission is controlled by the chairman, Lloyd Hunsinger. The other two members owe their jobs to him and pretty much do what he says. You and I need to get out into the mountains and urge your children's parents to come to the meeting and show their support."

"What if they won't come?" Nicolette said.

"I'm not going to worry about that." He stared straight ahead. "This is their school. If they don't care enough to save it, I guess it ought to close."

Nicolette touched the sleeve of his coat. "That's rather harsh for someone who's put so much into making the school work." She smiled. "As I recall, you hired the first teacher, rounded up the student body, and created the music department."

Abe glanced at her and chuckled. "But it's *their* school. If they won't stand up for it, why should we?"

"Because we know better, and we know how," she said.

"When do we start?"

"How about tomorrow?"

"I'll pick you up."

Sookey waited on her porch for Nicolette and Abe to return from the commission meeting. She rubbed her arms against the cool night air and rocked, lest she fall asleep. She had no idea of the time.

She recognized the sound of Abe's sedan, and watched the headlights wind down into the cove. Nicolette and Abe got out laughing.

"Y'all sound like you had a good time. How'd we do?"

Abe took Nicolette's arm and guided her up the steps. "We won't know for a while, but I feel real good about it. How about you, Nicolette?"

"Oh, Sookey. I wish you could have been there. You would have been so proud. Our parents stuffed the room full. There were so many, we had to move into the main courtroom. I think the commissioners were impressed." She sat beside Sookey and patted her arm.

Abe stretched both arms toward Nicolette. "This is the one you would have been proud of," he said. "She spoke as headmistress on behalf of the school. Aside from being stunning, she was articulate and persuasive."

Sookey place her hand on the back of her neck. "Hold on, Abe. What are you saying?"

He rubbed his small hands together. "I'm saying she was magnificent. I think she won them over."

"I'm so glad," Sookey said. "I thank you both."

"You're welcome," Abe and Nicolette said in unison.

Nicolette raised one hand. "One question, Abe?"

"Yes?"

"What were those documents you presented to the commissioners at the end of the meeting?"

Abe leaned against a porch post. "They were copies of overdue mortgages I hold in Sookey's portfolio on property owned by Hunsinger's two henchmen. I don't think the vote will be unanimous."

"Would you call that a threat, Abe?"

"No. I call it the American way."

CHAPTER 32

▼

When word came to Sookey in the summer of 1953 that Billy had been released from a prisoner of war camp and would be home in two weeks, she rode Maude to her special place high in the mountains. Billy's Silver Star was gone from the rock where she placed it two years before. Her mind told her that a curious raccoon could not stand the temptation of the shiny medal and hauled it off to its den. Her heart told her that God heard the prayer she left with the medal and sent one of his creatures to make the trade for her Billy. Her expression of gratitude was as heartfelt as it was short: "You've done right by me, Lord, and I thank you."

*   *   *   *

When the train pulled into Atlanta's Terminal Station, Sookey strained to see through its soot-dulled windows. Steam swirled around the platform, partially masking her view. Passengers peered from the cars, and her gaze flicked from face to face, searching for only one. Her stomach churned. Was he on board? Maybe he missed the train. What if he was hurt or sick somewhere?

When she did not see him, she hung her head and stepped back into the crowd, nervously fidgeting with the buttons on her new polka-dot dress. An elderly black porter tapped her on the shoulder.

"There's a soldier waving mighty hard at you, ma'am."

Sookey jerked her body back to the front of the platform. There he was, pressed against a window, grinning and all gussied up, looking fine in that green uniform with all those ribbons on his chest, waving both arms, and mouthing unheard words. She did not have to hear them. She had heard them in her heart for three years. The hope of hearing them again had kept her sane. He was calling her name. She could read his lips.

"Sookey. Sookey. Sookey."

"Are you his nanny?" the elderly man asked.

Sookey never took her gaze off of Billy. "No, Sir," she said. "I'm his mama." She knew the porter would not understand. No one ever did, but that did not change a thing. That was her son on the train. He was home.

"I want to carry his duffel, ma'am. Ain't no charge. Would be an honor."

When Billy fell into Sookey's embrace, she held her little boy once more. She clung to him, wishing their bodies would melt and fuse together. Her tears mixed with his in salty rivulets that wet their kisses and dripped from their faces like warm rain.

"Oh, Punkin, I've been watching the road for you every day. I just knew you'd come."

Billy wiped at his tears with the back of his hand. He laughed. "The devil himself couldn't have kept me away." He held her face in his hands. "You're my mama. Yes, you are."

CHAPTER 33

▼

Abe and Sookey watched from the sidewalk as Billy and his new wife, Christine Fortier, placed a sign in the window of a small office in the heart of Millersville. "Billy Briggs M.D." the sign read. Sookey's dream had come true.

The opening of Billy's office had not gone unnoticed in town. A knot of townspeople led by Clyde Truett gathered in front, protesting and demanding that Billy and "his kind" leave.

Abe raised his hand and waited for them to quiet. He removed a sheaf of papers from a worn leather briefcase. Peering over his glasses, he read aloud from deed after deed the corporate names of the owners of almost every parcel of property in downtown Millersville.

"Before you take any action," he said, "you need to know that the sole stockholder of every one of those corporations is standing beside me. In other words, folks, most of the business district of Millersville is really owned by..." He paused. "Sookey Shanks."

The dissenters gasped, traded blank stares, and drifted away.

Billy gasped, too, when he learned that Sookey was, in effect, Clyde Truett's landlord. Billy grabbed Sookey's arm and ushered her across the street. He entered Truett's store for the first time since he was a child and slapped a single penny on the counter. Without a word, the red-faced man handed him a piece of candy. Once outside, Billy gave it to a child on the street. Every Saturday morning he followed the same routine—for the rest of Clyde Truett's life. When the price rose to a nickel and then to fifteen cents, he still laid down a penny, and Truett rang up the sale without argument.

Abe's stock purchases for Sookey had made her a majority shareholder of the Bank of Millersville, and he sat on the Board of Directors. He had also acquired a considerable amount of land for her, both in Fortune County and elsewhere, including some in downtown Atlanta.

Sookey Shanks had become a millionaire several times over, but to her, Abe's greatest gift was a small parcel on the county line south of Millersville. Soon after the closing, Abe drove her and Billy to the site and let her watch while he and Billy chopped down a faded, vine-covered sign that had stood on the property for years.

"What if they put up another one somewhere else?" Sookey asked, when they finished.

"We'll just chop that one down, too," Abe said. "Own it or not."

The School at Shanks Cove flourished through the years, and Sookey opened it to all races. No one was ever turned away for lack of funds. Except for students living at the school, few black residents returned to Fortune County, but because of Sookey's fortitude and hard work and Abe Waxman's business acumen, no one ever bothered Sookey Shanks again.

✳   ✳   ✳   ✳

On the eve of her eighty-fifth birthday, Sookey called for Billy to come to her. She placed his hand in hers. "Take me to the top of the world, Punkin. It's my time. I can feel it. Just like old Methuselah."

Refusing all offers of help, Billy drove Sookey as deep as he could into the forest and carried her in his arms to her special place at the top of the rock bald in the mountains. Exhausted when they arrived, he sat against a pile of flat rocks and cradled her in his arms. Although her hair was a solid gray, her face was still shiny and smooth, as it had been since his childhood. Her eyes sparkled as she gazed at the passing clouds. A faint smile played across her face. Billy rocked her as he would a small child and sang softly to her the hymns she loved, but lacked the strength to sing.

When he finished, she was gone. He ceased rocking, but sat holding her for a while. He could envision her riding off into the clouds on the back of Maude, turning to wave, a broad smile flashing in the sunlight.

Billy returned from the top of the world without Sookey. He had buried her there with his own hands. He returned later to place a bronze plaque on a rock over her grave:

"In memory of my beloved mother,
Sookey Shanks
This world was not her home.
She was just a passing through."

978-0-595-79409-6
0-595-79409-2

Printed in the United States
34289LVS00005B/10